Reflections of a Stranger

Linda Hanna & Deborah J. Dulworth

Contact Information: titleadmin@pelicanbookgroup.com

Scripture quotations, unless otherwise indicated are taken from the King James translation, public domain.

Cover Art by Nicola Martinez

Harbourlight Books, a division of Pelican Ventures, LLC
www.pelicanbookgroup.com PO Box 1738 *Aztec, NM * 87410

Harbourlight Books sail and mast logo is a trademark of Pelican Ventures, LLC

Publishing History
First Harbourlight Edition, 2012
Print Edition ISBN 978-1-61116-190-8
Electronic Edition ISBN 978-1-61116-189-2
Published in the United States of America

Dedication

We dedicate this book to our Lord and Savior, Who has led us to start this venture and has seen us through.

Thanks to our husbands, Bill Hanna and Ray Dulworth, for your patience and encouragement.

And to our families, much love and many thanks. We appreciate the prayers of friends, the red pens of the Marion Writer's Group and ACFW critique groups 205 and 236. Your endless support has been a tremendous help.

And a heartfelt thank you to our editor, Jamie West.

1

Cora Timms was a three-wheeled trolley ride away from a nervous breakdown. Her neighbor, Patrick Hyde, warned her of a prowler in the neighborhood. She ran to lock the doors. Where was Ed?

He should've been home hours ago. The sharp ring of the phone cut through the air, and sent shivers jolting down her spine. Another ring. Was it Ed, or…the wretched man who'd harassed her for several weeks? The thunder of the Arizona monsoon fed her near-phobic state. She was worried about her husband. She had to answer.

Cora held her breath as the caller's gruffness accosted her ear.

"You look as pretty as ever in your white pants and purple shirt, Cor-rah."

Her nervous fingers punched the off button of the cordless phone as her throat tightened with pent-up screams. She wiped perspiration from her hands and dialed her friend.

"Three threatening calls in one day, Dahlia. How could it be a coincidence? He can see me because he knows what I have on. I'm scared. Ed's two hours late. Could you come sit with me?"

"My pie's pert near done, so give me five minutes and I'll be over, Sugar. Meanwhile, shut them curtains, and make us a pot of industrial strength coffee."

The living room draperies billowed as Cora yanked them closed. Why hadn't Ed taken the calls more seriously? Where was he, anyway? Had he drowned in a flooded ditch, like their daughter, Vanessa? Her stomach coiled. Determined to keep her mind off negative thoughts, Cora headed for the kitchen.

The rich scent of coffee grounds permeated the kitchen as she counted scoops. Cora filled the glass carafe with water, and wiped the bottom with a linen towel. She jumped as a loud thud outside grabbed her attention. What was that?

A movement on the patio. Lightning flashed and illuminated two obscured figures struggling in the torrential rain.

She gasped and choked back a cry. She set the carafe on the counter, and stretched across the sink to lock the window. Her elbow hit the glass pot and knocked it to the floor with a crash.

The next burst of lightning revealed only one person, his hooded face staring at her.

Cora screamed and jumped back in alarm. Her foot slipped. The world tilted and went dark.

ॐ◌ऽ

A baritone voice called through the muddled fog. "Cora?"

Her eyes fluttered. She heard her name again, inviting her back to consciousness.

"Can you hear me?"

Dazed, she blinked several times as her elderly neighbor came into focus.

Dr. Sam Richmond sat on the floor beside her, and

lightly smacked her hand. A mix of spicy aftershave and coffee hung in the air.

She turned. A coffee can rested beside them, its grounds strewn about with broken glass and water.

Dr. Sam's white shaggy-dog eyebrows bobbed above pop bottle glasses, which magnified his eyes. A shock of unruly white hair topped his forehead, where drops of rain beaded.

What was he doing here?

Why was she spread-eagled on the kitchen floor? Cora pushed a lock of wet hair from her face, touched the throbbing lump on the back of her head and winced. "Ow! What happened?"

"I hoped you could tell me." Sam's arthritic fingers shoved his thick-lensed glasses up on his nose. He held two fingers to the pulse of her wrist and cleared his throat. "Do you recall how you got this knot on your head?"

She squeezed her eyes shut, in an attempt to remember. Vague images materialized in a cloud of gray. A gut feeling suggested she had witnessed something horrible. Another burst of lightning made Cora flinch and grasp the sleeve of Sam's hooded windbreaker. The doctor's eyes bored into hers. "You remembered something, didn't you?"

She released the death grip on the older man's arm. Years of trust between them should've brought reassurance. Why did she feel so uneasy?

"I can't make sense of what happened. I saw someone outside the kitchen window." Cora turned away and changed the subject. "These lousy monsoons are the only thing I hate about living in the Arizona desert." She winced. "My back hurts, Sam. I need to get off this floor."

Another flash of lightning filled the room.

She covered her eyes while images popped into her mind, again.

Two men wrestled on the patio...and then, only one. Could one have been Sam or...her husband?

Cora shuddered at either possibility.

She struggled to get up. "Ed left and never came home. Where is he?"

"Calm down." He put his hand on her shoulder. "Ed's in the living room talking to the McGibbons's. They were too loud so I asked them to leave. We'll call him in a minute."

As Sam scooted forward on the rubber mat, caked mud fell from his shoes. Maybe he was one of the men outside the window. She suppressed the negative thought.

"Do you remember anything else?"

Cora hesitated. "One minute I was making coffee and waiting for Ed to get home with ice cream from Sugar Dips. The next thing I know, I'm on the floor with you staring down at me."

"So, you were at the window, and whatever you saw caused you to faint?"

Should she say anything else? One admission would lead to another. She covered her face, and whispered, "All I remember is slipping in the water."

"It'll come to you." He rubbed his nose with the back of his hand. "Any other pain?"

"Other than my tailbone taking root on this hard floor, no."

He smiled and patted her arm. "You and me both, Cora. Here, take my arm. Let's see if you can sit. Easy does it." Dr. Sam's manner, as always, was professional and dignified. He changed positions and braced her with his left hand.

The room doubled as Cora sat up. Two Sams and four magnified eyeballs swirled in front of her. "That's far enough, Sam." Her voice shook. "I'm woozy. Where's Ed?" She blinked and attempted another peek as Dahlia McGibbons's familiar Texas drawl came from the dining room.

"All I know is, the poor little thing was fit to be tied about ya bein' two hours late, Ed. Ya keep scarin' her like that, she ain't never gonna get her pluck back." Dahlia clucked her tongue. "Anyway, there was another one of them phone calls, like last week when ya was gone."

Ed cleared his throat. "Did she say if it was the man this time?"

"Yeah. He scared the puddin' out of her. I sent Wendell Floyd to Sugar Dips to fetch ya while I came on over here."

As Dahlia spoke, worry bounded through Cora. The bits and pieces of memory confused her, like two jigsaw puzzles in the same box. Oh, yes, Ed was late. Now that she remembered with great clarity. Her teeth clenched. 'Late' would've been twenty minutes, but two hours? That's more like…missing. She was glad he'd made it home safely, however, once her backside was off the floor, he was dog meat.

"Ed?" Her voice squeaked.

A gamut of emotions flickered across Ed's face, and his shoes crunched on broken glass as he rushed to her side. "I'm here, Toots."

"She'll be just fine." Sam shifted to face him. "We're trying to figure out how to get off the floor. Wanna give us a hand here, buddy?" He raised his arm for assistance.

"Absolutely." Ed used his foot to scoot shards of glass away before helping the wobbly doctor. Once Sam was steady on his feet, Ed knelt beside his wife. "How are you?" His voice quivered. "I've been worried."

Cora gazed into Ed's bronzed face, and her frustration melted. She loosened the hold on his golf shirt. "I'm fine."

He drew her into his arms and kissed the top of her head. "Dahlia was on her way over when Wendell and I got here. We found you unconscious on the kitchen floor."

Dahlia came into the room. Her signature flippy, dark hair, still damp, had been whipped and tangled by the storm's gale. "Like he said, ya was out cold. Wendell Floyd hot-footed it next door to get Sam." Her bracelets jangled when she placed a cool hand on Cora's forehead.

Equally wet and disheveled from the storm, Wendell Floyd McGibbons stood behind his plump wife, and patted down his meager comb-over. The pudgy security guard invested a lot of time to disguise his bald pate with a few surviving hairs. "Ya got glass all over the floor. Did ya have yourself an intruder?"

Ed stood. "Let her gather her wits before you go into interrogation mode, Wendell."

"Well, it's my sworn duty as senior secur'ty guard to ask questions," Wendell griped.

The kitchen window rattled with a crash of thunder and heavy rain beat against the house. Ed turned to the doctor. "OK to get her up, now, Sam?"

"Yes, but take it easy, Cora."

Her trembling hand reached for Ed. "I'm fine."

"You may experience more dizziness when you

stand." The doctor turned to Wendell. "Let's get a chair ready for her."

Ed put an arm around her waist as Cora took a deep breath and clung to him for support. Another thought resurfaced. The phone calls. That man threatened Ed's life and knew her secret. How could he know about that? Well, now wasn't the time to spring that little nugget on Ed, still, he needed to know his life was in danger. She tugged on his sleeve and looked up. "Ed, there's something I need to tell—"

Sam interrupted. "You might want to have her lie down for a while. Be sure to call me right away if you have any problems."

"Thanks, Sam." Ed shook his neighbor's hand. "Don't know what we'd do without you. Now, what can I give you for the house call?"

The older man waved. "Don't mention it. Glad to be of help." With his medical bag in one hand, he reached for his umbrella with the other. "I don't know why I brought this thing. The wind's too strong for it. 'Night, now." Lightning flashed as Ed opened the door. The doctor hesitated before stepping into the deluge.

Determined to stay on the subject, Cora waited until Ed returned. "I've been trying to tell you that wretched man phoned again."

Wendell moved forward. "Dahlia Sue told us about that when Sam was here."

"Is that when you passed out?" Ed lifted her hand and kissed it.

Cora's pulse quickened. "Just listen to me. It's hard for me to piece it together. I need to talk it through."

Ed shrugged and rubbed his forehead. "I didn't

mean to rush you. Take your time."

"Let's see. I was putting the kitchen window down, and then, I-I saw them." Weariness weighed her down.

Their home, in this gated community, had always been a safe haven. It certainly wasn't now. Not with the phone calls and two strangers fighting on her patio. She felt violated and vulnerable.

"You saw someone in our backyard? In this storm?" Ed handed her his hanky and tenderly smoothed her hair. "You've been so high-strung since those phone calls began. I don't mean to doubt you, but are you sure there were people out there?"

Wendell spoke up. "Every now an' again, Sam forgets to let his silly cat back in. I'm guessin' that was him out there lookin' for ol' Smudge."

A frown creased Cora's forehead. "I know the difference between a man and a cat, Wendell." She brushed coffee grounds from her stained pant leg.

"Now wait a minute." Ed went to the kitchen window. "Could it have been your own reflection?" He pointed. "There's mine. It would've been an honest mistake."

"You're not listening, Edward." Cora's eyes flashed. "It was not my reflection. I saw two people out there! They were fighting and one of them fell." She frowned.

Wendell's face lit with excitement. "Maybe he's dead. I'll go check for bodies." He hitched up his pants. "Dahlia Sue, flip on the outside light."

"Ya'd best watch your step, Wendell Floyd." Dahlia's pendulum earrings wobbled. "If there really was someone out there, he might still be prowlin' around. An' besides that, the lightnin' is bad, an' I don't want ya shish-kebobbed into Abraham's bosom."

"Now wait a minute," Ed countered. "Things are getting out of hand. Let's all calm down. Go ahead and check it out, Wendell."

The eager security guard snatched his Stetson and hustled outside.

Cora grabbed her husband's arm. "This nightmare started before I saw them. That caller phoned again. He was looking in the window because he knew exactly what I was wearing." Her breathing became rapid and shallow. She pressed a hand to her chest. "There's more. Patrick Hyde called before him, and, and…"

"She's gettin' too excited, Ed. She can't breathe."

2

The patio door slid open. Wendell stormed in and joined the others, now in the living room. "Didn't find no mortal remains out there."

"Well, that's a load off our minds." Dahlia headed for the kitchen. "I'm gonna go tend to the broke glass." She stopped in the doorway and put her hands on her hips. "Wendell Floyd, we're gonna need coffee, so hoof it on over to our place an' fetch our perc'lator."

"Horsefeathers," Wendell mumbled. "Ya 'spect me to go back out in the storm?"

"Yeah, an' wear your hood this time." She wiped her hand on a kitchen towel. "Oh, an' while you're at it, bring that apple pie sittin' on the counter."

Wendell perked up, rubbed his hands together and smiled. "Why didn't ya say pie in the first place? I'm on it, Dahlia Sue." The Texan ambled from the room.

Cora drew a deep breath. There were things Ed should know, but first, she needed time alone to reflect on the events of this nightmare. She scooted to the edge of the sofa. "I'm feeling much better, Ed, except my clothes got wet when the carafe broke. Even my scuffs got soaked. I'm going to change into something dry."

"Want me to help you to the bedroom?"

She slowly stood to check her balance. "No, I'm fine. Could you look for my old pair of black slippers in the spare closet?"

Cora entered the dark bedroom. Her vulnerability peaked when she closed the door. Her fingers felt along the wall to find the light switch. The bedside lamps came on and a tingle ran down her spine as a sense of being in the spotlight enveloped her. The caller could see everything. She raced to draw the curtains and dim the lights. No way would she provide one more peep show for that ogling ogre.

As Cora reached for an outfit in the closet, her gaze darted back to the window. She dressed and sat on the bed. Being alone hadn't freed her mind as she'd hoped. The haunting scene she'd witnessed on the patio was still disjointed. No matter how hard she tried, the pieces refused to come together. The only thing for sure was the caller wanted his envelope.

☙❧

Cora immediately felt safer as she left the bedroom and headed for the living room. Noises from the kitchen caught her attention. How embarrassing. Dahlia McGibbons was her guest, not to mention, the star of a popular cooking show. Even though they'd been friends for years, she shouldn't have to work like a scullery maid. Cora called out, "Let me help you, Dahlly."

Ed entered the room, fuzzy slippers in hand. "Oh, no, you don't. Stay put."

"Well, then *you* help her." She reached for her old scuffs and frowned. "Oh Ed, you brought me those silly duck slippers."

"It's all I could find." He reached out and playfully squeezed a duck. *Quack-quack.* "The kids would be so proud that Grandma's finally wearing their Christmas present."

Fear of the intruder was still fresh on her mind. Cora stared blankly at her husband as he plopped down on the sofa. "Stop clowning around, Ed. You should be more concerned about what happened tonight." She crossed her arms. How could he be so insensitive?

"What do you mean? Of course I'm concerned."

"You keep sidetracking me, and I've been trying to tell you something important."

Ed put his arm around her. "I'm sorry. I wanted to lighten the mood. Tell me, now."

"That man on the phone demanded his envelope back."

Ed frowned. "What envelope?"

"How should I know? But the man threatened your life if he didn't get it." Her lip quivered. "When you were so late getting home, I thought the worst."

"Nobody's going to hurt us." He pulled her close and kissed her temple.

Cora rested her head against his shoulder. If only he'd heard the harsh voice on the phone just once, or saw what happened outside their home, he'd understand the danger.

Ed rubbed her arm. "You know God has promised to protect us. You worry too much, Tootsie. Why can't you just trust in Him?"

"I once had all the faith in the world. I lost it when He didn't protect our daughter." She pulled away from him and wiped her eyes. "I can't imagine losing you, too."

"If the threats are serious, God will take care of it one way or another." His gaze focused on hers. "Look, we have to trust. He promised never to give us more than we can handle."

Cora bristled at the self-righteous comment. She wanted to shake him. Losing their daughter was more than she could handle. Now, *he* was in danger. His unruffled manner frequently grated on her nerves, but never more than right now. She stared at him. "Maybe you'll take the threats more seriously when you talk to Patrick. He was looking out his window and saw someone around our house. He called to warn us. Later, there were two people on the patio." She paused and waited for a response.

Thunder rumbled in the distance as Wendell clamored into the kitchen, coffee pot in one hand, pie carrier in the other. He stomped his boots. "I pert near tripped over that mangy Smudge. Can't hardly see a black cat at night unless he looks straight at ya." He hollered, "Hey Ed, best call Sam an' tell him his critter's here!"

Ed searched Cora's eyes. "Mind if we talk about this later? You know Wendell and his sleuthing. He blows things out of proportion. With his input, it would be easy for our imaginations to run amuck."

Imagination? Was that what he thought? Ed *still* didn't get it. Cora pulled away from him as tears threatened. She would not cry.

Wendell ambled into the living room and sat down. Thunder from the dissipating storm grumbled softly in the background, and rendered a more serious tone to the Timms's conversation.

"I want to know why you were at Sugar Dips so long, Ed." Cora narrowed her eyes into a critical squint. "It only takes a few minutes to get ice cream. You had to know I'd be worried when you didn't call home. That's one reason we have cell phones."

"The Pastor wanted to get in a round of golf soon. I tried to call you before we made plans. You didn't answer the house phone, or your cell." Ed kissed her cheek and offered a gentle, but cautious, smile. "George Shipley and Roger Clark were talking in the corner. Since I'd just fired one and replaced him with the other, I got nosy."

Wendell's forehead puckered. "Someone needs to draw an' quarter that George feller. Now, there's a maverick if ever I seen one." He crossed an ankle over his knee. "That varmint sure ain't got no business with your new feller. Did ya find out what they was jawin' about?"

"No, not really," Ed replied. "I want to give George the benefit of the doubt. He was probably giving Roger an earful about some of the rookies at the golf course. Still, their conversation stopped abruptly when I joined them, and George left in a hurry."

Wendell snorted. "If that don't beat all. Sure sounds a might fishy to me. There was always somethin' that didn't sit right where that feller's concerned."

"Go easy on the poor guy." Ed raised his hand to stop the negative blather. "He told me he's had a difficult time at home lately."

The Texan sneered. "I got me a gut feelin' he's just pullin' the wool over your eyes. Mama always said ya can put a boot in the oven, but that don't make it a biscuit."

Ed continued with his story. "Anyway, the strangest thing happened once I finished talking to Roger. I went to the car and discovered a flat tire."

Wendell scooted forward. "There ya are! George

had somethin' to do with it."

"I think George is smarter than that. He wouldn't do something so obvious."

Cora was bewildered. "We just bought those tires last month."

"I know, but it was flat just the same. I was in a hurry to put the spare on, and forgot to call. Simple as that. Can't we let it go for now?" He gave her a boyish grin. "Give me some credit, Toots. After all, I did remember the ice cream."

"Hey, y'all. I got the mess all cleaned up," Dahlia yelled from the kitchen. "Coffee's busy brewin' an' the pie's warmin'. It'll be ready soon."

"Great," Ed called back. "Ready anytime you are."

The cowboy's hands went up. "Wait a minute. I wanna know about that caller an' the guy at the kitchen winder."

Finally! Someone willing to listen to her. Cora turned to him. "Oh, Wendell, when he called, he said he'd been watching me all evening."

Ed cleared his throat.

She was determined to have her say. "The kitchen curtains were wide open. It took me a while to get brave enough to close them."

"Ah-humm!" Ed quickly cleared his throat again, this time with more oomph. Cora looked his way.

Being out of Wendell's line of vision, Ed sliced his finger across his own neck in attempt to quiet her.

Cora disregarded his less-than-subtle hint, and leaned closer to Wendell. "The caller knew I was alone. He even knew what I was wearing." Her voice escalated. "Worst of all, he threatened Ed's life."

Wendell's eyebrows shot up as he turned to Ed. "I can't hardly believe ya ain't havin' a conniption about this. An' why ain't nobody told me of this situation?" His jowls shook in frustration. "I *am* the senior secur'ty officer around here, ya know. If I'm gonna keep this place safe, I need to know all the comin's an' goin's. My daddy an' his daddy afore him was always tellin' me—"

Not in the mood for his tired yarns, Cora interrupted him. "Ed doesn't take it seriously."

"People get prank calls all the time," Ed explained as he sat beside his wife. "They didn't get threatening until tonight. We had no reason to say anything before."

"I'm afraid of what that man might do." Cora wiped her eyes, then, looked up. "Why would anyone want to hurt us? I don't feel safe here anymore, Ed."

"We're protected by the best home security system money can buy."

"An' ya can always count on me." Wendell added.

"Still," Cora pulled on her husband's arm, "I'd feel safer with another deadbolt."

Ed nodded. "We'll have a new one installed tomorrow." He patted her hand. "Try to relax and I'll call the police. We should've done that right from the start."

"No!" she cried out as a nauseating wave engulfed her. She leaned away from her husband and pressed a hand to her pounding temple. "You can't call the police. The caller was adamant about not contacting them."

"I don't care what he said. If you want this to stop, we'll have to call his bluff."

Her stomach continued to churn. It wasn't just the caller's threats that upset her. She'd taken great pains to conceal certain things from Ed. She couldn't let him find out. Not like this.

Excitement sparked in Wendell's eyes. "I gotta get to sniffin' around afore the cops get here." He jumped to his feet and eagerly rubbed his hands together. "Finally, an honest-to-goodness mystery that me an' my buddy, Jack, can sink our choppers into. I'll dig into my whisker disguises."

Ed tossed a frown Cora's way and whispered, "Oh great. I told you we should talk about this later. Now that you've got him worked up into a frenzy, he'll want to take over."

The security guard pointed to the phone. "Could ya gimme a few minutes afore callin' the po-lice? I'd like to go on out, an' do my prelim'nary look-see."

Ed came up off the couch. "Hold your horses, Wendell," he commanded. "You were out there before. Wouldn't you have spotted something?"

"I weren't wanderin' around doin' my full search. Didn't check the winders an' such. I just looked for bodies."

"If you go prodding out there now, you could mess up any evidence."

"Looky here, I know what I'm doin'," Wendell yammered. "My daddy's Texas Ranger blood is gallopin' through my veins, an' I'm hankerin' to start my 'vestigation."

Ed stared into the Texan's eyes. "This is my property, Wendell. I don't want anyone digging around until the police are finished."

The security guard slumped back in his chair. He huffed and laced his fingers atop his round midsection. "How are me an' Jack gonna crack this here case with just leftover clues?"

Dahlia appeared at the kitchen door. "Wendell

Floyd, folks 'round here got plenty o' things that need fixin'. That handyman needs to keep his mind on his job." She motioned for him to follow. "Now, make yourself useful. I need ya to tote the coffee into the livin' room for me."

He grumbled under his breath, then obediently uprooted himself from the chair.

Dahlia returned laden with a serving tray filled with pie 'a la mode and coffee cups. She set the tray down and wiped a dribble of ice cream from her bejeweled hands.

Ed's mention of the police worried Cora. If the caller was watching, he'd see the cruiser. She grabbed her husband's arm and pleaded, "Can't we wait and call the authorities in the morning? Please? It's late, and my nerves are shot."

He rubbed the back of his neck. "Oh, Toots."

"I don't think I can take any more stress tonight." Cora dabbed her eyes as angry thunder rumbled. "Besides, are you sure the police could find anything in this storm?"

"She's got herself a point, Ed." Dahlia's voice was filled with compassion as she added, "Look how pale she is, an' she's shakin' like a leaf, too. Bless her heart."

Ed raked his fingers through his thinning hair. "We shouldn't put this off, ladies."

"Nope, Ed's right as rain," Wendell agreed. "This has to be stopped afore them crim'nals get a foothold."

A charm bracelet jangled as Dahlia crossed her arms over her ample chest. "Men. Can't y'all see the poor li'l thing's just a bundle o' nerves? Don't ya 'member what Sam said? We can't be havin' her pass out again. Now, just leave her be."

Ed gritted his teeth. "Right, but like it or not, first

thing tomorrow morning I'm calling the police. Meanwhile, I'll talk to Patrick and see what he has to say."

As he dialed their neighbor, Cora was confident Patrick would back her up about the prowler.

It was hard to believe this whole mess began with one lone secret. Now, it spiraled into death threats and a possible murder. A shiver ran down her spine. At least she had all night to think it through. Maybe her nerves would settle when she got her story straight.

3

The living room closed in on Cora as they waited for Patrick to answer the phone. Her head throbbed from the kitchen fall and the confusion that followed. The awful scene outside the window seemed so vivid at the time. Did it really happen? Goose bumps dotted her arms. Where was Patrick?

With a shrug of his shoulders, Ed finally hung up. "Sorry, Toots. Doesn't look like he's home, yet."

"Prob'ly went to check on Letitia." Wendell stroked his chin. "He does that every time we have a nasty storm."

Dahlia rubbed Cora's back. "I think ya need to lay down, girl." She turned to Ed. "You fellers get started on your snack while I help her to the bedroom. We don't want to scrape the poor little thing off the floor again."

Cora's fuzzy slippers quacked as Dahlia led her down the hall.

Once in the bedroom, Dahlia pulled down the satin comforter, and patted the king-sized mattress. "Here ya go. Get yourself up here an' rest."

Cora couldn't wait to kick the noisy slippers off. She had to be in control if Dahlia was going to take her seriously, and the mallards on her feet didn't help. "I know I've been a little emotional, but I'm not crazy." The timbre of her voice rose. "There really was someone outside the window. It had to be the caller."

"What makes ya say that? It coulda been just a neighbor walkin' through the yard."

Oh, crud. She didn't believe her. Cora squeezed her friend's arm. "Listen to me. No one...*no one* would have a reason to be sloshing around my backyard in a monsoon."

"That's what we've been tryin' to tell ya, Sugar. Nobody with a lick of sense would be out there. Ed was prob'ly spot on about ya seein' your reflection. Now ya got it all built in your mind that the caller was out there an' you're freakin' out." Dahlia looked at Cora nose-to-nose while she fluffed a pillow. "Land sake's gal, ya could worry the warts off a frog."

Cora's voice was clipped. "Well, be-that-as-it-may. Patrick phoned and said to lock my doors because there was a prowler over here. The man who called earlier said he could see me." Her whole body shook at the thought. "He said, 'You look as pretty as ever in your white pants and purple shirt,'" she lowered her voice to imitate him, 'Cor-rah!'"

"Now calm down, Sugar."

"Calm down?" She held her arms out. "That's what I was wearing. Talk about being spot on!" Cora looked sternly into Dahlia's eyes. "He threatened Ed's life and then a few minutes later, I saw him at the window. And you want me to calm down?" She grabbed her friend's wrist. "He threatened us, Dahlly. He means business, and I have to figure out what he's after before it's too late. I could be a widow this time next week."

Dahlia leaned over and patted her hand. "I understand."

How she hated to be patronized. Anger and frustration welled as her friend kept talking.

"I'm thinkin' this has to be a prank caller who's gettin' his thrills from your reaction. If ya ignore him, he'll stop callin'. I know this here's a silly question, but have ya thought of unpluggin' the phone when Ed's gone?"

"Of course I have. He knows every nasty storm reminds me of Vanessa's accident, so he always calls me if he's behind schedule." She looked away. "It was flooding. He was two hours late. What would go through your mind if your daughter died in a monsoon?"

"Sugar, he was just two blocks away at the ice cream store. If it was me, I woulda thought his fans prob'ly kept him busy." The charms on Dahlia's bracelet jingled as she hugged her friend. "Wendell Floyd still bellyaches when I do apron signin's for my fans."

Apron signings? Where did that come from? Cora looked at her and frowned. "What on earth are you talking about?"

"Well," Dahlia said, "fans are always mobbin' me when I'm on the road, an' it's the same for Ed. He's a world-class golf pro. Steady Eddie Timms is a magnet to every duffer on the planet. Ya know guys are always peltin' him with questions. They come hustlin' out like red ants from a burnin' log."

A light tapping on the bedroom door caused Cora to jump.

Ed poked his head inside. "How are we doing in here?"

"We're just havin' us a heart-to-heart. Go ahead an' eat your pie. I'll be out in a flash." Dahlia gave Cora's shoulder a squeeze. "I always admired your spunk, but ya kind of let go of it since Vannie's death.

Ya been so jumpity lately. It's no wonder ya been forgettin' stuff, an' seein' things. I'd like to have my strong an' confident friend back again." She patted the pillow. "Why don't ya lay back, an' get some rest? You'll feel better once the storm passes." Then Dahlia took Cora's hand. "How 'bout we pray before I go back to check on the men?"

Cora's stomach knotted. Dahlia meant well, however prayers hadn't given her any noticeable relief during the past two years. What made anyone think it would help now?

Dahlia prayed for calmness to return.

Cora wasn't looking for calmness, although she wouldn't turn it down. She wanted clear-cut answers mixed with a healthy dose of validation.

"An' please, dear Lord, give Cora clarity of mind as she…"

Clarity of mind? Was her best friend implying she had an emotional breakdown? Or worse, that she was lying? Either way, Dahlia didn't have faith in her story. Cora's heart broke. She needed someone to believe her. Wendell-the-wonder-sleuth from Sweet Pickle, Texas was her only ally. The problem was no one ever took the correspondence-trained detective seriously, either. Her self-esteem took a nosedive. So much for calmness.

"Amen." Dahlia's quick hug brought Cora back to the present. "Just rest an' don't give another thought to those men-folk, I'll take care of 'em." She turned off the light. "I'll put your pie in the fridge, too. Be sure an' tell me what ya think, because it's a new recipe I form'lated for my next cookbook. Give me a holler if ya need anything, ya hear?"

Cora swallowed the knot in her throat. "Thanks, Dahlly."

With that, Dahlia closed the door.

Exhausted, Cora rested her head on the down-filled pillow and listened as raindrops pelted the bedroom window. Why didn't Ed and Dahlia believe her? They were the people closest to her. She rolled over and wiped the tears that trickled down her cheek. The caller must be someone from her past, but who? She pressed her eyes tight as her mind rehashed bits and pieces of that last phone conversation. There was the envelope he mentioned. That didn't ring any bells. It must hold something precious or he wouldn't threaten Ed's life over it. If she didn't give it to him, would he really expose her secret like he promised?

She groaned. Had Ed contacted Patrick, yet? He was her only proof of a prowler. A low rumble of thunder announced another wave of violent weather. Her problems were like the relentless monsoons. "I can't handle this, God."

Cora turned on the bedside lamp, plucked a tissue from the night stand and blew her nose. As she reached for another tissue, her eyes settled on the family portrait taken years ago when Vanessa was still at home and life was good. Their youthful images drew her into a rush of bittersweet memories. They were so happy, then. Why couldn't things have stayed that way?

She was drawn to Ed's handsome features, which reflected strength and character. His healthy appearance and athletic physique were evidence of the many hours spent on the golf course. It had been so easy to fall in love with him at first sight. Cora dabbed her eyes. How long had it been since they'd actually said, 'I love you'?

Between the PGA tour and running his own golf

course in Saguaro Valley, Ed was kept away from home, leaving her alone. Oh, if she had a nickel for every frozen dinner eaten with only reruns of the Andy Griffith Show for company. And the plethora of jigsaw puzzles she worked on until her eyes crossed. In spite of this, their marriage was based on trust in God and mutual respect and remained intact. Cora twisted her platinum wedding band and squeezed her eyes shut. Trust in God and mutual respect. The thought pricked her conscience.

Her secret defied both attributes, and she sensed Ed struggled with their crumbling marriage, too. There was nothing she could do about it. At least, not yet.

Cora wiped the tears, and looked back to the photo and the diminutive young lady standing behind Ed. She kissed her fingers and touched her daughter's likeness. Vanessa's death had strained their marriage to the point that it might never recover. Ed couldn't understand the pain and emptiness that continued to haunt her. She tenderly hugged the picture before returning it to the drawer. How she longed to hold her daughter close once more.

Again, thunder ripped through the atmosphere. The lamp flickered, drawing attention to the Bible beneath it. The Holy Book beckoned her to open its well-worn pages. For as long as she could remember, scripture had always offered hope and reassurance. Since the loss of their daughter, Cora's mind could no longer grasp its promises.

Sunday after Sunday, she and Ed returned to the same pew where they had once worshipped with Vanessa. Of course it was difficult, but Vannie used to sit there and Cora couldn't bear to be anywhere else.

Publicly, she sang hymns and kept up a spiritual

facade in spite of her grief. In private she couldn't talk to God. The words were no longer there. A void now existed where God's peace had once flourished. Life was meaningless. She was alone and it scared her.

The closeness she and her daughter shared was painful to remember. They couldn't have their cozy chats over coffee or laugh about the kids' antics. In spite of all that pain, she was still thankful for the precious memories. To let go would be a betrayal. The lingering grief threatened to smother her, especially after their son-in-law, James, remarried less than a year after Van's death. Cora gritted her teeth. She was trying her best not to be prickly about Jocelyn, but a father of three teenagers had no business with a twenty-four-year-old flirt.

The oft-quoted verse Romans 8:28 came to mind. *All things work together for good to them that love the Lord.*

She frowned. "How could anything good come from that tragedy, God? Why would You take Van when she had those beautiful children to raise? Is it good for them to be brought up by a self-centered girl?" She wailed. "What about me? I don't even get to see my grandchildren since Jocelyn had them move so far away."

Cora pursed her lips. Lashing out at God wouldn't change the situation. Was He even listening?

At that instant, lightning and thunder collided and shook the room. A nudge from God? A tingle coursed down her spine and brought on an intense shudder. She closed her eyes, determined to regain composure. Maybe getting ready for bed would get her mind off things. It was worth a try. She made her way to the adjoining bathroom.

Cool water on her flushed cheeks did little to help.

Secrets. Death threats. How did her life sink to this level? She took a deep breath, and glanced into the mirror at her own image, now the reflection of a stranger. "Who are you, Cora?" Her secret was bound to come out. Then what would happen?

She patted her face dry and looked into the mirror. Her blue-gray eyes were puffy from tears and fatigue. Faint worry lines on her paled complexion had become more obvious since the harassing calls began a few weeks ago. Well, a thick layer of Velvety Dew moisturizer would help with damage control.

Cora reached for the miracle cream, and braved another look at herself. She sucked in her cheeks and let them free fall back into place. A frustrated sigh escaped as she considered smashing the mirror with the jar.

She hurried to her bed and turned the light out as the brewing storm erupted full force. A tremendous burst of light exploded in the dark heavens as rain once again pelted the windows. Cora pulled the comforter over her head. Lousy monsoons.

In spite of her weary state of mind, she continued to dwell on the random pieces to the puzzle. Maybe once the fog lifted she could get more of the fragments to fit.

Minutes ticked by, and drowsiness drew her into a restless sleep. The jangling telephone startled her into consciousness. Cora was shaken and disoriented from being awakened so abruptly. Again, the phone by the bed vibrated with its harsh ring. Why didn't Ed answer it? She reached over and turned the ringer off.

Thoughts of the last call snaked into her confused mind. The crackling interference made his raspy voice barely audible, still, it was clear he knew her secret.

Her throat tightened as she relived the phone call. Her heart quickened, and she struggled to breathe as the gravity of the situation emerged. Who was this man from her past? How could he know about the secret? Only one other person knew, but he'd never tell.

Somehow this stalker could see her and even knew when she was alone. Was he looking in the windows or did he have cameras hidden? Cora shivered at the thought of television shows about voyeuristic perverts. She pulled the blanket tight under her chin, her eyes darting from side to side. Could he see her now?

Cora looked at the ceiling for telltale signs of cameras. Aha! Light fixtures. It couldn't be all that hard for her to take them down and check. Then again, she could see herself dangling from the chandelier, her legs violently thrashing about as electrical currents jolted through her body. No, no, no. The handyman was paid to do stuff like that.

Lightning flashed. The caller's menacing remark echoed in her ears. "Thought you'd get away with it, didn't you? After all those years and what you put me through, did you really think you'd never hear from me again?"

All those years? What on earth had she done to the man? Cora shook her head. Why couldn't she recall doing something so offensive that this guy would take years to track her down? The only reasonable explanation was that it had to do with her term as county treasurer. She couldn't think of any major altercations or scandals during that time.

How did the woman caller fit into the picture? Cora rubbed her temples as she groped for answers. Had she done some utterly despicable deed to her, too?

Both times she called, her voice sounded shaky and frightened as she delivered her perplexing message.

The man's phone call earlier tonight was just as cryptic. He wanted her to ask Ed about his very wicked slice—if he made it home. Then came his final ultimatum. "Get me that envelope in twenty-four hours, or I'll get Ed. You'll be hearing from me."

That didn't give her much time. How could she convince her doubting husband to help her look for the envelope?

Cora struggled to recall more information to plead her case. What about the manila packet? It had a red seal on it. That was probably a good thing to remember. The man insisted Ed put it in their safe. Why would he hide a stranger's personal belongings in there without telling her? Maybe he did tell her at the time. But that was so many years ago.

A thought hit her between the eyes. Wait a minute. The caller wouldn't have asked a mere *stranger* to put something in the safe for him. He had to know Ed. Could her husband have anything to do with this mess? However, if they knew each other, why wouldn't he just go to Ed and get his stupid envelope back? Why involve her unless...Ed had a reason not to give it back.

None of this made sense. Surely Ed couldn't be a part of it. There *had* to be more pieces to the puzzle she'd either forgotten or hadn't found yet. All the random pieces she had still didn't fit. *Come on, Cora, you're a puzzle worker. Get that border together.*

Another sickening notion hit her. The caller knew what she was keeping from Ed, and if Ed *was* involved, he would be aware of it, too. Icy fear twisted her heart. The calls only came when he wasn't home. If Ed wanted her out of his way, he could've orchestrated this whole thing.

Surely not. She hid her face in her hands. "Where are you, God?"

Disturbing thoughts circled in her mind until Ed came into the bedroom. A few minutes later, he crawled into bed and called to her in a soft voice. "Toots, are you awake?"

Cora's heart pounded as she feigned sleep. She was mentally and physically drained, and besides, there was nothing left to say, or do, at least for tonight.

The grandfather clock chimed eleven times. Eventually, Ed ceased to toss and turn and fell into a deep sleep. Hmmm. The sleep of the innocent? Maybe he wasn't involved. She'd just have to go on blind faith.

However, Cora's mind refused to shut down. A compendium of clues turned over in her mind. Into the wee hours of the morning, she continued to unravel the terrifying scene at the kitchen sink. Patrick called about a prowler, she made coffee, and locked the windows. That's when a thump on the patio grabbed her attention, and her eyes caught movement. Two hooded men were out there. The scuffle started.

She rolled over in bed, closed her eyes, and willed herself to see their faces. If only she could remember one feature, it would help.

Cora sat up. That's it. Before the one man fell, there was a flicker of light under his hood. He must've worn glasses.

She fell back onto her pillow. Big deal. She lived in a retirement complex. Who didn't wear glasses? Everyone wore hooded jackets during a monsoon, including the three men in her house tonight. Wendell lived for recognition. If he was involved, his daddy and his daddy afore him would spin in their graves. And Sam? Well, he was just too old and wobbly. Then there was Ed. He was two hours late. Blind faith, girl, blind faith.

Then something else nagged at her. Cora's stomach clenched as she strained to remember what her mind suppressed. Lightning lit the room. Then, it came to her. The hooded man on the patio held something. But what was it?

4

The aroma of their housekeeper's freshly brewed coffee filled the air and stirred Cora from a fitful sleep. Burning eyes and a desert-dry mouth gave her the first clue she'd blubbered too much the night before. She pried her eyelids open to see the glowing numbers on the digital clock and moaned. Eight-fifteen.

Cora threw the covers back, and dangled her feet over the side of the bed. Like it or not, it was way past time to get up. Ed was probably on his second bear claw by now.

Oh no. He was going to call the police this morning. She took a deep breath, and dreaded the thought of facing them. What could she tell them, anyway? Shadows tiptoed around the backyard…in the middle of a torrential storm…one had something in his hand. Of course, there was her big reveal, one wore glasses. Whoop-de-doo. In the clarity of daylight, her account of the events seemed farfetched. Even to her. Maybe Patrick was home this morning and would confirm her prowler story.

Cora yawned, reached for her silky robe, and searched for her scuffs with her foot. *Quack!* The sound made her jump. She kicked the duck slippers aside and trudged to the bathroom.

So many thoughts bombarded her mind. She didn't want the police to pry, but craved protection from a possible murderer. So, like it or not, more of her story had to be disclosed. Within reason, of course.

They'd have to know about the menacing phone calls and the caller's intent to harm Ed if she didn't hand over the envelope. Which brought up last night's unanswered questions. Why didn't he fork over that envelope to the caller? What made it so important? Money? Ed wasn't a materialistic person. It must be information. Was the caller blackmailing *him*?

She rinsed her soapy hands and dried them. No, the man specifically said he tracked *her* down. What did he call her? An accessory after the fact? Everything he said seemed to point back to her days as county treasurer.

Cora paced the bathroom floor. Surely she'd remember being involved in some misappropriation of funds. Wait! The caller said accessory *after* the fact. That means *he* stole money, not her. Maybe she inadvertently helped cover it up. That wouldn't be good, either. The manila envelope must hold some sort of evidence.

However, if the caller gave the evidence to Ed to hide, then Ed had protected her all along. Was he aware of the contents? If so, that meant he was the accessory to the accessory after the fact. Well, no need to mention any of *that* to the police. At least not yet.

If that wasn't stressful enough, she still had to tell Ed about her secret before someone else did. Obviously waiting for the right time was the wrong thing to do.

She glanced at her watch and thought of a million other places she'd rather be, at the bottom of a well, in front of a firing squad, even being the main attraction at the proctologist's office was more inviting.

Cora ran a comb through her hair and looked into the mirror. With so much tension in her life, she imagined a whole chorus line of wrinkles just waiting to make their debut. She smoothed an extra dab of Velvety Dew moisturizer on her face.

The enticing smell of French Roasted broke into her thoughts. A cup of coffee might clear out the cobwebs. She hoped Lupe made it good and strong.

A quick search for her scuffs was fruitless. She'd have to stick with the fowl footwear, which accessorized her peignoir so elegantly. Cora quacked down the hall, greeted the housekeeper and grabbed a mug of coffee. Then, she headed for Ed's home office. Cora stopped and poked her head around the corner when she heard Ed speak on the phone. She leaned in closer. What's a little eavesdropping between spouses?

Ed stood at the office window and scanned his adjacent golf course. "I'm glad you caught that on your calendar, Pastor Luke. That's no problem. We'll set up another golf date soon. I'd better let you go for now, the police should be here any time." He replaced the receiver and turned to Cora. With a warm smile he pulled her into his arms. "Morning, Toots. Feeling better?"

Cora's voice quivered. "Not really." She abruptly brushed aside Ed's attempts at being cheerful. "Why didn't you get me up before you called the police? And why did you tell the preacher? I don't want to end up as a sermon illustration."

"You're always up by seven. I figured you were getting dressed. Besides, you knew I was going to call them first thing this morning." He tossed his ink pen on the desk. "I tell Pastor Luke everything that's going on so he knows how to pray for us." He pulled her close. "And even if we are a part of his sermon, he won't use our names."

Cora's slippers protested as she stomped back to the bedroom. *Quack...quack...quack!*

"Hey Toots," Ed called. "You want a bear claw, or some duck chow with your coffee?"

"Arrrggh!" she growled and gave one final stomp. *Quack!* "Men." Time to slather on another layer of Velvety Dew.

"Just trying to help," he called after her.

❧❦

Vibrations rattled the window when Cora slammed the bedroom door.

Ed laughed and shook his head as he sat at the desk. "She'll get over it."

Lupe came to the office. "*Señor* Timms, the handyman is here."

A silver-haired fellow with a clipboard stood behind her. Ed invited him inside. "Good morning. I heard our former handyman retired. Nice to meet you."

"The name's Jack Thurston. Been here two weeks and I'm still finding my way around. Wendell McGibbons has been a big help teaching me who's who. He seems to know everybody." Jack's eyes widened as he shifted the clipboard to his left hand. "Hey! You're Steady Eddie Timms, the famous golf guy. I've seen you on those sports drink commercials." He shook Ed's hand. "The wife's name is Nora, right?"

"Well, you're close. It's Cora."

The handyman looked at his clipboard. "Oh, yeah, so it is. Sorry, I'm really bad with names. Wendell said she wanted new locks installed. From what I can tell, your security system has all the bells and whistles. Are you sure you need new locks?"

Ed nodded. "My wife's been a little edgy lately and thinks she'll feel safer. Could you come back later today to add deadbolts and chains to the doors?"

"Sure. I'll go buy them this morning." He scribbled on his work order. "Wendell told me about the strange calls your wife's been getting and how she thinks someone was killed. Think about it, murder in a gated community. A person just doesn't feel safe anymore."

"I'm not sure what she saw, but we didn't find a body. I doubt it was a murder."

"If there's anything else I can do, be sure and let me know."

"Now that you mention it, there is one way you can help. While you and Wendell are sleuthing around, keep a tight rein on him," Ed suggested. "Don't let him go overboard and turn my yard into an excavation site, especially before the police get here."

"I know what you mean." A grin crept across Jack's deeply creased face. "Wendell always wants to be the first rattler out of the box. He's determined to solve this before the police. It sure is a puzzling situation, though." He lifted his clipboard and shook it. "If we could just get our hands on that rat."

Ed sighed. "I don't want you and Wendell going too far with this and get hurt. It's better to let the authorities handle any dangerous situations."

"Right. Well, I'll try to get the locks in this afternoon. At least that'll be a step in the right direction." Jack glanced around the office. "Nice den. Anything else you need repaired while I'm here?"

A soft knock sounded at the partially opened office door.

Jack stepped aside and Ed motioned for the cleaning woman to enter.

Lupe's voice trembled and her deep brown eyes flashed in alarm. "*Señor* Timms, the *policía* just drove up." Her hands shook as she pushed back a strand of dark hair and secured it with a tortoiseshell comb. "*Señora* needs me. You let them in, *sí*?"

"Sure, Lupe. I'll be right there." Ed's heart went out to the anxious woman. Cora's ordeal was taking a toll on her, too. He walked Jack to the side door, and offered a handshake. "Thanks again."

Jack turned to leave. "If I don't get out of here, my van's going to be blocked in the driveway. Give me a jingle if you need any more help." The worker chuckled as he turned to leave. "I'll do what I can with Wendell, but no promises."

જ⊷⚬⊷

Her stomach churned at the thought of facing the police. Cora worried she'd inadvertently reveal too much information. She took a deep breath, and then joined Ed in the living room.

The older policeman seemed especially interested in the cabinet filled with Limoges china, Waterford crystal, and polished silver.

His partner squinted as he scrutinized the paintings, prints, and sculptures that graced the residence. "I'm impressed. You've got quite a collection here, Mr. Timms." The younger man removed his hat, and walked to a round table in the corner of the room. "What have we here?" He glanced at the bookshelf where several boxed puzzles were stacked.

Cora stepped forward. "Those are mine. Puzzles help me relax when I'm alone." She frowned. Badge or no badge, he'd better keep his grubby paws off the one in progress.

Ed threw his wife a reassuring smile and took her hand. "Honey, these are Officers Reed and Davis. Officers, my beautiful wife, Cora."

Reed, the rookie cop, looked up from the puzzle. His mouth twisted into a smirk as he flipped a puzzle piece onto the table and swaggered over to his partner.

Cora eased into a chair. So he was the bad cop in their little good cop/bad cop routine. She frowned as a warning echoed in her mind. *Be careful what you say...be careful what you say.*

5

A numb sensation engulfed Cora. This Reed fellow was tall and good-looking, still his smirk gave her the willies. She straightened her shoulders. If Officer Stud Muffin thought his attitude gave him power and dominance, he had another think coming. She looked up as he fixed his steely gaze on her. Cora swallowed. Well, maybe it did give him an edge.

Officer Reed's expression grew dark as Lupe entered the living room. The poor woman took one glance at him and set the serving tray on the nearby table. She handed a cup of coffee to Cora and quickly turned to leave.

Ed placed his hand on Lupe's shoulder. "Wait a minute, Lupe."

The woman stiffened, and her eyes widened.

"This is our housekeeper. Lupe and her husband, Mateo Santalis, are under contract for the Saguaro Valley complex. They go out of their way to make sure things are spic-and-span around here."

A double chin formed as Lupe bowed her head and mumbled, "¡Hola!" She excused herself and retreated to the adjacent kitchen.

Cora watched the housekeeper leave. "You'll have to excuse our Lupe. She's timid around strangers, especially when she doesn't understand what's going on."

With a slight nod of acknowledgment, Reed wrote

in his notebook.

Davis, the older of the two policemen, appeared to be close to retirement age. His goatee, and what was left of his dark hair, were heavily streaked with gray. He adjusted his reading glasses and nodded to his partner. "Officer Reed is going to scout around outside while I ask you a few questions, Mrs. Timms." He paused and clicked his ballpoint in anticipation of her answers. "Your husband tells us you saw a prowler and a possible homicide last night."

"That's right." She sighed and clutched her coffee cup tighter as the snotty-hottie cop cocked his hat and went out the front door.

Officer Davis's voice was calm. "Why don't you go ahead and tell me what happened from the beginning, ma'am?"

The strain of a sleepless night left Cora an emotional blob. She dabbed her eyes and sniffed into her napkin. "There's so much on my mind, it's hard to know where to start."

"Have a seat, Officer Davis." Ed cleared his throat. "This could take a while."

"Thank you. I think I will." The older cop pulled out a straight-backed chair, and bumped the puzzle table.

Cora grimaced as a rainfall of pictured fragments fell to the floor. The badged old billy goat didn't even notice. Humph, some detective. And this klutz was going to solve the murder? She hid her face behind the cup and tensed as the cop cleared his throat and looked in her direction.

"Mrs. Timms?"

Cora peeked over the rim of her security cup. She might as well get this over with so he'd leave. She lowered her coffee. "It all started with the harassing phone calls."

"Wait, ma'am. I thought we were called here for a prowler and a possible murder."

"That's half right." Ed spoke on her behalf. "She saw two people on our patio last night."

She glared at Ed. "And, the other half is, I think one of them was killed. It all started with those crazy phone calls."

"Did anyone else witness these phone calls?"

"No." Her face warmed. "They only come when I'm alone."

The corner of Davis's mouth twisted slightly. "Hmm. Let me see if I have this right. What you're saying, Mrs. Timms, is you think the caller and the prowler are connected in some way?"

"Yes, of course. He said he was watching me."

"Um, he was watching you over the phone?"

Cora arched her brow. Where'd he go to school? Keystone Kop Kollege? "More than likely he looked in the window. Doesn't that make sense?" She shifted in her seat and shrugged. "It makes perfect sense to me. Our neighbor, Patrick Hyde, saw a prowler, too. It was during the storm, and he called to warn me."

"What about this Patrick Hyde? Will he confirm your story?"

"I've been trying to call him, officer," Ed commented. "He doesn't answer. Pat often takes little road trips at the drop of a hat."

"Do you have any idea who this window peeper might be?"

Cora frowned. "Do I have any idea who…uh, no. Well, he says I know him, but I don't recognize his voice." Suddenly, incoherent phrases erupted with pent-up frustration. "Look, he tracked me down, because I did something to him. I can't remember him, or what I could've done. He saw my white slacks and purple blouse. Oh, and there was a wicked slice involved."

"Just a minute, Mrs. Timms. Let me catch up." Davis's pen scrawled across the notebook as he made a feeble attempt to record her statements. "Purple blouse, wick-ed sli-i-ice."

Cora ignored him and reached for her coffee. The floodgates were open, and there was no stopping it. "Sometimes it's a woman. I'm sure I don't know him. Oh, and the envelope has a red seal. I saw something in his hand." Her voice strained. "He even knows about my…" Shut up, Cora! Fortunately, her verbal diarrhea stopped before she revealed too much. Yipes. Did she mention the envelope? The coffee cup wobbled as she returned it to the table. "This is all so confusing."

The questioning wasn't going well. It wasn't going well, at all. There was a train on the horizon, and she was tied to the rails. She just *had* to be more discreet. Focus, Cora, focus. It wasn't time for Ed to know about her secret, and timing was everything. For now, it was nobody's business but hers. She twisted her wedding band and licked her dry lips. Taking a cleansing breath, she willed herself to get a grip on her runaway emotions.

The police officer stopped writing when Cora's words became disconnected. He scratched his chin and looked at Ed with an odd grin. "Can you shed any light on this?"

"Cora says the calls come when nobody else is here. She said they turned threatening last night. Then, she saw shadows outside the kitchen window after the neighbor called. I thought maybe it might be her reflection, or the neighbor's cat."

"I see."

Cora gritted her teeth. Would he ever stop with his stupid cat theory? She reached for her coffee, again. "It was more than shadows, Edward. I saw real, live people. Not my reflection, and *certainly* not Smudge." She lowered the cup to the table.

Ed patted her knee. "Yes, Toots."

This man was really pushing her buttons. She tried to regain a smidgen of dignity, and pushed his hand away with a disgruntled sniff. If she didn't know him better, she'd think he *was* involved in this whole mix-up.

He turned to the officer and continued. "Where was I? Oh yes, when I came home, Cora was out cold on the kitchen floor."

The officer flipped to a fresh page in his notebook. "Mr. Timms, why didn't you call us right away?"

Ed put a supportive hand on Cora's shoulder. "Like I said, she was in a state of shock when she came to. The constant storms we've had lately added to her stress, so the doctor said to keep her calm."

"Now, wait a minute," said the officer. "Where'd the doctor come from?"

"Next door."

"And, why didn't you call us?"

"Cora needed a doctor. She was weak and upset. All things considered, I thought it would be better to let her rest and talk to you this morning."

"I understand, but next time, don't put it off. Even if your wife is upset, you should call us, so we can check the area," he admonished. "Of course, the storm would have hampered our efforts, however, it's very important that we get every trace of evidence as soon as possible." The officer took a deep breath. "Could the calls just be a childish prank?"

Cora came up for air. "Look, I'm getting calls and it's not a child's voice. They're scaring me to death. I'm living this nightmare every minute of every day."

The officer's reply was monotone. "Yes, ma'am." He straightened his back. "Now these phone calls, can you tell me if you heard any background noise that might help pinpoint his location?"

"Uh, I wasn't listening for background noises. Besides, last night the phone line crackled with all the lightning and thunder." She shifted in her seat as Lupe milled around in the kitchen, and listened to every word. "I-I had my mind on what they were saying."

"Right. During any of these phone calls, did you happen to notice anything about the voice that sounded familiar? An accent, maybe?"

Cora searched the officer's face. Was that another hint of skepticism in his tone? "I told you there are *two* callers. That should be in your notes, by the way. One man, one woman."

"What do they sound like?"

"What do they sound like? Well, the man calls most of the time and his voice is gravely and raspy. It sounds a little forced. Do you think he's trying to disguise it?"

The monotone voice returned. "That would be my guess, ma'am."

"The woman sounded," she leaned over to whisper, "Hispanic." She cleared her throat. "But I didn't recognize it." She watched Lupe hurry from the kitchen.

"How old would you guess the man to be?"

"I don't know. I told you he disguised his voice, but he's not a kid." Before Officer Davis could ask, she added, "The woman has a clear, younger-sounding voice."

"Do you have caller ID?"

Ed muttered, "No, but it's about time we got it."

The officer made a few additional notes. "What about the threats the caller made?"

"He insisted I have something of his, and if I don't give it to him, he'll get Ed."

"That's where the envelope comes in."

She gasped. Oh no, he *did* catch that. "Yes." She bit her lower lip and looked at her hands. "I assure you, Officer Davis, I don't have a clue as to what that man is talking about. He also said something curious. He said that Ed was working on his wicked slice. I'm not sure what golf has to do with anything."

Davis turned to Ed. "What do you know about the wicked slice?"

He shrugged, unable to keep eye contact with Davis. "A slice is just a term golfers use. But I was at Sugar Dips getting ice cream, not giving lessons."

She'd known Ed for nearly forty years, and he was holding something back. Cora's eyes narrowed. What was it?

The cop rubbed the back of his neck. "Anything else either of you need to tell me?"

Cora piped up. "We had a flat tire—tell him about the flat tire, Ed." Without a second breath, she added, "They were new tires. Don't you think it's strange, Officer? A brand new tire flat already?"

"For Pete's sake," Ed replied. "We can't prove anything. It's probably just a coincidence. I could've run over a nail."

Davis sniffed. "Let's go ahead and make arrangements to tap your phone lines."

Her secret. "No." Cora's stomach churned. Her anxiety intensified. "I don't want that." Ed stared at his wife. "Why not? It'll help catch these people. We all want them caught, don't we?"

She paused. "Of course we do, but tapping is an invasion of privacy." Oooh, that sounded *so* lame. "I don't want someone listening in on my private conversations. Some things are personal."

Ed threw his hands up in a gesture of frustration. "We can't live like this. You're not thinking it through. If all this is true, these people are dangerous." He looked directly into her eyes. "You have me completely stumped. Where's your logic, Cora?"

She looked away. There was nothing she could say. Maybe she'd just plead the fifth or claim insanity. Let them figure it out.

Davis scratched his head and leafed through his notes. "We're not making any progress. Why don't we go over this once more? Slowly." He paused. "What about the prowler? Even though this will be difficult, we need to go to the kitchen. You can show me where you stood. Officer Reed will be outside the window, then you can tell me how far away the guy was."

They followed Davis to the kitchen and Cora stood at the sink. "First, Patrick called to warn me. I was right here making coffee. That's when I saw two men fighting on our patio, and I reached up to put the window down."

The officer asked, "Exactly where were they standing?" He called through the open window for his partner to move accordingly. "Is this right, Mrs. Timms?"

"Maybe back a few steps." She watched as snotty-hottie Reed followed directions.

"Stop. Right there."

"Great. Now close your eyes and think about the scene for a moment. I know it was dark and rainy, but did you see what they were wearing?"

Cora shut her eyes to recall the incident. "I remember they wore dark hoods, and there was something else." She snapped her fingers. "I know what it was. One wore glasses."

"OK, hoods and glasses." He jotted it down. "Now we're cookin'. What else? Did he have anything in his hand like maybe an umbrel—"

"Wait!" She blurted. "That's it."

"Breakthrough," Ed shouted. "He had an umbrella."

Cora stomped her foot. "No, no, no. Not an umbrella. It was a knife. I remember, now. He had a knife in his hand."

"A knife?" Davis questioned. "Are you sure that's what it was? Remember it was dark and stormy. An umbrella would make more sense."

"Would you forget the umbrella? I'm very sure. After the man with the glasses fell down, the knife reflected in the lightning." She lifted her hand to mimic the figure's pose. "He held it like this." She squeezed her eyes shut and shuddered. "He *did* kill him."

As Davis recorded her statement, Ed spoke up. "Why didn't you say anything about the knife last night?"

"I didn't remember it until just now." She felt her face warm. "In my defense, I did tell you I thought the man was killed."

"Wendell didn't find a body out there, Toots. Dead

bodies don't have a habit of walking away from the scene."

The officer stepped closer. "You didn't recall seeing a knife right after it happened?"

She fidgeted and rubbed the back of her head. "I was out cold. That probably has something to do with my faulty memory. I knew he was holding an object, only I couldn't picture it until now."

Davis scratched his ear and sniffed. He returned Ed's glance.

Cora caught their subtle reaction and grew frustrated. "*You* believe me, don't you Ed?"

He offered a non-committal shrug. "I'm really trying, but a murder? Here? In our quiet community?"

A lump formed in her throat. Her own husband didn't believe her.

"Ma'am?" The policeman lightly touched her shoulder. "I'm sorry to push you so hard, however, knowing exact details can make all the difference in a case. Is there anything else?" He looked at her. "Anything at all?"

Cora lowered her eyes and gave an anxious little cough. A tense silence filled the room. Her nervous hesitation was only for a moment. Did Davis notice?

"What more could you possibly need?" Cora carefully ticked the facts off on her fingers. "A man watches me, knows when I'm alone, and even what I wear. He threatened Ed. Patrick warned me about a prowler. Two men were outside my window. One had a knife. The other fell." She drew a deep breath. "Isn't that enough?" A rush of unexpected tears surfaced. She took Ed's handkerchief and wiped her eyes.

The officer thanked Cora for her time. "If you think of anything else, be sure to call right away." He motioned for Ed to follow him outdoors. "Let's check on Reed's investigation."

Coffee sloshed onto the counter as Cora nervously poured another cup. She stood at the sink and wondered where Lupe went.

The three men's voices reached Cora through the open kitchen window. She leaned closer.

Davis spoke. "I'm not surprised Reed didn't find evidence. If there had been tracks, they would've been destroyed, thanks to last night's rain. So that's about it, unless you have something else to tell us, Mr. Timms."

Ed cleared his throat. "About that flat tire I had."

Aha! She knew he was hiding something. By now, Cora's nose was all but pressed to the screen.

"What's so unusual about that?" Reed asked.

Davis replied, "You gave me the impression you thought it was a nail."

"Actually, the tire was slashed."

"Any reason you didn't mention this earlier?" the older officer asked.

"Wasn't trying to hide it. I wanted to wait until we were alone to fill you in, so it wouldn't worry my wife any more than necessary," Ed commented. "It's a good thing, too, since she's sure a man with a knife was out here. Then, with that wicked slice comment he made."

"Let's go check it out," Reed suggested. The men followed Ed into the garage.

Cora nearly choked on her coffee when she heard Ed's account. "The tire was slashed?" she whispered. Her hands went to her mouth as she recalled the hooded figure holding the knife. What else had Ed kept from her? Was it really to spare her needless worry? She left her cup on the counter, and hurried to the side door so she wouldn't miss a word.

She eased the door open just wide enough to get the lowdown, and watched as the three men studied the tire in Ed's trunk.

"It's been cut all right," Officer Reed said. "You say this happened at Sugar Dips?"

Ed nodded. "George Shipley and Roger Clark were talking. I was curious since I fired George a few weeks ago and Roger took his place. George rushed out when I went to their table. I hate to think that my damaged relationship with him was the catalyst for this vandalism."

Davis looked up from the ruined tire. "We'll check Shipley out. There's not a whole lot we can do, except maybe add another patrol car in the neighborhood. Since this is a gated community with a security guard, that hardly seems necessary."

"Wendell McGibbons for protection?" Ed rubbed the back of his neck. "That's it?"

"Is there a problem, sir?"

Cora didn't want to miss anything, so she opened the door a hair wider.

"Not really." Ed replied. "Wendell's a nice person and all, but considering his age, I think he was hired mostly for window dressing and not so much for security. Aren't you going to talk to the neighbors?"

Officer Reed answered. "I've already done that. Nobody noticed anything unusual happening last night. Probably because of the storm."

"What about Patrick Hyde, across the street? He saw something."

"I tried his house, but no one came to the door."

"Come to think of it, Wendell told me Pat was going to visit his lady friend sometime this week. He sure picked a great time to up and leave."

"Truth is," Davis said, "our hands are tied until the perpetrator gives us more to go on. We need substantial evidence." He pushed the front of his hat up with the end of his pen. "We have no actual suspects, no body, no knife, no blood. Sorry."

"Me, too." Ed's brow furrowed. "In the meantime, if my wife is right, we could be in danger, couldn't we?"

Reed piped up. "That's possible, sir. In all likelihood it's fear run amuck."

"I've tried not to dwell on my own nagging suspicions, and you've just filled me with more doubt." Ed slammed the trunk lid.

"Give us time to check it out from all angles." Davis closed his notebook. "We'll get back with you, later."

Ed frowned and rubbed his chin. "Let me give you a little background information. Cora's been withdrawn since our daughter died. She resigned as county treasurer. Then our former son-in-law quickly remarried and moved our grandkids to Vegas. She never complained about being alone, until the phone calls began. Now, she's downright paranoid."

Davis pulled his notebook out again and licked his forefinger. He flipped a few pages to read a previous entry and then looked up. "You know, Mr. Timms, your wife was so fearful of a prowler, her paranoia gave way to hysteria."

Ed released a deep sigh. "I'm worried about her, Officer Davis." He shook his head. "She's never behaved or talked so erratically."

This was ridiculous. It was all she could do to stay quiet behind the door. Why didn't Ed defend her?

Reed spoke up. "Is she in danger of hurting

herself?"

"What? We're not on a suicide watch, if that's what you mean."

A surge of exasperation filled Cora. She clenched her fist. The once solid ground of her life was now quicksand, and she felt herself sink deeper into despair. Did Ed know what she'd been hiding from him? Was he trying to get rid of her, or drive her to the loony bin? The cops weren't any help, either. She was the victim. They made it sound like she was a raving lunatic who needed to have her belts and shoelaces taken away.

Davis nodded to his partner. "I think we'll have another look on the patio before we leave." He shook Ed's hand. "Thanks for your time, sir."

Cora closed the door quietly and scurried back to the kitchen. She grabbed a dishtowel and innocently turned when Ed called her name.

"Hey, Toots. The officers are done with the questioning. That wasn't so bad, was it? They're going to check the patio for a few minutes, so don't let them spook you." He kissed her forehead. "I'll be at Wheels and Deals to get a new tire. Look for me in a couple hours."

"Thanks for the heads-up. See ya later." Cora waited until Ed left and then rushed to the kitchen window. No way would she miss what the cops had to say.

She heard Officer Reed complain to his partner. "If she didn't want us to help, then why did they bother to call us in the first place?"

"To be completely honest," Davis added, "I have a gut feeling she's hiding something. She had all the classic signs, like hedging questions, little eye contact, and repeating things."

Cora leaned in closer to hear Reed's reply.

"I noticed that, too. She kept clenching her teeth and fidgeting."

"She got really upset about putting a tracer on the phone. Talk about melodramatic."

"And what about this Hyde character? Why would he suddenly decide to go on a trip in the middle of a monsoon with a prowler on the premises? Doesn't add up, does it?"

"No, it doesn't. Hey, Reed, I just had a thought. What if Hyde *didn't* call? After all, we only have her word for that. He could've been out of town the whole time. Suppose she did all this for attention?"

The smug young Reed laughed. "Oh yeah, the ol' phantom stalker ploy. Come on, let's get back to work."

Phantom stalker? Cora fumed at their condescending remarks, and watched the officers leave. The phone rang. She gritted her teeth and turned to answered it. "Hello?"

It was a moment before the thick accent was heard. "You make big mistake, *Señora!* You had warning. You talk to *policía* and now you will wish you were not born."

Cora heard a click. Then silence.

6

Events of the morning left Cora discouraged and miffed at the cops' assumption of her mental decline. If Ed knew about the last phone call, he'd have a phone tap installed immediately. No way. Better to ignore the whole thing.

Since Ed returned from Wheels and Deals, he tagged after her like a hound on the hunt. Cora bumped into him twice in the kitchen. Agitated by his suffocating attention, she shut the cabinet door a little too hard.

"Ed, you know I love you," she frowned to add emphasis to her words, "but don't you have people to influence at the golf course?"

"Roger's covering for me this morning." He opened his arms to her. "I'm all yours, Tootsie."

She forced a smile. "Can't you find something to do while I make lunch?"

"Oh, well, I'll help get things out." He opened the refrigerator door. "Do we need anything in here? Hey! This Half and Half's turned to cottage cheese. Better add that to your list." He put the carton back and bent down to look deeper inside the fridge. "While you're at it, write down catsup and, umm, pickle loaf."

Cora shuddered. "Oh Ed, honestly. Wouldn't you rather have shaved ham instead?"

"I haven't had a good ol' pickle loaf and sardine on pumpernickel since before we were married. Yeah, add sardines and pumpernickel to the list, too."

The man had an iron gut. Pickle loaf and sardine sandwich, indeed. Cora marched across the kitchen and closed the refrigerator door. With hands on her hips, she stared him down. "Ed, if you really want to help, please go read the paper until I call you."

"You sure?"

Without a word, she pointed to the other room.

"You're a hard woman, Cora. A ha-a-a-ard woman." He turned to leave. "I've half a mind to go to the golf course after lunch."

"Then we have a meeting of the minds."

At her insistence, Ed left to check on Roger at the golf course after lunch. The peace and quiet Cora expected did not materialize. Instead she rehashed the policemen's embarrassing visit. Her story of a stalker hadn't convinced anyone. Their flip allegations of her fading mental competence might be true, but they were hurtful and degrading.

She wasn't delusional. The blackmailer's threats remained vivid in her mind. If she couldn't produce the envelope, or keep the police out of the picture...would the callers live up to their warning? With Ed gone, the walls of the house closed in on her. She had to get out. Away from the sinister calls, the prying eyes, and her vulnerability.

Cora put McGibbons' old coffee carafe on the top shelf of the dishwasher, and thought about the need for a replacement. Dahlia had urged her to get a BrewMeister Mach 1 Coffeemaker. BrewMeister sponsored her TV show. The southern cook promised it would give her one to twelve cups of perfect coffee in ninety seconds. Now would be the time to get one. She'd better remember to put it on the grocery list along with the pickle loaf.

Cora set her purse down and fished around inside. Car keys? Check. Cell phone? Check. She laid her keys and phone beside the purse, pulled out the grocery list, and quickly added pickle loaf and BrewMeister. Where was her debit card? She made a beeline to the bedroom dresser. What she wouldn't do for a soothing cup of vanilla coffee about now.

She snatched her purse and headed for the door as the house phone rang. Startled, she took two steps towards it, and then stopped. If it was Ed, he could wait, but what if it was the kook? As Cora punched in the code for the security system, the phone went quiet, and she made a mad dash for the Lincoln.

The car door slammed shut. Cora realized something was missing. Where were her keys? She grumbled, dug in her purse again, and pulled out a spare house key. Ed would never let her hear the end of it if she lost them again. Cora groaned, climbed out of the car, punched in the code, and marched back in the house. "Better leave a note for Ed while I'm at it." Her pen scratched across the notepad. "Going for pickle loaf."

The phone rang once more. "I'm not going to answer, Bub." She stomped back to the car in a huff. Was there a way to mainline vanilla bean cappuccino? It was definitely something to look into.

By the time she arrived at the store, her last cup of breakfast coffee caused her to squirm. A restroom search was top on her "to-do" list. Hopefully, Dalton's was clean.

The entrance to the store was blocked by a giddy troop of Wilderness Scouts busy with their annual cookie sale. She rushed past the Scouts and their display.

Desperate, Cora bulldozed her way through the crowd and into the five-stall bathroom, only to find a young mother and her toddler already waiting in line.

"Mrs. Timms! Wait up." A young girl opened the door and called. "You forgot your cookies the other day."

Cora recognized the freckle-faced scout from church. "Oh, hi, Brandi. Cookies? I don't remember buying cookies." She tried to conceal her frustration of yet another occurrence of forgetfulness. "Are you sure these are mine, sweetie?" Two stalls became available and Cora rushed into one.

Brandi held onto the door. "Well, sure I'm sure, Mrs. Timms." Her rusty curls bounced as she nodded her head. "Don't you remember last week at the mall?"

"Excuse me, Brandi. I *really* need to go." Cora quickly locked the door while the scout continued to chatter.

"Oh, sure, Mrs. Timms, go ahead. Remember, you weren't feeling well when you paid me. Then you walked off and left the cookies on the table. I called you. I guess you couldn't hear me, 'cause you didn't even turn around. Here." The girl shoved the shopping bag with the cookies under the stall door.

Cora sighed and rolled her eyes. "Just a minute, honey. You hold them for me until I wash my hands. I'll be right out."

She left the bathroom and thanked Brandi for the cookies. As the pig-tailed scout smiled, Cora caught a fleeting gleam of braces before she peeked into her bag.

"You got two boxes of Mint Pit-a-Patties," the girl said with pride. "And one box of Coconut Whippersnappers."

Puzzled, Cora glanced at Brandi. "Why did I buy Whippersnappers? Ed and I don't like coconut." She laughed and gave the young scout a hug. "Well, I must've had my reasons."

"You said something about getting them for your son."

"I did?" Cora's smile faded "Well, then, how much do I owe you?"

The girl giggled. "You already paid for them, remember?"

Embarrassed, Cora laughed. "Thank you, Brandi. I'm glad you remembered. I sure didn't." An icy grip curled around her heart. Her son? What other little tidbit had she mindlessly blurted out? And to whom?

"No problem." Brandi's voice brought Cora out of her thoughts. "I was going to give them to you, or Mr. Timms at church." She gave Cora a bear hug, waved good-bye and scurried back to her chatty friends at the cookie display.

The warm squeeze triggered a rush of memories. Cora choked back a sudden flood of tears as she recalled her daughter's last embrace. Would the pain ever cease? She didn't think so.

Another troubling thought assailed her. Why couldn't she remember something as simple as buying cookies? These forgetful episodes were more frequent. She pressed her index fingers to her head and massaged her throbbing temple.

Sarah Carpenter, from church, said she'd been ignored at the Christian bookstore. Yesterday, her neighbors, Dixie Firestone and Sylvia Drake, both griped about being snubbed at Java Joe's Coffee Shoppe.

Stomach still in knots, Cora rooted through her

purse for the grocery list. Where was it? Probably with her cell phone back home on the kitchen counter. Maybe Officer Davis was right and she *was* wandering on the wrong side of sanity. She wove her way between other shoppers to the snack bar, and parked her cart next to another.

Sizzling hot dogs on the rotisserie caught her attention. For some reason, Cora felt she had a lot in common with those shriveled franks. Perhaps it was because she, too, felt old, crinkled and dried up. Yep, that was it.

A small voice called out from behind the counter. "Would you like a Dalton Dog?"

Cora searched the length of the snack bar. Her eyes lit on a short gal with a hair net-covered ponytail, all but hidden behind the counter. "I'll pass. Just a bottle of water, please."

With drink in hand, Cora slunk down in a nearby booth, and tried to recreate her shopping list. What was on it? Oh, yes, BrewMeister, Half and Half. Ed will want a piping hot cup of coffee with Brandi's scout cookies. Thank goodness, the girl hadn't spoken to Ed. How could she explain buying coconut cookies for a son they never had?

A white-haired couple sat in the next booth. The husband cut a hot dog into small pieces and fed his frail wife. The poor woman was slumped in her seat, while he dutifully wiped mustard from her mouth. Cora turned her head as tears blurred her vision. Would Ed do that for her?

The thought was pushed aside as she added Pumpernickel and Ed's pickle loaf to her list. Her stomach knotted in revolt. Time to think of something pleasant.

The Scout bag fell against her arm. Oh yeah, the Mint Pit-a-Patties. Maybe when she got home, Dahlia would help her attack the scout cookies. Then again, a quiet afternoon was what she needed most, and quiet wasn't in Dahlia's vocabulary. Cora sighed. Nope. Better to relax with a pot of coffee, and scarf a box of mint cookies on her own.

First things first. Finish the shopping, relax later. Cora smiled at the older couple and went to get her cart. Ahead of her, a young man with red hair set up a gherkin display. Oh…she almost forgot. Pickle loaf and sardines. Well, pickle loaf, maybe. She shuddered. Sardines? Never!

By the time her shopping was done, Cora was exhausted and couldn't wait to get home to put the new BrewMeister Mach 1 to the test. She turned into the driveway, pushed the garage door opener, and pulled the Lincoln into their two-car garage.

The overhead door closed with a bump. With the cumbersome BrewMeister box balanced on one hip, Cora juggled the two grocery bags and headed for the door to the house. She clenched her purse strap between her teeth to free one hand, but before she could get the key in the lock, the door eased inward. Cora hesitated. Had she left it unlocked when she went back to get her keys?

She barely processed the thought when a dark blur shot through the open door with a wild shriek. Cora screamed and dropped the BrewMeister box. She slapped her free hand over her pounding heart. Smudge, Dr. Sam's cat, hid behind storage tubs in the corner and refused to leave his hideaway.

Cora moved the stack of mail aside and put her packages on the kitchen counter. Something crunched beneath her shoe. "Where'd this dirt come from?" She bent down to look closer, and followed the gritty trail across the kitchen. With her hands on her hips, she released a disgusted sigh. "Those are footprints. Edward Bruce Timms, you tracked the whole back nine into the house."

Her irritation grew as she put the groceries away. With a huff, she stomped to the broom closet for the hand vac. Why didn't Ed clean up after himself? Where was he, anyway?

Cora quickly maneuvered the vacuum across the Spanish tile, and managed to suck up most of the dried mud. Then, it dawned on her—the prints were too small to be Ed's. Maybe he wasn't to blame. A cold shiver ran down her spine. Who, besides Smudge, could've been in the house while she was gone?

Wendell had a key. Surely he wouldn't sleuth for those leftover clues without permission.

The telephone interrupted her thoughts. She put the hand vac aside and answered it. "Hello?"

"Cor-rah!" the demanding voice growled. A shiver ran down her spine. "Did you pick up milk at Dalton's? I noticed you were out."

She panicked as reality sunk in. Her stalker had been in the house. She started to hang up, but then, remembered that Officer Davis said to pay attention to background noises. Cora listened intently. The loud bark of the neighbor's dog interrupted her concentration. She took the cordless phone into the living room where it was quieter.

The ragged voice brought her out of her thoughts. "Naughty, naughty Cor-rah has been to the Pegasi

Café again."

She reached for a nearby scratch pad. "What? Where did I go?"

"The Pegasi Café, as if you didn't know, you trollop."

"No-o-o, I've never even heard of that place." She quickly scribbled down the name of the restaurant. Wait, did he just call her a trollop?

"Can't fool me. I followed you."

The hair on the back of her neck stood at attention. Her first priority was to prove this was no phantom stalker, and no one could do this but her. She had to concentrate on background noises, any clue to his location was all-important. Her back straightened. She could do this.

It was time to stop being the victim. Cora rolled her eyes. Easier said than done.

She jumped when Tinkle-Belle yapped outside the window. Why didn't Letitia shut her dog up? Cora fought to keep her mind on track.

Since the man's location proved vague, Cora decided to hone in on his identity. Maybe if she asked real nice, he'd throw her a bone. She cleared her throat. "You'll have to excuse me. I've been having a terrible time with my memory." Did that sound convincing? "Now, where did you say we knew each other? Was it school?"

"Nice try," he quipped. "Aren't you tired of playing games, yet?"

"What do you mean?" Cora listened for something distinctive in his voice. No accent.

No lisp. No speech impediment of any kind. This bozo wasn't helping her at all. She had to keep him talking.

"Really living in the lap of luxury, aren't you, Cor-rah?"

"I don't see how that's any of your business."

"Oh no? It became my business when you came into your vast fortune. We both know where you got it."

"And where might that be?" she asked with pen poised.

"Art, of course."

"Art? Is that what this is all about? Art?" She scribbled the word down and looked around the room at their modest collection. "We might've invested in a few paintings and some small sculptures over the years, but no big-ticket items like you're suggesting."

He swore. "I've about had it with this stupid act! You know what I mean." The sound of psychopathic rage filled his voice. "I didn't serve that dime to get cheated by you. You have six hours left. Get me the envelope, or Ed gets hurt."

"Envelope? Wait a minute. I thought we were talking about art." Her mind swirled in confusion and stymied her concentration. Cora ripped another filled page from her small note pad and quickly scrawled his last statement. Her voice quivered as she warned, "I'll call the police."

"And tell them what? Looks like we're at a stalemate. This is serious. You can't go running to the cops again because you're in it up to your eyeballs, and you know it."

She quickly wrote—"eyeballs." It suddenly dawned on her.

Tinkle-Belle's constant barking not only came through her window, but she also heard it on the phone.

The caller was *outside*.

The menacing voice on the phone spewed death threats. Cora jumped when the doorknob rattled. Breathless, she fled into the shadows of the hallway as the door opened and closed. She flattened herself against the wall.

"Are ya here, Sugar? I brung ya a plate of fried chicken."

Cora's mind reeled at the sound of Dahlia's familiar twang. Her hand shook as she covered the receiver and offered it to her friend. "Listen," she whispered.

With her bracelet jingling, Dahlia set the plate down. She grabbed the phone and put it to her ear. "Oh, Cora. Nobody's there, Sugar."

Humiliation burned Cora's cheeks.

"I'm as sorry as can be." Dahlia's expression grew serious as she shrugged her shoulders. "But just have yourself a listen."

She took the phone, unable to look directly at Dahlia. "I don't understand. He had to be close, I heard Tinkle-Belle on the phone. Did you see anyone?"

"No. That scoundrel prob'ly saw me an' it scared him off." Dahlia cackled. "I tend to do that to men, don't ya know?" She put her hands on her hips. "Why didn't you use your cell phone? Ya shoulda called 9-1-1 while he was on your landline."

"My land *what*? Oh, never mind." Crestfallen, Cora released a long sigh. She desperately wanted someone to hear the man's voice. Her gaze gravitated hopelessly to her friend. "It doesn't matter, now."

"Well, it matters to me! Wendell Floyd an' Jack was talkin' about your problem at breakfast. Ya know, I believe them calls are for real. What all did he say this time?"

"Let me sit down first. I'm shaking inside and out." She slumped into her recliner and fumbled with her notes. "I wrote some of it down like the cop said. Oops!" Papers fluttered around her feet. "I'm so nervous, I'm dropping everything." Cora leaned over to pick them up, laid them on her lap, and studied her hastily scrawled chicken scratches.

"Here's one ya missed." Dahlia said. "It says six hours. What's that mean?"

Tears pooled in Cora's eyes. "When he called last night, he gave me twenty-four hours to find the envelope, or he'd get Ed. Today, he reminded me there were only six hours left."

"I'll tell Wendell Floyd to get his squirrel gun ready an' he can be watchin' out for Ed. If he sees anything strange, he'll give the police a jingle."

Cora grimaced. She could just see the headlines now. "Golf Pro Mortally Wounded With Squirrel Gun." She looked up. "Tinkle-Belle's been yapping all morning. I wish Letitia would let her in."

"An' that crazy dog's been scratchin' at her garage door, too," Dahlia said. "Letitia must've cleaned out her fridge again. She always puts all that smelly stuff in the garage way before trash day." She leaned forward. "Now, what's on the rest of them notes?"

"Well, they're out of sequence now. I remember he mentioned something about swerving on a dime. What on earth does *that* mean?"

Dahlia threw her head back and let out a hardy laugh. "I think ya mean servin' a dime. That's prison talk. A dime is a ten-year sentence. A nickel is five-years an' so on. He must be an ex-con." She smiled mischievously. "Just how many do ya know?"

"Ex-convicts? I don't think I know any, Dahlly. How do you know all that stuff?"

"I learned a lot from Wendell Floyd. Ya know how my man likes to keep up with cop an' prison lingo."

Cora nodded. Uncertainty about her friend's teasing response lingered. She looked down at her notes. "He said we were out of milk. That means he was in here, Dahlly. Inside our home. And he mentioned our art pieces, too."

Dahlia frowned. "Who all has access to this place?"

Cora slowly counted on her fingers. "Well, you and Wendell." She paused, and with an arched brow looked for her friend's reaction. Nothing. "And of course, Lupe and Mateo, but they've always been as honest as the day is long." She thought for a moment. "Then the complex office. They let us know when someone is coming to make sure it's convenient. Besides, they don't have the security code. I think that's it."

"Ya sure?"

"Oh, wait, there's the new instructor at the golf course. Roger something. Back when I worked at the county treasurer's office, Ed had an emergency one day. He gave the last instructor, George, the security code and his keys. Oh, Dahlia!"

Dahlia's eyes popped. "Cora! Sugar! Do ya hear what you're sayin'? Ed-fired-George. George-had-your-hubby's-keys-an'-code." Her earrings sparkled and swayed as she shook her head. "Now, it sure don't take a genius to spot a goat in a flock of sheep. Ya'll are too trustin'. That rascal could've made copies! Maybe we should call the cops again."

"Absolutely not!" she said emphatically. "I don't

want them back here. They didn't believe me last time. Phantom stalker, indeed. How could they help, anyway?"

"What do ya mean, phantom stalker?"

"The police have convinced Ed that I don't have any cows in my herd."

Dahlia cackled. "Ya don't have *what*?"

"Cows in my herd. Oh, you know what I mean. You say it all the time."

Dahlia's forehead creased into a frown. "Ya mean one cow shy of a herd?"

"Yes. They all think I'm nuts." Cora narrowed her eyes. "The young cop said I'm so lonely, I'm just imagining stalkers and prowlers to get attention."

"Horsefeathers. I know ya better than that. What's wrong with Ed, anyway? He knows ya better, too."

"You'd think so." Cora looked around the room, "It won't help to call the police. They won't believe there was an intruder. He's long gone by now, and nothing seems to be out of place, no stolen items to report."

"We got us a bona-fide crime, here. Someone broke into your home, maybe an ex-con. Don't ya realize how risky it is to let him get away with it? He wants somethin' from ya, so he's not gonna stop 'til he gets it. He'll be back."

"I know breaking and entering is a crime." Cora threw up her hands. "Still, without evidence, they're not going to believe me."

Dahlia stood. "Maybe there's some proof around the door."

"When I got home from Dalton's, the back door was ajar. It's the second time this week. So nobody had to actually *break* in." Cora sighed. "I don't remember leaving it open, and I can't believe Ed would."

"Maybe Ed wasn't the culprit."

"Since you brought it up, do you think Wendell might've come in search of clues? He's so determined to solve this case."

Dahlia nodded. "Could be. He leaves more clues than he finds. Still, did ya take a close look at the door? It just mighta been jimmied."

"I didn't look. I was loaded down with groceries and stepped on crusty footprints. The phone rang and then you came."

"Back the train up! Footprints? Ya never told me about that."

"What's to tell? After all that rain we had. Someone walked in with muddy shoes, it dried, and I haven't had time to think beyond that."

Dahlia sighed. "Why don't we have us a look-see?"

They quickly headed down the hall.

Cora stopped short. "Oh, I didn't put the vac away."

"Wait a minute. Ya mean to tell me ya cleaned up the footprints? That was evidence."

Cora's mouth flew open as she contemplated the likelihood. "All I could think of was not tracking the dirt through the house."

Dahlia looked heavenward in disbelief. "Cora, Sugar, how can a smart cookie like you be so rock-ribbed about catchin' the stalker; yet so slow on the uptake in findin' the partic'lers?"

"Everything happened at once." Cora's eyes began to puddle. "Smudge was in the house, and I blamed Ed for the dirt...and I feel so stupid, Dahlly."

"Now, now, don't fret so, Sugar. Bless your heart.

You're goin' through a lot of craziness right now. Everybody's got their limits. Are ya sure ya punched in your code when ya left?"

"I was in and out a couple times," Cora rubbed her head. "Anything's possible."

"I'll tell ya what, let's go ahead check the door for jimmy marks just to be sure."

The two women went to the side door to examine the casing. A loud thump followed by a clatter of metal on metal startled them. They turned and followed the noise.

Dahlia stepped down into the garage. "What was that?"

"It sounded like Ed's golf clubs fell over." Cora's voice lowered. "Oh Dahlly, someone's out there."

"Calm down, Sugar. Turn the light on an' I'll go check."

Cora watched as her friend tiptoed away from her. A scream came from the same direction. "What is it, Dahlly? What's wrong?"

Dahlia's raucous laugh resonated off the walls. "Mystery solved. Doc's crazy cat jumped out at me. You get outta there, Smudge."

"That's a relief." Cora headed for the golf bag. "You get the cat, I'll pick up the clubs." When the clubs were gathered, Cora said, "Oh. I know how he got in. I closed the overhead and noticed the door to the house was ajar."

"That's right, we were gonna check for pry marks, weren't we?" The duo went back to the door. "Naw, no marks at all."

Cora's eyes welled. "If only I hadn't cleaned up those footprints."

Dahlia patted her shoulder. "Forget about that. Ya

have to move forward from where ya are. The stalker's gonna slip up somewhere along the line, an' then he'll be bear bait." She led Cora back to the kitchen where they sat at the counter. "Let's give our minds a break an' relax."

Cora sighed. "Sounds good to me."

Dahlia moved a box out of her way and noticed the label. "Hey, ya got yourself a BrewMeister. Let's try it out."

"OK, I'll get the coffee. Would you wash the new carafe for me?"

The women got busy and ninety seconds later the aroma of coffee filled the kitchen. They'd finished half a pot before the scout cookies entered Cora's mind. "You were right about the BrewMeister. The coffee's delicious and I have something to go along with it." She brought the Whippersnappers to the counter and hoped her friend would gorge herself. Cora deliberately omitted the story of her encounter with Brandi at Dalton's. Would Dahlly still defend her if she knew about the escalating mental lapses? Why chance it?

Dahlia filled their cups for the third time. "Best get them scout cookies put away before I gobble 'em all up. Ed would tan my hide."

"Oh, he can part with a few Whippersnappers." Cora smiled. "He won't miss them at all. Thanks for the tip on the BrewMeister."

"You betcha. I only take cream o' the crop sponsors." Dahlia looked at her watch. "Listen, it's three-thirty. Wish I could stay longer, but Wendell Floyd invited his buddy to eat with us, again. Those two have been burnin' the midnight oil tryin' to solve your mystery. They'll get to the bottom of it soon. Ya just wait an' see! Remember, ya can count on my prayers too."

Cora hugged her friend and whispered. "Thank you, Dahlly." She was consoled and gratified to know the three of them backed her.

࿇

Once her friend was gone, Cora looked down at the sparkling clean floor. Dahlly was right. The only possible evidence of her phantom stalker's existence had been swept up. She sat at the counter and buried her face in her hands. How would the authorities ever be convinced without proof?

Her eyes caught sight of the morning mail still on the counter. She halfheartedly sorted through it. Big surprise. It was all for Ed. Why didn't he take it to his office?

Cora rubbed her forehead and headed for Ed's office with the mail. You just can't depend on men. Whoa! With that thought in mind, could she depend on Wendell to keep Ed safe through the night? Squirrel gun indeed. A shiver ran down her spine. What else could she do? This would *not* be a peaceful night.

The phone rang.

Crud. Why hadn't she turned the ringers off when Dahlia suggested it? She determined to take her friend's advice after this call. The receiver felt heavy as she lifted it to her ear. Cora took a deep breath, and waited for him to make the first sound. She swallowed. "Don't worry, I'll be there."

7

At breakfast the next morning, Cora yawned at least a dozen times, nibbled at her prune Danish and watched the steam curl from her husband's freshly filled mug. Ed was oblivious to the chaos that hampered her sleep the night before. The normal night sounds were bad enough, but when police lights swirled on the bedroom wall, she nearly came unglued. Ed snored right through the cops questioning Wendell outside the bedroom window.

Ed sniffed the Half and Half before he added it to his second cup of coffee. He popped a bite of coffee-soaked Danish into his mouth, licked the goo from his fingers, and grabbed the newspaper. He tossed her a playful wink over the top of his half-moon reading glasses, and was soon lost in the sports section.

Cora's heart melted. Was he really capable of plotting against her? Surely not.

The clock hands seemed to move with unhurried calculation. She tapped her manicured nails on the table as Ed reached for another Danish. Why did the man have to pick today of all days to dilly-dally over breakfast, when she had special plans for the day? He'd have to leave soon, but if she hurried him along, he'd suspect something. Cora blew on the rim of her cup, then sipped the vanilla coffee. Patience was a virtue, right?

The commitments for later that day made her

stomach plunge. Like it or not, the decision was made, and it was time to get it done.

The grandfather clock chimed and pulled Ed from the wonderful world of sports. He took the last swig of coffee and pushed his chair from the table. "I gotta get moving. Why didn't you tell me it was so late? I have a lesson in fifteen minutes."

She smiled and cleared her partially eaten breakfast. "I didn't want to rush you, dear."

As he left the house, Cora spied the latest stack of mail left on the counter. With the exception of their church newsletter, all of it was Ed's...again.

Time to get a life. When she took the bundle to his office, her eyes were drawn to a blue folder on the desk. The temptation was too great. A peek inside revealed a new life insurance policy. Made out in *her* name?

"Well, well, well. The plot thickens."

Why hadn't Ed mentioned it? That wasn't like him. They always made those decisions together. That booger just replaced George at the top of her suspect list.

Cora headed for the master suite to lay out her favorite turquoise pantsuit. Melodious strains of Vivaldi's Spring gently swelled in the background while the deep garden tub filled with water. She sank into a mound of luxurious bubbles. If this didn't relax her, nothing would.

The bath water swirled down the drain as she patted dry. Why couldn't her problems vanish that easily?

A muffled thump from the bedroom sent a shiver of panic through Cora. "Ed? Is that you?" She hesitated a moment and listened. No answer. "Lupe?" The housekeeper wasn't due until later. Why would she come early? Her heart rate soared. She threw on her satin robe and peeked out the bathroom door.

At that moment, the phone rang. This could be a lifeline if someone was in the house. Her bare feet slapped on the tile floor as she hurried to answer it.

"Good morning, Cor-rah," the gruff voice greeted her. "Were you surprised to see your husband still alive this morning?"

Shock held Cora speechless as a wave of apprehension swept through her.

The caller continued. "I'll admit you threw me off with the Lone Ranger standing guard with his gun. But he won't be in my way much longer. How much do you treasure your friends?"

She stood frozen to the spot and struggled to regain a sense of balance, the phone still clutched in her shaky hand.

"So, did you find my small memento in your top dresser drawer?"

How was he able to see inside the house? Her gaze traveled to the bedroom windows. The blinds were closed, draperies drawn. Maybe there *were* hidden cameras after all. She slammed the receiver down, and clasped the robe tighter to her chin. Should she dress in the closet? No, that would be too Superman-ish.

Cora ran to the dresser. The drawer was open a crack, and a strap of her slip hung out. Wait. She didn't leave it like that. It could only mean one thing. The noise hadn't been her imagination. Someone had been there while she was in the tub. The thought brought an involuntary shudder.

Her hand reached into the top drawer. A photograph lay partially hidden beneath her rumpled lingerie. She stared in disbelief at the image of herself in the arms of another man. On the back of the snapshot, the block letters read: "Does your old man know?"

Cora felt violated. In her frenzy, she emptied out the whole drawer and chucked the silky contents into the laundry hamper. "He touched my things. They're all soiled," she said through gritted teeth. "And, where did he get that old picture?"

She struggled to shove the empty drawer back in place, and remembered there were two callers. The man's accomplice was a Hispanic woman. Lupe? Her knees weakened, and she leaned against the dresser for support. Lupe was the only other person who could be in her dresser without causing suspicion.

Thoughts bounced around as Cora dressed and plotted an immediate escape to Phoenix. She rubbed her forehead. That left a lot of time to kill until 2 p.m.

The bedroom door swung open with a bang, as Ed entered the room. Startled, Cora snatched the photo from the dresser top and threw it into the emptied drawer. She slammed it shut and turned to face him with a fake smile.

"What are you doing, Cora?"

Was he accusing her of something? As nonchalantly as possible, Cora walked to the bed and sat down. "I have a few errands to run, dear. I was going to call you." She slipped on her knee-high stockings and looked at him. "Were you in here a few minutes ago?"

"Of course not." His eyes narrowed. "What kind of errands?"

Of all the times for him to start prying. "Well, if you must know, Mr. Nosy Parker, there's medicine and dry cleaning to pick up, and I have a hair appointment. If there's time, I'll stop at the library, too. There's a book about American citizenship Lupe wants to read."

When Ed didn't respond, she changed the subject. "What happened to your shirt?"

"Pastor Luke brought his new puppy to the clubhouse. Little Skipper got overexcited when I picked him up." Ed opened the closet door, pulled the stained golf shirt over his head, and reached for a clean one.

Cora shook her finger. "Don't you dare put that smelly wet thing in the hamper."

"Would I do that?" He laughed. "You know me pretty well, don't you? I'll toss it in the tub. Listen, why don't you go into Phoenix with me? I need to pick up those trophies for the tourney on Saturday. We can run your errands and grab a bite to eat."

Cora rubbed lightly scented lotion into her dry hands and watched him in the mirror. "I'd rather go alone this time." That wasn't entirely true. She needed him now more than ever, but she couldn't bring herself to confide in him, yet.

He called from the bathroom. "Any particular reason you don't want to come with me?"

The suspicious tone grated on Cora. She had to think fast. "Didn't you say Hank Arthur is lined up for a golf lesson this afternoon?" She retrieved her purse, and dropped a handful of breath mints into the zippered pocket. "I have a hair appointment and won't be home until later. You'd be too late for Hank's session."

"Oh, I guess you're right."

"Look, Ed, I'm not running away from you." Cora

turned to face him. "Please understand, I'm stressed out and need to get away from the phone."

As Cora backed away, he caught her arm. His voice lost its harsh edge. "Level with me, Toots. Something isn't right. I feel you're holding back, not telling me everything. We've never kept secrets from each other even when things were tough." Ed took her hand and kissed it.

Never kept secrets? Well, there was a questionable insurance policy on his desk that said otherwise. Not telling him everything? Cora sniffed. Maybe not, but one thing was for sure, today would begin a new chapter in her life. She desperately hoped for a positive outcome.

Cora hated to build a wall between them, but she had to leave before this last surge of fortitude waned. "I've got to go, Ed." She grabbed her purse and hurried to the door.

He pointed to her feet. "Aren't you forgetting a little something?"

Cora looked down. "Oh, hush, and tuck your shirt in." She put her shoes on and stomped out the door. So much for dramatic exits.

8

Ed paced the floor. When Cora left in such a huff, concern got the better of him. Under normal circumstances, they respected each other's privacy. However, her actions this morning led him to reconsider that agreement. His jaw tightened. It was obvious she was hiding something. Maybe the answer was in the drawer she slammed shut. Did he really want to know?

His stomach knotted as he approached the dresser and pulled the drawer open. It was empty, except for a lone snapshot. He focused on the image of his wife wrapped in the arms of an unfamiliar man.

Stunned, Ed lowered himself onto the bed. Who was this man? He knew all her family members. A friend of the McGibbons? No, the bell-bottom pants dated the picture before they'd known Dahlia and Wendell. Besides, the man didn't hold her like a mere acquaintance. This was a more familiar embrace. Ed stiffened as he noticed a date stamped on the edge of the photo. He won first place in the European Pro Golf Tour during that summer.

His hands trembled as he turned the photograph over to examine the message. He read it aloud. "Does your old man know?"

This wasn't like his wife at all. He considered her self-imposed isolation, forgetfulness, and how skittish she was with the police. Now her clothes were gone, and in their place was this suspicious picture. Had she meant for him to find it? Frustrated, he combed his fingers through his hair, and added up the evidence against her. Had she renewed her relationship with this man? Did they have a rendezvous planned today? No, it couldn't be.

Ed struggled to remain calm as he headed back to the dresser. A yellow highlighter lay on a road map. She had a habit of marking her route. His hands shook as he picked up the Phoenix map to examine the charted course. What was at the end of her trail?

Her yellow marker was drawn from Saguaro Valley to a street in close proximity to Apache Trophies and Awards, where he was to pick up the golf trophies that afternoon. What on earth would possess her to go to that part of Phoenix, and why did she insist on going alone?

Agitated, Ed remembered a note in Cora's handwriting that he'd found on the living room floor. He pulled it from his shirt pocket. *Pegasi Café* was all it said. The name sounded familiar. Might as well check that out, too. The phone directory was in the bedside table. He found the address, and was hardly surprised at the location. He kicked one of Cora's duck slippers across the room. *Quack!*

ॐॐ

Cora slipped the Lincoln into reverse, armed with her carefully written directions. A Phoenix map was in the glove compartment as a backup. She inched her way out of the driveway, and honked hello at Dr. Sam, who was cleaning the windows of his dark blue Caddie.

Lupe and Mateo Santalis's cleaning cart was at the recently vacated condominium directly across from the Timms. Old man Gunther had recently moved. Lupe often complained about the bachelor's slovenly habits, no doubt, they would have a busy day to prepare for the next owner.

Saguaro Valley was home to a growing number of retirees from all over the country who happily found their way to this easy-living complex. The gated community was located next to the desert-style golf course designed and owned by Ed. The residents seemed to reflect the overall contentedness of living in the peaceful environment. It was beautiful, and also well planned to meet their ever-increasing physical needs.

Several neighbors returned her friendly wave. Cora smiled as Letitia Bockman walked her Standard poodle. Tinkle-Belle pranced in pink boots and hooded parka. The pooch controlled the pace of the eighty-eight-year-old woman as they trotted through the neighborhood.

Letitia was a slightly stooped woman, and always wore a polyester dress with vintage beads and matching earrings. The frail widow never wore slacks, probably never had. She lived alone and was starved for human companionship. If the dear soul ever cornered an unsuspecting victim, she could, and would go out of her way to wax lyrical.

Cora slowed to stop at the security gate, and waved to Wendell McGibbons.

He motioned for her to roll down the window.

"Me an' Jack, have been workin' hard on the Saguaro Sidewinder."

"The what?"

"Ya know, your case. The first lead didn't pan out, but Jack found us another clue. We'll have this crime solved in two shakes of a lamb's tail."

Cora wouldn't be surprised since Wendell and Jack put in more effort than the police. Their mutual fondness for detective work and mysteries was key to their friendship. Should she mention this morning's intruder, or the picture left in her drawer? Nope. She didn't want Team Wendell to root through all her dresser drawers. Cora waved, closed the window, and pulled closer to the exit.

After a short wait for a break in the traffic, she merged onto Shifting Sands Avenue. Fortunately, the first part of the trip was routine, so Cora could almost drive it in her sleep. The familiar route gave her racing mind a chance to slow down. She passed Chug-a-Mug, her favorite coffee shop. A vanilla cappuccino sure sounded good. Maybe she'd reward herself on the way home.

Home. A shiver ran up her spine. Her mind returned to the threatening phone calls and the turmoil that waited for her there. Did she really want to go back home?

A soft voice stirred within. *I will go before you and make the crooked places straight, Cora. Call on Me.*

"You weren't there when I needed You the most, Lord."

I promised never to leave you nor forsake you.

Cora contemplated the divine words for a few minutes before she pulled into a parking space at the local mini-mall. Reluctant to surrender to God's voice, she cried out, "It's too hard. I can't." She fought back bitter tears, and struggled to compose herself until finally another wall was raised to silence the Inner

Voice.

She lifted her chin and marched into Nancy's Gift Shoppe to select a few greeting cards. Before breakfast, she'd called in their prescription refills at Montgomery's Pharmacy next door. Cora glanced at her watch. The medication should be ready for pick-up, and she'd still have an hour to kill before her hair appointment. Plenty of time to grab lunch.

She placed her parcels in the car, and glanced around for a place to eat. Tammy's Tea Room. This would be a great time to catch up with the owner, Tammy Marsh, who'd been Vanessa's best friend. She was in the passenger seat on the fateful evening of the accident, and had suffered critical injuries, too.

Cora hesitated, and then entered the establishment. The last time she'd eaten here, Vanessa was with her, and now the Tea Room brought back so many memories. Some good. Some bad.

Tammy looked up when Cora walked through the door. With an enthusiastic wave, she rushed over to give her friend a hug. "Long time, no see. So, how've you been?"

"Oh Tammy, it's so good to see you. I had some time before my hair appointment and thought I'd stop in for lunch."

Dense red scars ran from Tammy's eyebrow to her jaw line and were vivid reminders of their shared tragedy. Her dark hair draped down to conceal much of the disfigurement.

Tammy offered her a menu. "I'll give you a few minutes to decide, then I'll be back so we can chat."

It didn't take long for Cora to choose a chicken salad sandwich with raspberry iced tea.

Several minutes later Tammy returned with her

friend's order and a cup of tea for herself.

Stories of Tammy and Vanessa's years together were lovingly recounted with both laughter and tears. Cora missed sharing memories of her daughter. It touched her heart to find someone who didn't shy away from it. She needed that. Until the topic turned to the accident.

"For months I struggled with flashbacks of that night." Tammy self-consciously pulled her hair over her scars. "Van didn't respond so I don't know if she heard me, but I prayed with her until she lost consciousness. It was an hour before the life squad could get to us because of the flooded roads. And Cora, I want you to know that I held her hand until they got there."

Cora could only nod as a lump formed in her throat. She struggled to fight back tears of remorse. Ed told her Vanessa had already passed away when the life squad arrived. Would she have lived if they'd gotten there earlier? The nails in Cora's clenched fists dug into her flesh as she inwardly ranted. *My baby needed me. She needed You, too, God. Why didn't You help her?*

Tammy continued, "Ed talked to me a few months later, and assured me there was nothing else I could've done to help. Your husband was a Godsend, Cora. Because of his encouragement, those horrible nightmares finally stopped. Be sure to thank him again for me."

"Yes, I'll do that." Cora smiled. "He'll be happy to know you're doing better."

"The paper had a good article about him taking second place in the Senior Invitational. I'm so proud of him." She leaned over for a quick hug. "Thanks for stopping by. You've always been like a second mom to me. I've relied on your prayers and you're always in mine."

Cora's conscience pricked as Tammy wiped a tear. She hadn't thought to pray for her, or anyone else for that matter. Who cares? God wasn't listening.

"So, tell me about your grandkids, Cora. I'll bet they're almost grown by now."

"We haven't seen them since last Christmas." The words accentuated the anger she felt. "They moved all the way to Las Vegas."

Tammy set her teacup down and searched Cora's eyes. "Las Vegas? Why would James move the kids so far away?"

"Dear James remarried, and rather quickly, I might add."

Tammy gasped. "Oh Cora, please tell me you're kidding. Who is she?"

"That super model, Jocelyn Cassell. She wanted a big house in Las Vegas, and James knuckled under to please her. We don't get to see the kids much at all."

"*The* Jocelyn Cassell? Isn't she only in her twenties?" Tammy frowned. "And how old are the kids?"

"Heather is fourteen, and is taken in by all the glamour. I just imagine Jocelyn slinking around the house turning the boys' heads, too. It's gonna be their ruination." She shaded her eyes to hide the tears.

Tammy patted her hand. "James won't let that happen. He's always had very high morals. God will give him the wisdom he needs in this situation. You and Ed need to visit those grandkids more often." The sound of laughter entered the Tea Room when the door opened. Tammy looked up. "Oh there's a group of Red Hatters. I'd better get back to work." She stood and hugged Cora's shoulder, then picked up the bill. "Lunch is on the house. Oh, and please come back."

Unable to finish her sandwich, Cora pushed the uneaten portion aside. She gathered her things and left a nice tip. Good memories were all that were left of Vanessa, and she wanted to build on that. Instead, the conversation turned to the accident, and alienation of her grandkids.

Within a few minutes, Cora had arrived at the Salon de Belleza. The intense odor of a new perm accosted her nostrils as she scanned the room for her hairdresser. A plume of hairspray quickly fogged the cubicle as Andre finished his client.

He smiled and waved. "Cora, love of my life!" He motioned for her to take a seat at the shampoo bowl.

Soon the warm water and Andre's soothing scalp massage eased Cora's pent-up tension. Her mind drifted back to the conversation with Tammy. It was true, she and Ed *should* have more involvement with Vannie's children. However, the kids wouldn't be wowed if they took them from the flashy lights of Sin City to Prune Acres, USA. Still, they all needed new memories. Oooh, a trip to Hawaii sounded good. *Without* James and Jocelyn. That worked. The thought of the grandkids all to herself was a great boost to get through the day.

"...and don't forget to tell Dahlia. She likes a good bargain." Andre's voice snapped her back to reality. He wrapped her head in a warm towel. "Cora, did you hear me?"

What had he been talking about? There wasn't enough time to have him reprise his whole monologue, so she wiped water from her neck and smiled. "Oh yes, she likes her bargains."

A short time later, Andre gave her the hand mirror, and turned the chair to let her see the end result. The bell above the shop door jingled. Andre turned and looked. "There's Anne, my one-fifteen." He unfastened the cape and shook it. "See ya next week, dear." He turned to the new customer and held out his arms. "Annie, love of my life!"

Cora paid for the wash and set, along with a jar of Velvety Dew. The wall clock indicated she had forty-five minutes to get to Phoenix and follow through with her plans.

She wasn't accustomed to the heavier traffic on the Phoenix highway. It was like being on a souped-up conveyer belt with no controls. Valley Metro buses snaked into the stream of traffic, and belched their exhaust. She had left her comfort zone far behind.

Cora's heart raced. She sat ramrod straight and maneuvered into the turn lane. The red light gave her enough time to pull the slip of paper from her purse and confirm the address of her destination. So far, so good. Only one more turn after this. The directions she'd written were accurate. She glanced at the dashboard clock. Ten minutes until two.

With little time to spare, she pulled into an empty space in the parking garage, and looked into the visor mirror. "Well, Cora, this is it. Your last chance to back out."

∽◦∾

It was nearly noon when Ed stopped at a downtown intersection. He knew this was the area Cora had marked on the map and he began to look for

Baxter Boulevard.

A prominent sign came into view. "Would you look at that, there it is. Pegasi Café." Ed seethed as he looked in vain for a place to park. Was she in there now? He circled the block and made another pass, in search of his wife's car. Not a Lincoln in sight. He decided to pick up his trophies and return.

The clerk at Apache Trophies and Awards spent several minutes sharing his latest golf jokes. Ed wasn't in the mood for Chester's corny style of jocularity, but for the sake of their business relationship, he had to endure it.

With his purchase finally loaded, and dour disposition intact, Ed quickly reset his course for Baxter Boulevard.

The Pegasi parking lot was still filled to capacity. After Ed made several laps around the block, he eventually found an empty spot across the street. What should he do now? Go inside? If he did go in and found her…he couldn't finish the thought.

Ed remembered the first time he met Cora at a Stuckey's gift shop. He was with his sister, Judy, as she bought fudge. The pretty honey-blonde behind the counter caught his attention right away.

Judy said, "This handsome man with red ears, is my big brother, Ed, and he thinks you're groovy. He didn't take his eyes off you all through breakfast."

Heat rose in his face as he selected pecan logs, and fumbled for change. His mind raced to strike up a conversation with Cora. "Do you like pecan logs?"

The pretty blonde said, "Yes, but I favor Tootsie Rolls."

Ed smiled. That's when he decided to call her Tootsie. When she took his money, their hands lingered, and he instantly knew she was "the one." His whole life changed in that moment, and he longed for her to be a part of it. In nearly forty years, the longing was as strong as ever.

A scream from an ambulance siren jerked Ed from the past. His mind reverted to the condemning picture he'd found in Cora's drawer. Had he lost his Tootsie for good? What would life be without her?

Ed resumed his watch of the Pegasi entrance and prayed, *"Oh Lord, what shall I do?"*

The wait was long and he had nearly lost his patience when a taxi pulled up across the street. His jaw dropped as a lady and a distinguished younger man, walked arm-in-arm out of the restaurant. The man pulled her close, and she nestled her head on his shoulder as they walked to the cab.

"Cora?"

Still in shock, Ed quickly reached for the snapshot in his shirt pocket. Was it the same man? He leaned forward and squinted, unable to get a good look at him. Where were they going? Wherever it was, he was going to follow them. He put the car in gear and edged forward.

Tires squealed and horns honked.

Ed slammed on the brakes and punched the steering wheel as the passing traffic blocked him in. The cab sped off and left him behind to stew in his misery from this unexpected trauma.

The disturbing scene at the café was etched in his mind. Ed fumed as he drove aimlessly through the busy streets, and peered at every taxi in sight. He continued to weigh the gravity of the situation. The shock of Cora's unfaithfulness cut him to the quick.

The only thing he could do was go home and wait.

For all these years, he thought he knew his beloved wife. Obviously, Cora had a secret life. He had to contrive a way for her to have no other option, but to admit the truth.

In his anger, Ed finally came up with a plan to "innocently" lure Cora back to the café for lunch the next day to check her reaction. There he would challenge her with what he had discovered and demand a full explanation.

9

Cora headed home in the hectic rush hour traffic. A Valley Metro bus pulled up beside her at the stoplight, and blocked her view of the exit sign ahead. Her eyes frantically searched the area. Convinced this was her turn, she flipped on her signal in anticipation.

"I hate driving in heavy traffic," she grumbled. "Now, Mr. Metro bus, if you'll let me get over, I'll be all set."

The bus driver motioned to her. She pulled into the turn-only lane in front of him, and waved a thank you. Cora saw the exit sign. She gulped and an iron weight fell on her shoulders. I-10 E. This wasn't right. It was one turn too soon. Fear, combined with worry, quickly knotted inside. Her head began to ache. "It's too late," she cried. She was headed for the wrong freeway and couldn't turn back.

Heavy traffic clamored around her which made it impossible to change lanes. Road signs whizzed past and not a single one mentioned Saguaro Valley. Where was she, anyway?

Both lanes slowed and finally came to a standstill. Cora could see red lights flashing in the distance surrounding an overturned semi. This had all the earmarks of a long wait. She put the car in park, but kept it running for the air conditioner.

With a heavy heart, she mulled over the day's erratic events. She left home early in order to get a break, however, her worries had more than tripled. Now, this new wrinkle topped it all. Would she be able to turn around and get home before dark? Ed must be pacing the floor.

She reached for her cell phone. No signal. There was nothing more she could do at this point. The cell phone was his idea. He'd just have to pace.

Cora groped in the glove compartment to retrieve the Phoenix area map. Maybe she could find her location. Feverishly, she poked her hand deeper into the compartment. Where was it? A flashlight loudly thumped to the floor quickly followed by a bulky pair of wrap-around sunglasses. She grabbed a handful of golf pencils along with wad of restaurant napkins. The glove compartment was now empty except for the diver's manual and a lone straw. Everything else lay heaped on the passenger seat. Cora remembered marking the route in yellow, and was sure she'd put the map back in the glove box. Had she dropped it in her haste to escape Ed's third degree? Her impatience intensified. Cora growled and stuffed the motley mix back into their cramped confinement.

She slammed the compartment door shut and angrily began to second-guess herself. Her hand searched the pockets on the doors. The map had to be there somewhere. Maybe it was in the back.

When she turned in her seat, she caught a glimpse of the growing string of vehicles lined up at least a mile behind her. She appreciated being near the front of this untimely parade.

Her appreciation quickly waned as a rhythmic beat emanated from the car next to her.

The grizzled, unshaven driver sported a pencil thin braid down his back. Obviously, the man was a remnant from the flower-power generation. He joyfully convulsed in sync with the vibrating noises, which had to register at least a point four on the Richter scale.

It had to be his favorite song since he played it for twenty minutes. Even then, the only recognizable words were: *gotta have peace, gotta have peace.*

How could a body find a smattering of peace with that racket?

The monotonous pounding droned nonstop. She'd reached her limit of harsh boom-diddy-booms, yet, was surprised when the repetitious lyrics got to her. The words emphasized her need for the peace that seemed to elude her.

The verse she memorized as a child came back to her. *John 14:27. Peace I leave with you, my peace I give unto you: not as the world giveth, I give unto you. Let not your heart be troubled, neither let it be afraid.* She turned on the radio to ignore the Voice, and cranked up the volume—to point five on the Richter scale.

A calm voice came from the radio and flooded the Lincoln. "When we place our worries and concerns into God's hands, He faithfully rewards us with His magnificent peace."

Cora turned the radio off and then covered her face with trembling hands. If only she could believe that once more. For two years she'd turned her back on God. Would He hear her cry? Even after all this time? The Holy Spirit was wearing away her resolve. A tear fell onto her wrist as she whispered, "Help my disbelief."

The cars in front of her inched forward. The accident scene took nearly an hour to clear. Cora was relieved to finally escape the head-throbbing rock music. However, she couldn't dodge the Holy Spirit.

The flow of cars and trucks eventually thinned. She'd turn at the next exit. There had to be a place to get directions. Cora's stiff hands gripped the steering wheel as tightly as possible. The minutes dragged and seemed like hours.

The lush foothills yielded to monotonous desert terrain. On every side of her, diverse varieties of cactus intermingled with a scattering of mesquite and creosote bushes. Scraggly underbrush had joined with free blowing tumbleweeds. Isolated, withered, forsaken. Like her life since Vanessa's death.

I've promised never to leave you, nor forsake you, Cora.

The scorching heat waned as the sun descended on the horizon. Tears spilled down her cheeks as a magnificent display of taupe, red-orange, and mauve filled the western sky.

Cora sniffed. Her heart longed to reach out to God's promise, but her mind still wasn't convinced. She leaned over and fumbled for a tissue. The car swerved and interrupted her concentration, and the crucial off-ramp whizzed by. She decided to make a U-turn. However, as she looked into the rearview mirror, the three roaring semis on her tail helped her reevaluate.

Several miles passed before another exit sign was visible. She successfully turned off the active freeway, and her tires hit the slow-down–rumble strips of the sloping ramp. The speed of the pulsating Lincoln slowed. Relieved at her return to civilization, Cora pulled into the parking lot of a gas station and convenience store. Two big floodlights illuminated the area.

Cora entered the store. A youthful attendant stood

on a small step stool, to fill the soda fountain with ice. Cora stood in his line of vision. "Excuse me, young man. I'm on my way home from Phoenix and trying to get to Saguaro Valley. Am I close?"

"Saguaro Valley?" He pushed up the bill of his cap. "Never heard of it. Is it in Mexico?"

"Mexico? No, it's near Phoenix."

"Wow, lady, you're not even close." He shook his head. Water dripped down his arm as he continued to fill the machine. "The huge sign for the Mexican border should've clued you in."

There was a sign? Good thing she stopped for directions before being frisked by the border cops and snuffled by guard dogs.

"I didn't know I was *that* lost." She lifted her hands from the counter and momentarily pressed them onto her aching temples. This was one more secret to keep from Ed. "Could you help me, please?" she asked the young man. "I lost my map and took the wrong exit."

"Just a minute. Let me finish what I'm doin'." The young man wiped his hands on his ripped jeans as he stepped off the stool. He pulled an Arizona map from under the counter and looked at the list of cities and towns. "Hey! There really is a Saguaro Valley. OK, first, you want to get back on Sasabe Highway and go about ten or twelve miles until—"

Cora held up her hand to stop him. "Wait. Could you give it to me in landmarks? I don't know my directions very well." She pulled a napkin from a nearby dispenser, and prepared to jot down the information.

He huffed. "I can get you to the Interstate, but after that you're on your own with the landmarks, grandma." The smart-alecky kid pointed outside. "OK, see this road right here?"

Cora nodded, and felt a surge of vexation at his condescending tone.

"Go that way until you come to the Bacadillo Hut. Hang a right at the light and that will get you back on the highway. Got that? Now, take the..." he paused to count. "Take the fourth exit, no wait, make that the fifth exit, then turn left. That road will take you right to I-10 which should take you close to Saguaro Valley." He looked up with a smirk and added. "Eventually."

"Bacadillo Hut. Got it. Now, what was the rest?"

He took the napkin and scrawled the directions as he mumbled, "Old people shouldn't be allowed to drive."

At that point, Cora couldn't have agreed more. Wearied, she thanked the impertinent teenager, grabbed the napkin and hurried to her car. She drove off. At least she could make it to the Bacadillo Hut with no problem. After that, who knew?

She unwrinkled the makeshift map and read out loud. "Right at light. Boy, Junior. I hope you know what you're talking about and not sending this old lady on a wild goose chase."

A Bucket o' Cluck restaurant and a few specialty shops were located by the highway's on- and off-ramps. She was finally headed in the right direction. Cora breathed a little easier and relaxed. She adjusted the rearview mirror to block the glaring, uneven headlights of the car behind her.

Mile after mile, she cautiously ventured deeper into the low hills. The terrain continued to change as the hills became more prominent. It was so late. Why hadn't she called Ed back at that convenience store when she had the chance? He was probably worried sick about her.

A sign came into view. "Iguana Bend!" she shouted. "I know where I am now." That's where she visited Letitia in the local heart center. Encouragement lifted her spirits.

New housing developments had sprung up, hiding the old landmarks she had once relied upon. Before long, she came to a recognizable stretch of road. Almost home.

The relief was short-lived.

A quick and disturbing thought continued to plague her as she glanced into the rearview mirror. It was crazy, but she couldn't shake the feeling that the same dark car with misaligned halogen headlights had followed her for several miles.

Cora slowed so the car could pass. It slowed, too. She picked up speed, and it kept pace with her. Uh-oh. Was he really following her or was this her overactive imagination kicking into high gear?

A sudden turn onto a side road with the mysterious car in hot pursuit brought the truth home. His brights flashed and momentarily blinded her. Phantom stalker, indeed! The malicious driver pulled up close behind her, only inches from her car. A jolt rocked her as his car made contact. Once, then twice. His horn blared.

Did he expect her to pull over? In the middle of nowhere?

"Not on your life, weirdo. There have been too many people on my phone, in my house, and in my dresser."

Dahlia's advice echoed in her ears. "It's time to stop bein' the victim."

Temper forced her usually timid disposition to change. It was either fight or flight. Cora chose both. With empowerment, determination, and adrenaline pumping, she sped up to put some distance between them. Under normal circumstances she'd never drive at this perilous speed.

The chase continued for another two miles. Cora had to keep her wits about her. It would be too dangerous to be isolated off the main road with a maniac on her bumper. She peered into the mirror again. The vehicle had fallen back considerably.

As the Lincoln rounded a curve, Cora could see a small house in the distance. If she turned her lights off and backed into the darkened driveway, the unshakable predator might not notice her and drive by.

Wow! Where'd that thought come from? It didn't matter…she was going to do it. Cora stepped on the accelerator to widen the gap more. Then, she approached the house, killed her lights and backed into the private drive. She parked the Lincoln beside another car, and waited.

At long last, the maniac's car zipped past. She sighed. Now was her opportunity to make a beeline back to town. Cora turned on the lights and stomped on the gas. Tires burned rubber. Her car fishtailed on the gravel as it turned onto the road. She hung on to the steering wheel and fought to bring it back under control without losing speed.

"I did it! I did it!" she yelled out loud, and basked in her own glory. "I *can* take care of myself." The exhilaration of the moment spurred her on. She drew a deep breath, and loosened her death grip on the steering wheel.

However, several minutes later, Cora's glory-basking moments dissipated as the intimidating lights crept up on her again. A moan escaped her lips. What would she do if he stayed on her tail?

Another idea came to mind as Cora approached the main drag. Her heart pounded as she pulled into the drive-thru lane at the Grill-n-Chill Root Beer stand.

Tires screeched and a horn blared. Cora twisted in her seat. The stalker's car tried to nose ahead of a van that pulled in behind her. He'd found her.

There she was, stuck in the drive-thru lane. She couldn't get out of the car now even if she wanted. Several cars snaked around the building. Her side mirror revealed the damaged fender of the pursuer's car. Well, duh, of course, it was. He'd rammed into her a few miles back.

The Lincoln inched forward so she could get a better view of the car. Dark blue. Ah-ha! Another clue. The only dark blue car she knew belonged to kindhearted Dr. Sam. She shook her head. Preposterous.

She zipped right past the squawking speaker that asked for her order and pulled up to the pick-up window. Without hesitation, Cora rolled her window down.

The lady poked her head out. "You didn't give us your order, ma'am. Would you like our Quarter Pound Slimer or our new Double Chubby Cluck?"

"No-no-no! I need directions to the police station."

"I'm not good with directions. I'll have to ask the manager. Hold on a sec."

The lady left. Cora anxiously tapped her left foot on the floorboard. She readjusted the side mirror, to focus on the drive-thru window and the honking vehicle two cars behind.

A few moments later, an older man with a stained apron leaned out. He rested his burly forearm on the frame and turned his attention to Cora. "I'm Max. Now, what can I do for you?"

"Directions to the police station, please."

"No problem. Go on Bilger to the second stop light." The store manager grunted and leaned out the window. "Will ya stop blowing that stupid horn, before I make ya eat it?" He looked at Cora. "Where was I? Oh, yeah, Bilger. Then turn east and go five blocks.

"There's a small bridge you go over on Braddock and then go straight to where the old high school used to be. That'll be Bradford. Now, Bradford is divided so you have to go around the water filtration plant. The police station is the big building on the south side of the street."

Cora was once again lost in the jumble of testosterone-laced directions.

"Can't miss it," he added with a wink and a smile.

Wanna bet? With an uneasy gulp and an anemic smile, Cora thanked the man. Logic told her the previous ten minutes had been a total waste. She sped out of the restaurant's drive, onto Bilger Street, and swerved to the right so there would be no need to brake. The dark car pulled out from behind the van to follow her.

This was no time for fear to take over. Cora risked a backward glance. Her clammy hands strangled the steering wheel as she impulsively raced through an intersection on a yellow light. Forced to stop at the second corner, she took a deep breath and exhaled slowly.

Eerie halogen headlights gleamed in her side

mirror from a few cars behind. Her stomach plummeted. In spite of the red light, her foot stomped on the accelerator full force. The Lincoln shot across two lanes of traffic. Angry drivers blasted her with a cacophony of horns. Two blocks later, she made a hard right turn, much to the annoyance of a livid taxi driver who shook his fist.

The previous ninety seconds were a blur. It was as though someone else had control of the car. She shivered.

The access to a strip mall was conveniently on her right, and Cora made a sharp turn to enter. Maybe she could get a signal on her cell phone to call Ed. Her heart sank. The parking lot was nearly empty and the store windows were dark. With the stalker only one stop light behind, she was desperate to find a place to hide the Lincoln. Cora drove to the back of the mall and jerked the car to a stop between a maxed-out dumpster and a delivery truck.

Ten minutes should be enough time for Marvin Maniac to pass by. Apprehension, mixed with sporadic headiness from the narrow escapes, made her tremble.

The mouth-watering pictures on the truck grabbed her attention. Oooh, Dolly McElf snacks! Her stomach growled and reminded her it had been nine hours since lunch. She turned off the lights and cut the engine, and dreamed of wolfing down a box or two of ooey-gooey, golden Twinkle Cakes. Focus, Cora. Focus.

She should've ordered a Slimer at the Grill-n-Chill, and why didn't she have sense to tell the manager to call the police instead of asking for directions? Lost, alone and hungry, Cora buried her head in her arms and sobbed. She had to get home.

Several minutes passed as she put time between her and the dark car. Both physically and mentally drained, Cora sighed and wiped her eyes and nose. She scanned the area. No off-kilter lights. She slipped out of her hidey-hole.

The rest of the trip home proved uneventful, although she continued her vigil for vivid blue headlights. Cora turned into the cul-de-sac. She pulled into her driveway, took a long, deep breath and slowly exhaled. Home at last.

Without warning, blue lights glared from across the street, and brazenly pierced the darkness.

Cora screamed and desperately jabbed the garage door opener. The door went half way up, lurched, and came back down. Up, down. Up. She waited for the garage door to fully open, then pounded on the horn with hopes it wouldn't deploy the airbag. She drove in with one long sustaining blast of the horn.

Ed stood in the garage, and frantically waved his hands. "Cora, stop. What's wrong?"

She flew from the car and into his arms. Her body quaked as he pulled her close.

"What happened?" Ed held her at arm's length, and looked directly into her eyes. "Cora?" He sternly, but gently shook her shoulders.

Between sobs, she shrieked, "Car—b-blue lights— followed me home!"

"Someone followed you?"

Her head bobbed as she pointed to the door. "Out there." Cora ran into the house.

❧❧

Ed scanned the garage for a weapon. Storage

boxes, bicycles, golf clubs. He grabbed his Big Bertha titanium driver, and rushed out into the night. Glaring lights hit his face. A car pulled out of the driveway and sped from the cul-de-sac. An alarm sounded in his head and shock registered as the vehicle disappeared. "That's George's car." he responded in disbelief.

10

Cora had locked herself in the bathroom by the time Ed came into the house. He tapped on the door. "Cora?" His voice grew soft and gentle. "Come on out, Toots. You're safe, now. He's gone."

Her muffled voice asked, "Did you see the car?"

"Yes, I saw it. Are you sure that's the one that followed you?"

The lock turned and the bathroom door opened slowly, then Cora flew into Ed's arms. He held his sobbing wife close and kissed the top of her head. "Shhh. It's going to be fine. Let's go to the living room and talk. We'll try to work things out." He offered his hand.

Cora nodded and took his hand. They walked to the sofa where Ed tossed a throw pillow aside so they could sit. "Are you feeling better now?"

"I think so."

"Good." He drew a ragged breath. "I'm sorry to bring this back up, but are you sure the car outside was the one that followed you?"

She swallowed hard. "Well, it was an older car, with those awful halogen headlights."

"A lot of cars have those lights."

"Yes, but these were lopsided, Ed." Her stomach growled. "Let's go to the kitchen, I need something to eat."

He followed after her. "You want to eat at a time

like this?"

"I only had half a sandwich at noon. My thinker might work better on a full tummy. Would you start a pot of coffee for me? Make it strong." Cora opened the fridge and eyeballed Ed's disgusting lunch meat. Naw, she'd *never* be that hungry. She grabbed the pickle jar and set it on the counter. "My hands are too shaky. Would you open this for me?"

Once the lid hit the counter, she crammed a dill pickle in her mouth. With great delight she crunched and swallowed. "I forgot how good a pickle could be. Come help me over here."

"You sure are bossy when you're keyed up."

The jars and bottles on the refrigerator door wobbled and clinked as she jerked it open. Ed waited while she filled his arms with various foodstuffs.

He shook his head. "Cora if you eat all this, you'll dream of your great-aunt Gussie!"

With pickle-stuffed cheeks, she looked back at Ed. Pickle seeds flew from her mouth as she asked, "You fink I'll be fleeping fometime tonight?" She swallowed, grabbed the loaf of bread and began to build her sandwich with shredded chicken and cheese. The butter knife slipped from her fingers and dropped to the floor. "I'm still a nervous wreck." Tears formed in her eyes, and she wiped them away. "I need some fortitude. Would you pour the coffee, please?"

Ed complied and went to the refrigerator for the Half and Half. He gave it a quick sniff before adding some to her cup. "I know this is hard, but we need to get back to the subject. Tell me about the car that followed you. Do you know what kind it was? Or the year?"

"What do I know about cars, Ed?" She added

sliced onion to the gastrointestinal nightmare on her plate. Cora enthusiastically gulped a bite of sandwich, stepped away from the counter and grabbed his arm. "Now, wait. I do remember something. He followed me to the Grill 'n' Chill. The area was lit up enough for me to see that the car was dark blue and the front was dented in. Did you get a glimpse of it? Was it the same one?" Her forehead wrinkled as she waited for his answer.

"Yes, I'm afraid so." Ed smoothed back his thinning hair. "It was George Shipley."

"Dahlia thought it might be him right from the start." She paced the floor. "He had access to our house before you fired him. Why didn't you change the security code?"

Ed eased onto a kitchen stool. "That's when I was in Scotland at the Senior Open. It never entered my mind when I got home. Besides, George is so tenderhearted, I can't believe he'd be a part of all this."

"If he's such a Boy Scout, why did you fire him?"

He rubbed his chin. "Wendell told me George took money from the Pro Shop. It was hard to believe. When he showed me the security cam tape, I had no choice."

"You didn't tell me that." Cora's coffee cup shook as she set it down. "Why would he torment me? I only met the man once at a Christmas party."

"I guess he used you to get back at me." Ed shook his head. "George had a bout of hard luck and I helped him out a few times this past year. Then he made some wrong choices, but I didn't press charges. So why would he retaliate?"

"He must've been desperate to steal from you."

Ed seemed a thousand miles away as he

explained, "His mother has terminal cancer and begged them for weeks to pull the plug. His wife, Marcy, was the main breadwinner and his mom's primary caregiver. On top of that, she worked nights. When stress overwhelmed Marcy, she took off and left him financially strapped with a dying mother to care for. That led him to take desperate measures."

Cora laid her sandwich down and studied Ed's profile. "How sad. Those poor people."

"George once told me he had a gambling problem before I knew him, so I was under the impression he got the help he needed. When Marcy left him, there went most of the income. That's when his old habits started again." Ed looked at his wife with sincerity. "I didn't realize he was so deep in debt."

"So what happened?"

"Well, understand George couldn't make it on one income. One night he took some money from the golf Pro Shop. He thought he could make a killing at the casinos, then pay it back before I found out." Ed raised his hands in frustration. "What really disappointed me was, he flatly denied the theft. If he'd just come to me instead of gambling, we could've worked something out."

Cora spoke after a brief silence. "Do you think George is the caller?"

He reached over and took her hand. "I think there's a good chance he is."

If George was the caller, the case would soon be solved. However, what if he *wasn't* the culprit? Her body shook with a cold chill. The caller told her that he'd taken years to track her down because of what she did to him. George had been around forever. So why would he wait until now to make his move? Other than giving him a Christmas fruitcake, she had never done anything to the man.

Cora looked at her husband, who was lost in his own thoughts. "Ed, I remember the caller insisted he gave you a manila envelope to put in our safe. Do you remember George doing that?"

"No, I really don't. It must've been a long time ago and I just forgot."

"So, now what are we going to do?" Cora questioned.

"You won't like this, Toots." He squared his shoulders. "We have to call the authorities again. Let's do it now and get it over with."

Cora's heart did the river dance. Her toes coiled and a cold sweat erupted from her forehead.

The police were coming again. They had their own expectations. Everything had to fit in a box with a big red bow and if it didn't they'd write it off. On the plus side, this was evening and Davis and Reed weren't on duty.

Tonight Ed could do all the talking. Surely they'd accept his account of the mysterious car. She wouldn't let her mouth run amuck this time. Phantom stalker, indeed.

Stillness permeated the room, except for the constant ticking of the grandfather clock. Cora glanced out the patio doors to the far edge of their property where Ed's golf course was located. It was a beautiful, clear night with a sky full of stars. Peaceful and serene. If only her world mirrored that tranquility. At least the caller's mask of secrecy was replaced with an actual face. It was a step in the right direction. The next hurdle was to tell Ed where she went today.

Ed returned and broke her train of thought. "The

police will be here soon."

"Let's sit in the living room." Cora took a deep breath and bit her lip as he settled next to her. "I'm sorry about storming out of the house this morning. I didn't mean to worry you."

"So, where were you and what took you so long?" A frown creased his forehead as he waited for her reply.

She swallowed hard. Her voice wavered as she spoke. "I told you there were errands to run. Then I got lost downtown in all the traffic and needed the map. But it was gone."

"I saw it on top of your dresser when you left."

"You did? I was sure it was with my purse. Well, anyway," She paused. This was the time and place to reveal all. Her shoulders raised as she gathered her courage. "Oh, Ed, please be patient while I think of the right words to explain. This is one of the hardest things I've ever had to tell you—"

The doorbell interrupted her confession.

Ed huffed in exasperation. "Well, you be thinking of the right words while I let the police in." He went to answer the door.

She vacillated between torment and relief. A mere blink away from going berserk.

The stern-faced policeman stepped inside. Ed briefed him about their previous complaint of the backyard prowler and then added today's events.

As Officer McNulty gathered information from the couple, Cora mentioned that the stalker rammed the back of their Lincoln. Twice.

She held her breath, as a deep frown creased Ed's forehead. If he couldn't tolerate a dented fender, how would he handle the whole truth?

Ed and Cora described every detail as best they could. The officer assured them that George would be picked up for questioning.

Once the policeman left, Ed inhaled and released it slowly. "Well, that part's over with. I'll call the insurance company about the damages to the Lincoln tomorrow morning. At least we know that George is the culprit. You won't have to worry about him calling, anymore. We can put it all behind us."

Cora rubbed the goose pimples on her arms. "I'm not sure when I'll ever feel safe again." Her gaze once again drifted out over the finely manicured golf course. "Thank you for backing me up about seeing George's car. I was beginning to feel you'd never believe me."

He sat next to her and patted her knee. "Now, if you remember, you were trying to tell me something before we were interrupted."

Second thoughts gnawed at Cora. He'd just regained his confidence in her, could she now dash his hopes of a happy future together? She looked at him and quickly lowered her head.

An uncomfortable silence hung in the air between them. He took her hand in his. "Obviously, you still need some time."

Riddled with guilt, Cora twisted in her seat. She couldn't muster enough nerve to continue with her confession. It would have to wait.

Ed finally stood and cleared his throat. Then, he walked behind her and squeezed her shoulders. "Think it might help if we went out tomorrow, just the two of us?"

"Where do you want to go?"

"I thought we could take the Lincoln into the body shop." He quickly snapped his fingers. "Hey, I know!

While I was in Phoenix getting the trophies for Saturday's golf tournament, I noticed a great restaurant. It's called the Pegasi Café."

She felt the color drain from her face. "The Peg-Pegasi?"

He leaned over her shoulder and whispered, "Have you ever been there?"

Cora immediately looked to the floor. Her hands shook as she recalled George's menacing words: *"Naughty, naughty Cora has been to the Pegasi Café again."* Her mind raced with uncertainties. The Pegasi? The very name filled her with alarm.

Ed joined her on the sofa. "Well, Toots, have you been there?"

"Uh, n-no," she stammered. "Well, I've heard of it, in fact, the caller mentioned it, but I don't remember being there." A chill ran up her spine. Was Ed's suggestion merely a coincidence? It seemed innocent enough, however, she sensed a smidgen of trickery.

He cleared his throat. "What do you say we go there tomorrow and get away from this place? It'll be something different for us."

She gave a feeble smile. "I guess we could do that."

The look on Ed's face suggested he knew something, but not another word was said.

11

Ed paced at the bathroom door. "Cora, I told them we'd have the car at the body shop this morning." He glanced at his watch. "You about ready?"

She peeked out the door. "Yes. I just have to get my shoes on. Oh, and change purses."

Rushing a woman was an exercise in futility, and Ed had learned the hard way. He sighed. "Fine. I'll be in the car."

The car radio kept his mind engaged during the wait. The news report, weather update, a stock market summary and five songs later, Cora finally made an appearance. He forced a smile as he leaned out the window. "You follow in the Lincoln."

They pulled out of their cul-de-sac and made their way to Shifting Sands Road.

Ed squinted and lowered the visor to block the Arizona sun from his eyes. Once he made a left hand turn, he glanced in the rearview mirror to make sure Cora was still behind him.

There are moments when one decides between pursuing a plan or letting it go. Did he really want to go through with this stupid strategy at the Pegasi? The restaurant seemed to be the hub of the problem. Cora's initial reaction would either vindicate or convict and then she'd have to explain her involvement with other men and why she lied to him.

Anger made his stomach churn. The night before,

she trembled in his arms. Their embrace was awkward, and he didn't feel like protecting her. George Shipley had betrayed him, and he feared Cora had done the same. All things considered, he chose to stick with his plan.

Ed raked his fingers through his hair and frowned. He had so little time to come up with a coherent theory about Cora and George. Either she had done something to him or she had done something and he found out about it. Ed rubbed his forehead as the inner debate relentlessly boggled his mind. Then a thought hit. Maybe George saw Cora and the man at the Pegasi. Ah-ha, that *had* to be why he blackmailed her.

First things, first. Drop the Lincoln off at the body shop and then let her face the music. By the time Cora joined him in the car, Ed still wrestled with second thoughts. Would this be the end of their relationship? How would he cope without her? He cleared his throat. Sure he'd been on the PGA tour a lot through the years, but Cora unfaithful? The thought never entered his mind. Their drive across town was silent.

Ed pulled into the rear parking area, helped Cora out of the car, and together, they walked to the front of the restaurant. Cora stopped dead in her tracks. She took a deep breath and looked up at the sign. He inwardly smiled. Good, she hesitated. Her guilty conscience finally kicked in. This ordeal shouldn't take too long and, with any luck, they wouldn't even need a table. Heh, heh, heh.

He clutched her elbow, and firmly led her into the ornate restaurant foyer where small fountains bubbled on either side of the entrance. Archway insets on the walls depicted bountiful vineyards which stretched into the landscape.

Ed was aware of Cora's discomfort as she licked her lips and nervously scanned the room. How long until she buckled and asked to go home? After all, her friend might be here, and she wouldn't want to linger in their rendezvous place. His pulse quickened as the tawdry thought sank in. Their rendezvous place. He mentally smacked his forehead.

A cheerful hostess, with a flaxen French braid, welcomed the couple as they walked to the podium. Ed nodded and smiled. "Reservation for Timms."

"Timms." She checked her list. "Yes, here we are. Since it's a cool day, would you folks like to be seated in the courtyard? We still have one table open."

Cora's response was monotone. "That would be nice, wouldn't it, Ed?"

He nodded and silently pleaded, C'mon Toots, give in, already.

The young woman smiled. "We use it primarily during the evening hours, but it's nice to take full advantage of it on days like this."

The hostess escorted them through the indoor dining area. Cora stopped for a second and took in the mural which illustrated a panoramic view of Greece's brilliant blue Mediterranean waters.

They followed the girl through large Corinthian columns that led outside to a canopied courtyard. Gurgling water trickled from the Pegasus fountain bordered by white wrought-iron tables. She took them to the vacant table in a far corner, and Ed held a chair for Cora to be seated.

The perky blonde handed them small festive menus and stated that Ben, their waiter, would be out soon.

Cora adjusted her posture and perused the list of

Grecian delicacies. "Look at the names of these dishes." She smiled and pointed. "How do you pronounce this? Spa-nak-o-pie-tees?"

"Prob'ly." What an actress. Ed peered over the top of his menu. She sat stiffly as her eyes darted about the courtyard. He held his breath; wild anticipation grew in his chest. Was she about to break?

Their eyes locked. "Why haven't we tried this place before, Ed?"

He grunted. His plot was falling apart at the seams. No, more like obliterated.

"Ooh, they have vanilla bean cappuccino. I've gotta have some of that." Cora tapped on a menu item. "Now, this looks good. Chicken Souvlaki. Marinated and grilled chicken breast. Comes with a choice of soupa, salata or French fries. I'm guessing the salata is salad. I think I'll go with that."

Disgruntled, Ed didn't look up this time. "Whatever," he mumbled and flipped the menu over. Cora was certainly giving an award winning performance. It was *almost* believable. He rubbed the back of his neck. This was going too far. Who's stupid scheme was this, anyway?

As if to answer his question, she said, "Look honey, it was *your* idea to come here." She leaned closer. "You've only said a few words to me since we left the house."

He tried to quell the rising anger, and gritted his teeth. "Obviously not one of my stellar ideas." How was he going to keep his temper? Cora acted so nonchalant. Did the woman have no shame? Or, was she playing a game, confident he wouldn't confront her in public?

Cora continuously kept her eye on the other

patrons. He felt for the photo inside his breast pocket. Was she looking for *him*? Or the young stud she left with yesterday?

Then she turned and studied Ed's face. "You don't like it here, do you? We can leave, they haven't taken our order, yet."

"Would you mind?" Ed looked up. A muscle worked in his jaw. "I see the waiter coming. I'll just tell him we have to go."

The young man in black slacks and white dress shirt with the Pegasi logo came to their table. Before Ed could get a word out, the waiter said, "Hello. My name is Ben. I'll be your server today." When he turned to Cora, his face lit in recognition as he poured water into their blue goblets. "Well, hey there, good lookin'. Sure didn't expect to see you back so soon. I'll bet you'd like your Vanilla Bean Cappuccino, wouldn't you?"

Cora's face revealed shock at the young man's question, and she cast a startled glance at Ed. She simply nodded in response while her foot tapped against the table leg. He settled back in his wrought-iron chair and scowled. This was a new wrinkle. How would it play out?

The waiter casually shrugged and turned to him. "And you, sir?"

Ed threw hot eye daggers in her direction. The waiter knew her. If that wasn't proof positive that she had been here before, he didn't know what was. She was toast. He cleared his throat several times to keep his temper at bay.

"Sir?" the waiter stepped closer, leaned down and raised his voice. "Would you like something stronger than coffee?"

Ed looked at Ben's commiserating smile. "I'm not

deaf, son, and as tempting as your offer might be, I'll just take regular coffee, with cream." Then as an afterthought, he added a terse, "Please."

Ben nodded in compliance. "Thank you. I'll be back in a few minutes to take your order. He threw Cora a puzzled look, and promptly left to get their coffee.

They sat in silence for several minutes.

Cora's face suddenly contorted. "Oh no. Ed, we have to get out of here, right now."

Ed stymied a smile. Showtime!

"*Now*, Ed."

"Why?" He fought the urge to stand, and crane his neck in all directions like an owl on the hunt. Who did she see? Was he coming this way?

"It's that busybody, DeeDee Hockenheimer, from the county treasurer's office." Cora donned a plastic smile and returned an enthusiastic wave as the woman in a mini-skirt rose from her seat. "She's coming over here. Listen, we have to act like we're having a good time or she'll spread rumors all over the county."

Ed smirked. "Wonder if she was here yesterday?"

"What?" Cora shook her head. "Aw, never mind. Here she is." Cora stood and her voice raised an octave. "DeeDee-e-e-e! How long has it been?"

"Since you stepped down as county treasurer." DeeDee lightly hugged her and kissed the air beside each cheek. "It's been almost two years. What have you been doing?"

Ed sipped his water, choked, and sipped again. That was the million-dollar question.

Their anorexic tête-à-tête was thankfully interrupted when DeeDee glanced over her shoulder. "Hogan's tapping his Rolex. Looks like he's in a hurry to leave. Well, it was good to see you again. Give me a call, we'll do lunch. Bye." She turned on her five-inch heels and carefully teetered her way to her husband.

A large entree was presented to a middle-aged couple seated near Ed and Cora. The server set the platter down. "As with Greek tradition," he announced, "Cheese Saganaki is flamed before your eyes." With a soft click of his lighter, the main dish was instantly ignited in a fiery whoosh. The courtyard diners were enthralled with the glowing display.

In spite of approving cheers from onlookers, intermingled with rousing ethnic music, a brittle silence once again loomed between Ed and Cora.

ॐॐ

Cora toyed with the cloth napkin on her lap. "I'll bet that burning cheese dish is good." She looked at her husband. "Have you decided what you want, yet?"

When no answer came, Cora made no further attempts at small talk. She stared at the prominent Pegasus fountain. This pretense was becoming more difficult, and Ed's sour attitude only fed her discomfort.

She took another glance around the dining area and shivered. Were they being watched? Would the caller show up and confront them? Her stomach clenched tight. She felt like a caged animal, confined, and scrutinized.

"I can't take this any longer." Cora dabbed her eyes and left the table, her fragile composure at its breaking point. The heels of her cream-colored pumps echoed on the stone floor as she stormed toward the powder room.

Relieved to be alone, Cora dropped her purse on the counter and mumbled under her breath, "That man. I hate it when he clams up." She stared at her reflection in the mirror and was taken aback at how the dim lighting accentuated her wearied appearance. Her face was pale and pinched thanks to weeks of fatigue.

Cora roughly unzipped her handbag. She rooted around for lipstick, and added the light matte tint to her lips. The minute Ed mentioned coming to the Pegasi, her instincts screamed "no," so whatever possessed her to agree to it? She ripped a tissue from a nearby dispenser, leaned over the sink to get a closer look in the lavatory mirror then blotted her lipstick.

She'd been resolved to take advantage of their day away to finally unload what had been gnawing at her conscience. Ed was so testy right now, she couldn't tell him anything…let alone something of *this* magnitude.

Suddenly her heart skipped a beat as a new thought occurred to her. Was he acting that way because he suspected something? Or, had George disclosed her secret after all?

Her mind continued to process different ways of clearing the air. How she dreaded the impending consequences.

12

The brisk rhythm of a Greek folk song encompassed the dining room. Ed wasn't prepared for the intensity of emotions that overwhelmed him when they entered the Pegasi. He had recognized hurt and anger over Cora's infidelity. However since they arrived, jealousy and resentment reared their ugly heads, along with the implication of his inadequacy as a husband. Ed recovered the old picture from his breast pocket and released a troubled sigh. Was he to blame somehow? Was it something he did, or something he didn't do?

Ed's brow furrowed as he focused on the impending problem of how to confront Cora. He tapped his fingers on the table, and brooded over the increased tension in their marriage. His determination grew to find a reason for her betrayal of their wedding vows. Ed wanted to believe that the sum of their union wasn't a complete loss. Still, all he could visualize was his wife at a corner table, holding hands with that young gigolo. He slowly twisted his linen napkin, and dreaded the moment of Cora's confession.

Ben, the waiter, came to Ed's table with the hot drinks that were ordered earlier. "Here's your coffee and complimentary breadsticks," he said. "Would you like to order, now?"

"We'll order when she gets back, but I'd like to ask you a question. You seem to know the lady quite well.

Has she been here before?"

The waiter lowered the serving tray to his side as he answered. "Are you kidding? She comes in at least once a week."

"Are you sure it isn't someone who just resembles her?"

"Absolutely, sir. That lady's one of my favorite customers, and I always look forward to seeing her. We enjoy giving each other a hard time. She has trouble pronouncing some of the Greek words so I tease her about butchering the language." The young man chuckled. "Her usual order is the Chicken Souvlaki Plate with Salata and Vanilla Bean Cappuccino. She complains about the coffee being too strong, but gets it, anyway."

"Does she come alone?"

The waiter cleared his throat and lowered his voice. "Well, I really couldn't say, sir."

Ed leaned forward and retrieved his wallet from his back pocket. He folded a couple bills and discreetly placed them in Ben's hand.

The young man's eyes popped, then he lowered his head. "Wow! Well, everyone knows she comes in here with Dr. Morgan, but that's all I'm gonna say." Ben turned and scurried off.

Ed bristled at the information and felt as though he had been punched in the stomach. Lively background music bounced with a lighthearted spirit, which only served to increase his animosity. He reached for the cream, and hoped the coffee was strong enough to ease the pain in his temple. How was he going to tell Cora that her promiscuous affairs were no longer secret?

৵৶

The indoor dining area quickly filled with hungry lunchtime guests. Voices buzzed and water-filled goblets clinked with ice as Cora slowly weaved her way through the maze of tables to where Ed was seated outside.

The hour of reckoning had arrived. Unable to put it off any longer, she was determined to get everything out in the open.

As Cora approached their table, she heard the ting-ting-ting of Ed's spoon as he mindlessly stirred his coffee. She laid her hand on his to end the irritating noise. "That's enough, Ed." She sent a perfunctory smile to the couple closest to them. Still, he seemed to be in another world and continued to move the spoon, oblivious to everything around him. "Edward. Stop."

"Stop what?" he asked.

"That crazy habit of yours. The endless stirring." She sat across from her husband whose ears colored as he eyed the other diners.

He set his spoon down. "Sorry."

A mixed bag of emotions assailed Cora when she saw Ben, the brazen server, coming.

The waiter threw her a mischievous smile and nudged her shoulder. "Looks like you bagged yourself another beau. You can take that ad out of the paper, now." He paused with the look of expectancy on his face. When Cora offered no lighthearted comeback, he changed the subject. "Ooo-kay, guess my timing's a little off today. Do you want your usual?"

"My usual what?"

"Your usual order." He licked the tip of his pencil

and eagerly waited to mark it down.

Cora shifted in her seat, and frowned at Ed. "I don't know what he's talking about."

The waiter looked at Ed and then back to Cora. "I'm sorry. My crazy sense of humor gets me in trouble, sometimes. What can I get you this afternoon, ma'am?"

She folded her menu, pushed it to the edge of their table and acknowledged his apology with a slight nod. "I believe I'll try the Chicken Souvlaki Plate."

"Very good choice, madam." The young waiter grinned at Ed. "That comes with soup, salad or fries."

She wrung her hands nervously in her lap. "Salad, please, with a couple crackers."

The overconfident young man turned his attention to Ed. "And what will you have, sir?"

"I'll have the same, but make mine with fries." He laid his menu on top of Cora's. The waiter quickly scooped them off the table and left with their food requests.

Cora waited until Ben was out of hearing range then said, "Well, I never. Can you believe how fresh that young man was? You should complain to the manager." Her husband sat motionless, his eyes fixed on the nearby fountain. "Ed, did you hear me?" When he failed to respond again, she touched his arm. His muscles tensed beneath her fingertips. Worry seeped into her voice. "What's wrong?"

He leaned back in his seat and lowered his voice. "Let's go ahead and ask the Lord's blessing for the food, first."

After his prayer, Cora asked, "So are you going to tell me what's wrong?"

Time seemed to stand still before Ed spoke. He

shook his head and broke the uncomfortable silence. "Cora, we need to talk," he muttered in a low voice.

"Yes, I know." She fumbled self-consciously with the napkin on her lap. The longer she tried to ignore the truth, the harder it had become to tell him. Her mind was a tumble of confused thoughts and emotions as she struggled to begin.

He scowled. "So, do you want to start?"

She forced herself to calmly sip her cappuccino. "Oh, this is terrible, it's much too strong." Cora looked up at him. "No, you go ahead and say what's on your mind."

He threw her an ominous look. "Very well. This isn't going to be an easy thing to say, and you probably won't like to hear it, either. After all these years of marriage, I feel I have the right to know what's been going on with the doctor." He took a drink of the strong coffee and set his cup back on the table with a heavy *thunk*.

Stunned by the abruptness of his statement, Cora gasped. "How did you find out?"

13

Mortified, Cora hung her head. She waited too long to tell Ed. How much did he know?

He glared. "So, is it serious?"

Cora couldn't deny the truth any longer. Her doubts returned to the Pandora's Box she was about to unlock. "I-I'm afraid it might be." Her hand shook as she rubbed her forehead.

"You're afraid it *might* be? You mean you don't know?" He helped himself to a breadstick. "What does he say?"

"He's going to tell me later this week."

"What? He's not sure, either?" Ed's breadstick broke in half. "Cora."

"Well, he's pretty sure, but for heaven's sake, Ed, he doesn't want to tell me something like that until he's positive. He doesn't want to give me any false hope."

"Are you playing some kind of game, or did you think this wouldn't matter?"

"I'd hardly call it a game." Cora boldly met his eyes. "Of course, it matters."

"Why haven't you told me before this?" He sounded beside himself. "Your nonchalant attitude has me totally baffled. Have we really grown apart that much?"

Cora sighed. She felt exposed and transparent, as if he perceived she was lying. "Oh, Eddie, I'm so confused, I can't think straight with that crazy man calling and all. I didn't know how to tell you. I mean it's not something I wanted to blurt out over morning toast and coffee, you know?"

Ed's vexation was written all over his face. "I guess you're right. Please pass the marmalade. Oh, and by the way, Ed, I'm having a torrid love affair."

Cora's jaw nearly hit the table as she stared at him. Once she gained a wisp of composure, she yelped, "I'm what?"

"Having an affair with Dr. Morgan." He sat back awkwardly, and scrutinized his wife.

Cora gritted her teeth, eager to keep the shocking conversation strictly private. "I-am-not! And will you keep your voice down, Edward? People can hear you." She paused. "And who is Dr. Morgan?"

He leaned forward, placed the palms of his hands on the table, and growled, "Your lover. As if you didn't know."

Heads turned. Silverware clinked on the china plates as the courtyard became quiet except for the splashing fountain.

"Shhh," she hissed. "What on earth are you talking about?"

Ed kept his voice lowered. "I heard that you've been meeting Morgan here in this very restaurant every week." He motioned around the dining area.

The waiter had just approached their table. He raised his eyebrows, set the food down and quickly left them alone.

She crossed her arms. "And just where did you pick up this choice bit of information? Wendell, the dynamic detective?"

"I saw you walking out of here yesterday. In

Morgan's arms." The photo Ed had found was now on the table in front of Cora. His voice shook. "And while we're on the subject, who's *this* Lothario?" He poked it with his forefinger for added emphasis.

Her face reddened with embarrassment when she saw the incriminating photograph. Her eyes narrowed into angry slits. "Where did you get that?"

"In your dresser drawer. Right where you left it. Now, I demand some answers."

"How can you sit there and humiliate me like this?" Cora began to cry.

"You were here yesterday, right?"

"I've n-never been here before."

"The waiter said you have a usual order, Cora. And you just ordered it."

"I can't possibly have a usual order since this is the first time I've been here. I wouldn't forget the courtyard or that fountain. Don't you think I'd remember a place like this? And I don't know any Dr. Morgan."

Ed studied her face for a moment. "Then what have *you* been talking about?" He paused. "Why have you been acting so strange lately? And, there's still the matter of that man holding you in this picture."

Cora blinked back tears and scooped up a bite of souvlaki. With her fork paused mid-air, she fixed her eyes on Ed. "Dr. Brant sent me to see a specialist for a few tests." She set her fork down and wiped her mouth. Then she pulled out her billfold and removed a receipt. "Here, you can check it out if you don't believe me. It's my receipt from the doctor's office."

When Ed refused to take the paper, she released a sigh. "Here. I insist. You need to see it." She slammed it on the table in front of him. "Look at it, Ed."

He picked up the piece of paper and quickly read it, then pushed the receipt back to her. "Even so, I saw you come out of this café yesterday. Can you explain that?"

"I can't. I wasn't here. I was hooked up to monitors all afternoon."

"All right, then, just what kind of tests did you have?" Ed chomped off a bite of crisp breadstick and brushed fallen sesame seeds from his black trousers. He crossed his arms and settled back with a smug look, as if she were hopelessly cornered.

She toyed with the salad and measured her words carefully. Her voice quivered. "Oh, Eddie. I'm so scared. I'm either in the early stages of Alzheimer's or I'm losing my mind."

The muscles tightened around his mouth. "That's ridiculous, Cora."

"Oh, is it? Let me tell you what's been going on." The words tumbled out of her mouth as she told him of her short-term memory loss, of forgetting people's names and trouble completing things that were once second nature. "I can't even concentrate on simple mathematical procedures and I was the county treasurer for years."

"What did Morgan say about it?"

"Not Dr. Morgan. Remember, I don't know him? Dr. Keith. Let me finish." She took a drink of water. "Brandi Fisher said I bought coconut cookies for my son, Ed. *Coconut.*"

"Your son?" Ed picked up the photograph and waved it. "Is this the father?"

"Don't be obtuse." Cora spouted. "You're my one and only. There's never been anyone else."

"If you say so." He waved the picture for

emphasis and set it down.

Their heated exchange was suddenly interrupted when a large, swarthy man in his early sixties ambled to their table in full Greek regalia.

"I'm Mikos Pagonis, owner of this fine café," he announced to Ed with heavy accent. The Greek restaurateur wiped his large palm on his red embroidered vest and offered a hand in greeting. Mikos turned to Cora, and his face immediately brightened as he offered a big smile. "You feel better today, yes?"

"Well, I've had better days."

"Sorry to hear this. We at Pegasi have been very concerned." He stretched his arms wide. "But souvlaki is to your liking today, yes?"

Cora nodded and dabbed her mouth with the linen napkin. "Delicious, Mr. Pagonis."

He threw his arms open again. "What's this? *Mr. Pagonis?*" He placed his hands on his chest. "It's Mikos, your friend. Mikos!"

A pronounced blush inched its way onto her cheeks. "All right, Mikos." The unrelenting stares of the other diners drew her attention. "I'm sorry we've disturbed your other guests."

"No matter, dear lady. You eat before souvlaki gets cold. Mikos will serve baklava for his favorite lady customer. On the house." He summoned Ben with a commanding wave of his hand.

Ed and Cora were speechless as they watched their host speak to the waiter, then make his way between white Corinthian columns into the main dining area.

Ed glared at his wife over the top of his glasses. "You can explain, yes?" His voice oozed with sarcasm.

"Look, I don't know that man." Cora stabbed the salad with her fork.

"Right." The Greek music ended and Ed lowered his voice. "Just like you don't know the waiter, or the man holding you in the picture, or the one holding you yesterday?"

"See? Welcome to my crazy world," she whispered back. "Nothing makes sense any more. Let me tell you about the picture." She took a drink of water.

"I'm waiting."

"Remember yesterday morning when I was getting ready to go to Phoenix? I got another phone call. The caller said he left something in my dresser. I was scared to death because he'd been in the house. That picture you're holding was in my drawer. That's when you came into the room and I put it back. It's me in the photo, but I don't remember having it taken, especially with that man. He's a complete stranger to me." She wearily reached for her cappuccino and finished the last of it.

Cora shook her head, and placed a hand over the cup as their waiter came by with a steaming carafe of coffee and the promised dessert. He quickly turned and left.

Ed tapped his fingers on the table. "So, exactly what did you do in Phoenix?"

"I told you, I went to see the doctor."

He arched an eyebrow "I guess that's one way to put it."

"Dr. Brant already ruled out a mini-stroke, brain tumor, and thyroid problems. He sent me to see a specialist, Dr. Keith, and that's where I was."

"You're not answering my question. You were

gone a long time. What else did you do?"

"I did some shopping at Nancy's Gift Shoppe, picked up medicine at Montgomery's, ate lunch, and had my hair done at Salon de Belleza. Oh yes, I was stalked on my way home, too."

"Where did you have lunch and with whom?"

Her annoyance with Ed's continued disbelief finally reached the breaking point. Her voice cracked with angry frustration. "I had a chicken salad sandwich at Tammy's Tea Room. Since you're interested in all the details, I had a glass of raspberry iced tea, as well. And except for chatting with Tammy for a few minutes, I was alone, Ed. Very alone." She paused. "After getting my hair done, I went straight to the doctor's office. I don't know what else to say. Either you believe me, or you don't."

Ed was quiet for a moment. "To be completely honest with you, Cora, I know what I saw yesterday. I also see how sincere you are, and how you'd be worried about having Alzheimer's." He reached over and patted her hand. "Why don't you tell me what the doctor said?"

Cora grasped his hand, relieved her husband was ready to listen. "They ran more tests." She nervously traced the Greek key design on the rim of her dinner plate. "He said all things have to be ruled out before Alzheimer's can be determined."

"Why didn't you tell me you were going through this?" He pushed his silverware away, and softened his voice. "I should've been with you."

"Look Ed, it's difficult enough to accept it myself. How was I going to tell you? I'm scared and didn't want to be put away in some secluded home. Remember, Mom had Alzheimer's and I've heard it's hereditary."

Ed rolled his eyes and leaned back in his chair. "Oh, for crying out loud, Cora, it can't be hereditary, at least not for you. I know you were awfully young at the time, but how could you forget she was your *adopted* mother?" He crunched into another breadstick. A brief silence followed as his statement sank in.

Her hands flew to her cheeks. "I guess because she's the only mother I've ever known. See what I mean? It isn't clicking up here anymore." She lightly tapped her head. "I keep forgetting things, Ed. *Important* things."

He chuckled. "Well, that's understandable, you were adopted at the age of two."

"But Ed, it's more than that. If it is Alzheimer's, I'll be wandering around in public, lost and confused. Maybe even *au naturel*. Or walking into rooms full of strangers, feeling like I should know them, and I don't. I saw it with Mom." Cora shut her eyes and promised herself she wouldn't cry. "Look what happened here. They know me, but I don't know them."

"Toots, you know your mom had the best care possible. God loves you, and He promised He wouldn't lead you anywhere He can't take care of you."

"I'm so frustrated," she said with clenched teeth. "How can I believe that promise? After all, God didn't take care of Vanessa in her hour of need. Why would He take care of me?"

Ed scooted his chair closer. "What do you mean He didn't take care of her?"

The waiter brought more water and then quietly removed their plates.

Once Ben left, Cora explained. "Tammy told me

that Van lived an hour after the accident. She suffered in that pile of twisted metal."

"Tammy went through a lot of agony because she couldn't help Van. She came to me and apologized." Ed patted her hand. "Sure, Van was alive, but God intervened. She was unconscious the whole time and didn't suffer."

Cora nodded as she allowed tears to fall into her napkin.

The Lord did take care of her.

Van didn't feel pain. The grief in her hardened heart eased a bit with this new revelation.

"We can count on God to take care of us through all of our problems, including our health." Ed wiped his salty fingers, and brought the subject back to her physical needs. "You still should've told me about these tests. I am your husband, after all."

"I wanted the diagnosis before burdening you with it."

"That's what our wedding vows were all about. For better for worse, in sickness and in health. We promised to be there to support each other through the difficult times."

"If it's Alzheimer's, I'll end up like a helpless baby and die in a very degrading way." She looked unflinchingly into his eyes. "Maybe I thought that you wouldn't love me anymore."

"Not love you? Now who's being obtuse?" He spoke in a gentle tone as he continued to pat her hand. "We'll take it one step at a time. Even if you get to the point where you don't know who I am, I'll still know and love you, Cora. That'll never change."

"Oh, honey," she whispered. Her tears displayed deep love for her husband. If only he could clear the other uncertainties in her heart.

Ed paused. "Well, now that we've established my undying love for you, what should we do about your Dr. Morgan?"

"He's not my Dr. Morgan. I don't even *know* a Dr. Morgan. That might be him in the picture, for all I know." Cora pursed her lips and added. "Well, you know what? Maybe I do know Dr. Morgan and I just don't remember. Or maybe I have a multiple personality and it's one of my alter egos having souvlaki with him. I don't know anything anymore. People tell me I've been here and there, saying all sorts of senseless things, buying coconut cookies, and I just don't remember. If what everybody says is true, then I must be crazy." Tears streamed down her cheeks. "Do you think I'm crazy, Ed?"

His stare dropped to the floor. "Well, this visit to the Pegasi has been one wild encounter after another."

Their eyes met.

"Do you believe what I've told you, Ed?"

Another one of those all-too-familiar stretches of silence followed.

Hurt was still apparent in his eyes as he turned and studied her. "You've got to admit there's a lot of evidence stacked up against you, but I believe that you believe."

Once again, large tears welled up in her eyes and spilled down her cheek. "I need you, of all people, to trust me. I don't care what anyone else thinks." She quickly wiped the dampness from her face, and glanced timidly at the unfinished baklava on her plate.

He watched her for several minutes, and contemplated the situation. "I've got an idea."

She sniffed. "What? I'm ready to do anything."

His jaw flinched, and Cora knew a battle waged within.

He reached for her hand and their fingers interlocked. "Well, it's a pretty gutsy thing to do, Toots. You're the love of my life and I want to trust you with all my heart." He took a deep breath. "Let's go to Dr. Morgan's office and see if we can get some of this cleared up."

Apprehension swelled in her chest. "Let's do it."

Ed paid the bill and they quickly vacated the premises. He took Cora's hand as they walked to the car. "If I never hear Zorba the Greek music again, I'll die a happy man."

Although no rain was in the forecast, ominous clouds began to veil the sun. Cora's state of mind was as unstable as the weather. Her stomach filled with Pterodactyl-sized butterflies that had become her constant companions. She glanced over at Ed in the driver's seat.

What would the next hour bring? What if Dr. Morgan knew her? If she recognized him, should she speak up or remain silent? Would their marriage survive the strange events of the last few weeks?

14

A couple blocks away, Ed pulled into a convenience store parking lot and maneuvered the car close to the public phone. "We'll look Dr. Morgan up in the directory." He brought the chained phone book to the car window and thumbed through the well-worn yellow pages.

Cora sat in silence as diesel fumes of a passing Valley Metro Bus permeated the car. The noxious smell and sight of the Phoenix bus was a reminder of yesterday's harrowing experience. She retrieved a tissue from the outer pocket of her purse and lifted it to cover her nose against the unpleasant odor.

He ran his finger down the list of doctors names and slowly recited, "Ma-jors...Mel-cher...Moore...here it is. Dr. Jefferson Morgan." He peered at his wife. "He's a neurologist. What a coincidence, his office is even on this very street." He pointed north. "Seems it's only a few blocks that way."

Her resolve slipped another degree. Cora was about to hyperventilate. She drew a long, deep breath and slowly released it. A mixed bag of emotions, ranging from curiosity to outright alarm swelled within her. She simply couldn't wrap her mind around the bizarre lunch with all the confusion and onlookers. The waiter and the owner both knew her, but she couldn't place them. To top it all off was Ed's firm accusation of her extramarital affair. And now, they were about to come face to face with Dr. Casanova himself.

Cora licked her dry lips, and silently prayed, *Heavenly Father, I've ignored You and don't deserve Your protection, but please hold my hand through this.*

A comforting voice answered from within, *I've promised to go before you, Cora. I'll make the crooked ways straight. Put your hand in Mine.*

She'd taken a step closer to God, and closed her eyes in an attempt to embrace His promise.

"It must be up here on the right." Ed turned his signal on. "Well, there's the sign."

When they arrived at the medical building, Ed pulled their car into the parking garage. He immediately grabbed the first available spot, turned off the engine, and bowed his head. "We're unsure of the outcome, Lord, but we're placing it in Your hands. Have Your way and use it for the glory of Your kingdom. Amen."

Ed's car door closed with a jarring thump, and brought Cora out of her daunting thoughts. He helped her from the car and then held her close. They walked in silence and a lump formed in Cora's throat as she contemplated what might be in store for them.

༺᠂᠂᠃༻

They noticed the roster of the medical staff, and looked for Dr. Morgan's floor. Cora also found the name of Herschel Keith.

"There, Dr. Keith. He's the one I saw yesterday."

Ed was perplexed as he pushed the button for the elevator and nodded. "Yeah, I saw it." Cora hadn't recognized the very building she was in the previous day and yet, hadn't forgotten the doctor's name. Was this inconsistency a part of Alzheimer's? His stomach knotted. Had the tension and trauma of the last few weeks caused the onset of the disease to accelerate? She seemed to forget actual events, and even people in her life.

Once they reached the right floor, Cora whispered, "I need to stop in the ladies' room for a minute and gather my thoughts. This is all happening too fast."

Ed understood since he fought his own battle with Satan's trap of doubts. However, he *did* see Cora with Dr. Morgan at the Pegasi. The next few minutes with the doctor would test their marriage. "While you powder your nose, I'll go on down to Morgan's office and tell them we'd like to have a word with him. Just don't take too long? They might fit us in between patients."

He entered the crowded waiting room. The pleasant receptionist looked up from her computer screen as he confidently walked to the window. "I wonder if it's possible to speak briefly with Dr. Morgan? I understand he's a busy man, but it's imperative that we see him. I promise it won't take long."

"It might be a few minutes, sir. Fortunately, we had a cancellation. May I tell him your name and the nature of your visit?"

"The name is Timms, Ed Timms." He paused. Being a celebrity did have its perks. "We're here to speak with him on a very personal matter. We'll wait over here."

He turned and found two empty seats next to a middle-aged man with curly red hair. The man had a gnome-like appearance and was dressed in bright plaid walking shorts. His pale legs were stretched out and ankles crossed. This drew attention to his over-sized, light blue athletic shoes and black socks. He nodded as Ed sat down.

The eccentric man's eyes widened as he eagerly sat up straight. He wiped his hand on his rumpled shirt, and then held it out. "Squeak Flannigan, here. I heard you tell Betty your name is Ed Timms. I know who you are." His Mickey Mouse voice sounded like an adolescent. "I'm a big fan of yours. Folks are always telling me I should be a pro golfer like Steady Eddie. Our styles are so similar." He poked Ed in the ribs. "Once my carpal tunnel heals, I'll give you a run for your money."

Ed stared slack-jawed, and wished he hadn't been so quick to stress his famous name to the receptionist. "Thank you. Always nice to meet a fan." With Cora's problems on his mind, the last thing he wanted to do was to become entangled in a petty conversation. The man had pink shoelaces, for crying out loud. Ed picked up a *Golf Digest* from the table in front of him, and rolled it into a tight cylinder. The rusty-haired man rambled on about his triumphs on the links.

A few minutes later, Cora walked into the waiting room and searched for him. Ed stood to get her attention as the receptionist peered out the office window and waved at her.

"Hey hon," she called to Cora, "I'm glad you're feeling well enough to be out. You sure gave us quite a scare yesterday. Dr. Jeff's with a patient. I'll let him know you're here."

Ed and Cora exchanged glances. His eyebrows rose as he stared at his wife. Cora had been so adamant about not knowing Dr. Morgan. How could he believe her version of the story now? Pushing his doubts aside and trusting her wasn't getting any easier now that the receptionist knew her, too.

A glazed look of discouragement spread over Cora's face as she took a well-worn magazine from the rack. Ed moved over so she could be a buffer between him and his flamboyant fan. She sat between the two, and pulled on Ed's arm. "That lady knows me, too. I feel like a Ping-Pong ball bouncing around the Twilight Zone."

Ed took her hand and kissed it reassuringly. The possibility of Alzheimer's had become a painful reality, and he was determined to be strong and supportive. "Everything will be fine. It'll be over soon and we can go home." He wished he had more faith in those words.

Soft giggles came from behind the window at the front desk. Ed noticed Dr. Morgan's staff witnessed their romantic exchange.

"So, is this the wife?" Squeak nodded to Cora. "She's quite a looker, Steady." He grabbed her hand and juicily kissed her palm. "They call me Squeak. I've seen you here before. What's your name, Doll?"

She pulled her hand away. "Hello, Mr. Squeak, I'm Mrs. Steady."

"Ooh, a sense of humor. I like that in a dame." The high-pitched voice rang out. "Hey Doll, you got an available sister?"

She turned to Ed's Technicolor fan and gave an icy reply. "I don't have any sisters."

Mercifully, the nurse called, "Mr. Flannigan."

"Oh no," he whined. "I've gotta go, just when we were getting to know each other." He licked two fingers and reached into his shirt pocket. "Here's my card, Steady. Squeak Flannigan, used car salesman. If you ever need new wheels, I'm your man." Squeak stood and vigorously shook his idol's hand. "Gimme a call, buddy, and we'll play a few rounds." He winked at Cora, and turned to follow the nurse.

Ed shook his head, relieved to see the man leave the waiting room and disappear down the hallway. He leaned over to Cora, and whispered, "We're broadening our Twilight Zone, Toots. In a single afternoon, we've gone from a cheeky Greek to a squeaky geek."

His lighthearted comment brought unexpected snorts of laughter from Cora. Ed matched her, snort for snort. The onlookers exchanged glances and the waiting room erupted in laughter.

Nearly a half hour had passed as Ed feigned interest in the dog-eared pages of *Golf Digest* and Cora flipped through a nine-month-old *Ladies' Day*. The waiting room had thinned out considerably.

Finally, a nurse called to them. "I'll take you to Dr. Jeff's office."

"Thank you." Ed helped Cora stand, and hand-in-hand, the two of them followed the petite young lady back to the doctor's private office.

"He'll be with you in just a minute." With a sly grin and a giggle, the nurse quietly closed the door.

Ed glanced around the physician's highly polished retreat, and tried to envisage the man from the objects displayed in his office. His numerous diplomas and certificates told of his impressive educational background. Together, they studied the neatly framed document from Harvard School of Medicine.

They settled into the wing-backed chairs to await the doctor's arrival. Tension mounted at every little noise outside the door. Cora gulped. "Think it's too late to join the Witness Protection Program?"

Ed reached over and softly brushed his fingers against her cheek. "Won't be long now," he said. "We're going to face this thing together, whatever it is." Once again he wrestled with his anger. Was he prepared to confront the man who wanted his wife? Another thought hit him. Or was the good doctor taking advantage of her illness to get to her wealth? In either case, it would be good to get to the bottom of it.

The dignified-looking Jefferson Morgan, with a neatly trimmed salt and pepper beard, entered the room. A maroon necktie added a splash of color against the stark white of the handsome physician's shirt and medical coat. "Mr. Timms?" He stretched out his hand in formal greeting. "Wait, aren't you Steady Eddie, the golf pro?" His eyes reflected the admiration of a true sports fan.

Ed got to his feet and reluctantly stepped closer to his wife's supposed Lothario. "Yes, I am." He glanced over at Cora, concealed behind the wing of her chair.

"Well, this is a real pleasure," the doctor said. "My nurses said there was a big surprise waiting in my office. I never would've guessed it was you." He pumped Ed's hand. "Dad and I used to watch your tournaments all the time. Please sit down. Now, what can I do for you?"

Ed chose to remain standing. "We hope you can answer some questions." He nodded in the direction of his wife, who timidly peeked from behind her cushioned refuge.

Morgan's gaze followed the older man's stare. The chair's oxblood leather upholstery creaked as Cora slowly stood and faced him.

As he took a deep breath, Ed waited for his world to crash down around him.

The neurologist stared in shock. "What on earth are you doing here, Mom?" He quickly closed the gap between them.

15

"Mom?" Ed and Cora asked in unison.

The twinkle in Dr. Morgan's hazel eyes disappeared as he took a closer look. "Wait just a minute." A confused expression filled his face. "You're not my mother."

The trio stood dumbfounded as impeding stillness swept through the room.

Jefferson Morgan motioned for them to take their seats. Without a word he walked over to the bookshelf, removed a framed photograph and handed it to Cora.

She stared at the photograph and gasped. Her mind reeled. How could this be? She looked into Dr. Morgan's face, her eyes pleaded for some kind of explanation. "I don't understand. How did you get this?"

Ed reached over and took it from her trembling hands. "Oh, my."

The young physician perched on the corner of his desk. "That, folks, is a picture of my mother, Emily Morgan."

"This is your mother?" Cora snatched it back from her husband's hold. "Look, Ed. This could be me in the picture, but it's his mother. She really looks like me, do you see a resemblance?" Cora could hardly catch her breath. "We have the same blue eyes and a dimple in our left cheek."

Had they stumbled onto a blood relative? A

cousin, maybe?

Ed strained to get a better view of the photo gripped tightly in his wife's hands. He straightened in his chair. "Cora and I had a very confusing lunch at the Pegasi Café today."

"I'll bet everyone thought she was Mom, right?"

"You guessed it. Cora said she'd never been there before, but the waiter knew exactly what she was going to order. He said she goes there all the time with a doctor. So, I persuaded him to give me your name. When the owner of the restaurant claimed to be a good friend, too, I knew we had to get to the bottom of this mess."

"Mom's made friends with several people at the Pegasi. We make a point to meet there every week. It's become our little tradition."

A hearty smile stretched across Ed's face. "Well, it's all beginning to make sense, now, isn't it, Toots?"

She tenderly traced the image in the photograph with her fingertips.

Dr. Morgan smiled. "Mrs. Timms, were you adopted?"

Ed gently nudged her elbow. "Cora?"

She looked at him. "What? I'm sorry...now, what did you say?"

"The doctor asked if you were adopted." He shared a grin with Morgan.

Too emotional to do more than nod, Cora handed the picture to Ed. She rummaged through her purse and pulled out a tissue to wipe her eyes. Her puzzled mind raced to make some kind of connection with the woman in the picture.

The doctor rose from the corner of his desk. He knelt down and gently placed his hand on hers. "How old were you when you were placed?"

"I was about two at the time, maybe a little older."

"My mother was adopted at the age of two and a half. How old are you, Mrs. Timms?"

She told him.

"Your birthday is April tenth, right?" An infectious smile lifted the corners of his mouth. He clasped her hands in his. "That's Mom's birthday, too. You're identical twins."

She searched the doctor's features. *"Twins?"* The impact of the discovery hit Cora full force. Her hand flew to her mouth and tears ran freely. She jumped to her feet. "Did you hear that, Ed? He said I'm a twin."

"Yeah, this is something you'd expect to see in a schmaltzy soap opera."

"Even so." She shook his shoulders. "The point is, I have a sister, Emily, and she's my identical twin."

Ed's eyes brimmed as he stood and embraced her, then twirled her around. "God is so good."

Cora nodded and cried into his shirt. She turned to her nephew, who now stood by his desk. "After all these years, I found my family. So, where is she? When can I meet her?"

Dr. Morgan gave a hearty chuckle. "I'm pretty busy right now, but maybe we can arrange something for this weekend."

Her spine stiffened. "What?" She plopped into her chair. Did he actually expect her to wait? This was wrong on so many levels.

"Fair warning, Doc. I'm afraid this weekend isn't going to be soon enough for my wife." Amusement crinkled the corners of Ed's mouth. "So, unless your mom lives in outer Timbuktu, Cora will insist on seeing her today."

The doctor smiled and took his seat at the desk. "Good news. No air travel for you."

"That's good news, then tell me"—Cora tilted her head—"Exactly how far away is she?"

"Mom lives only an hour from here, however she's staying at my house here in Phoenix until she's feeling better."

Cora tensed as she grasped the rolled arm of the wing-backed chair. "What's wrong with her? Please tell me it's nothing serious."

A concerned moan escaped Ed's mouth. He sat down and patted her arm as they waited for the doctor's reply.

"Mom recently found out she has angina. She had an episode yesterday while we were having lunch together."

Ed leaned forward. "At the Pegasi?"

"Yes," Dr. Morgan acknowledged. "The nitroglycerin pill she takes for the angina helps, but it gives her a severe headache. I took her to my house right away and my wife—"

"Oh, no." Cora interrupted. "I hope she's all right."

Dr. Morgan nodded and continued, "The headaches only last about an hour or so. My wife takes very good care of her. June said Mom was quite perky this morning and feeling like her old mischievous self."

Ed smiled. "You've cleared up another point for me. When I saw Cora leaving the Pegasi yesterday in the arms of another man, it was actually you and your mother." His ears brightened. "I should've known there was a logical explanation." He reached over to take her hand. "I made an idiot of myself, embarrassed you, and ruined a perfectly good lunch."

"Oh Ed, think of the scene we made at the Pegasi. What must all those people think? I can just see the *Inquirer* headlines now: *Pro-Golfer's wife caught playing a round.*"

"Will you forgive me, Toots?"

"Well, I suppose. You tried to believe in me even when there were no answers. I'm so thankful you stood by me long enough to figure it out. Some men wouldn't have. But, Ed dear, don't forget, you do owe me a souvlaki dinner."

Her mind grew more at ease since they discovered the disturbing experiences she endured were due to a simple mistaken identity. Was the fear of Alzheimer's disease unfounded, too?

Casually, the doctor glanced at his Rolex. "I really hate to break this off, but I've got patients waiting for my attention." He rolled the executive chair away from his desk, which indicated the end of their impromptu meeting. "Why don't you leave your phone number so Mom can contact you later this afternoon?"

"Dr. Morgan, I can't wait to see my *sister*." The word was foreign to her lips, yet the sound of it thrilled her. Joy bubbled in her soul. Sister. She wasn't about to let the doctor go before they found out where Emily was.

He reached for her small hands and gently pulled her up into his strong embrace. "Please call me Jeff." He smiled. "Of course you want to see her right away. What was I thinking? She'll be just as thrilled to see you. I'll call June to see if they're home. She can prepare Mom so it won't be such a huge shock. I have a couple things that need my attention first, so it'll take a few minutes. Take a seat in the waiting room and I'll get back with you as soon as possible." The young doctor grabbed a notepad and wrote his home address and telephone number.

"I'm so nervous. Ed, isn't this exciting? I have a sister—Emily!" she exclaimed with intense pleasure, and then looked at her nephew. "Sure wish you could go with us."

"There's nothing I'd rather do, but I've probably got a waiting room full of impatient patients. Besides, June will tape this reunion and I'll watch it later. And if I know my mother, you'll still be there when I get home." He hugged her once again. "I'm so glad to meet you, Aunt Toots," he said with a mischievous grin. "And you, too, Uncle Steady."

Cora chuckled and relaxed in his hug. They walked to the door, and then Cora looked at her nephew. "Tell me Jeff, do you like coconut cookies?"

16

They entered the waiting room and found a seat. Cora's mind processed the new revelation. She had a twin, which confused everyone.

Even that creepy guy on the phone.

Her heart skipped a beat. Was poor Emily involved in something dangerous?

After a short wait for Jeff to make his phone call, the receptionist motioned for them to come to the window. "This is such an amazing story. Dr. Jeff said that June and Emily are pacing the floor to meet you. They want you there as quickly as possible." She gave them a friendly smile. "It was nice meeting you. Enjoy your reunion."

Cora could hardly contain herself as they drove to the Morgans' home. She rattled on about a new future with her sister. "Oh, Ed isn't it wonderful? I still feel like I'm dreaming."

A wicked thought slithered into her mind. *Enjoy it while you can. Emily will be the only one with memories.*

She threw back her shoulders and refused to let the notion take root. Nothing was going to put a damper on this burgeoning relationship with her sister. Not monsoons, not George and his ominous phone calls, and certainly not the possibility of Alzheimer's disease.

"I'm so relieved there's an explanation why so many people thought they saw me. And you even witnessed some of it, too. See, I'm not so flaky after all."

Ed's grin was wide. "Well, now, that's still up for deliberation." He pulled the car to a stop at a red light. He reached for her hand and squeezed it.

His gentle gaze sent ripples of pleasure through her. She lifted his hand to her lips. "I love you, Eddie."

A tear gently slipped down his cheek. "You don't know how much I needed to hear that, Toots." He cleared his throat. "I love you, too. More than you'll ever know."

Her eyes moistened. Cora realized this was the second time her reserved husband had bared his soul today. Romantic feelings reawakened in her, and she embraced the moment. Who said romance was only for the young?

As they pulled up to the Morgans' stately home, Emily bounded out the front door. The air seemed to exude a sense of excitement as Cora studied her sister's features. Without a word, she pulled Emily into her arms and they swayed in a tight embrace. Cora released her hold to reexamine the tear-streaked face that mirrored her own.

Cora held a tissue to her eyes as they separated. "Ed, come meet my sister, Emily."

"Oh, call me Em." Her eyes brightened as she stepped forward with her arms outstretched. "You're the famous Steady Eddie." She turned around and pointed to the lady behind the camera. "This is my daughter-in-law, June Morgan."

"Hi, June. Pleased to meet you." The late afternoon sun danced off Ed's sunglasses as he leaned over for a hug.

A warm wave of pleasure rose in Cora's heart as

she treasured every word and gesture. She realized this was a far-better ending than the one she and Ed had feared just hours before. Her voice trembled. "I have a million questions to ask you, Emily."

"I've got at least that many for you, too. Let's go inside for coffee. We have so many years to catch up on."

Ed held the door open for the three women and followed them into the house. A few minutes later, the foursome gathered in the formal dining room around the large oak table. The aroma of fresh coffee mixed with the scent of hot cinnamon rolls was a welcomed treat after the sparse meal at the Pegasi.

Several of June's photo albums were stacked on the table near Ed. He busied himself with the variety of neatly preserved photographs while the women jabbered nonstop.

Between bouts of joyful tears, questions and answers flew from one sister to the other. Their early years were amazingly similar in many aspects. Each had wonderful, God-fearing adoptive families; both adored the humorous writings of Paige Turner, and they discovered a joint passion for mint Wilderness Scout cookies.

"You know," Cora said, "Seems odd to me that we're identical twins yet our names aren't the least bit similar."

"Well, actually Sis, my birth name is…are you ready for this? Eudora."

June's head shot up. "I never knew that. Eudora, huh? Oh, gag."

"My thoughts exactly. My adopted mother wanted to spare me great humiliation, so she thoughtfully gave me her mother's name, Emily. So, our original names do sound alike."

Ed added his two cents. "And you thought being named Cora was a bummer."

"Yeah. You'll hear no more complaints from me." Cora wrapped her fingers around her coffee mug. "I wonder why neither of us remembers the other? After all, we were toddlers, old enough to have memories."

"I have snippets of memory about what I perceive to be the orphanage. Being placed in a washtub with another child, which I now realize was probably you, and getting soap in my eyes. Again, probably you." Emily cleared her throat and took a drink of coffee. "This might sound off the wall, but all my life, there have been times when it felt as if a part of me was missing."

"Oh, that doesn't sound off the wall because I've experienced that empty space, too. Kind of like a missing piece to the puzzle." Cora said. "I assumed it was because I was adopted."

"Exactly." Emily nodded in agreement. "I thought once I married and had my own family, that lonely feeling would go away." She shrugged her shoulders. "It never did. In fact, it's only grown more intense over the years. I just wanted to be found."

"Now we've found each other."

Cora hugged her sister intensely. This time was precious and how she longed to protect this memory. She pushed aside the negative thoughts that pried into her mind and attempted to ruin everything. "We're together now. Let's keep this special moment in our hearts forever."

June and Ed quietly took in the emotional exchange. Soon, the conversation naturally progressed into early adulthood and marriage.

Emily married her childhood sweetheart, Philip, a week after high school graduation. Jeff was born the following spring, Reece and Rebecca came along a few years later.

Ed sipped his coffee and set the cup down. "Why don't you tell us about Philip?"

"Dad was the most patient and caring man I've ever known." June smiled and looked at Emily. "Don't you think Jeff's a lot like him?"

"Absolutely. My life with Philip was about as perfect as can be." Emily dabbed her eyes. "I still miss him."

Cora sympathetically rubbed her sister's back.

"He died so suddenly that my world stopped and depression overwhelmed me. I made it through his funeral only by the grace of God." Her hands shook. "Grief became a way of life and for four years, pain was my constant companion."

"Four years?" Cora gasped. Emily's sorrow was so much like her own, but *four* years?

June's voice was filled with compassion. "Yes, we did everything to pull Mom out of that depression. It still seemed like eternity. We were so worried." She reached over and hugged her.

Emily fidgeted with her coffee cup, then, cleared her throat. "You might not have liked me back then, Sis. I was far from the bubbly princess you see today."

Ed grinned at his comical sister-in-law, and then gave Cora's hand a reassuring squeeze. His voice turned serious. "Emily, do you mind if I ask how you got through your grief?"

"It was so bad I had to quit work because my thinking and memory became muddled. Depression had me smothered in self-pity for three years. Think about it, how could I enjoy life when my husband was buried in the ground? After speaking with our pastor, he urged me to go into grief counseling. I was reluctant at first, but couldn't stand any more.

"The counselor asked if I thought my pain was the only way to honor Philip. I knew he wouldn't want me to be miserable. Yet, I was, and figured nothing would ever change."

Cora sat dumbfounded as her sister's admission hit home. A short lull in the conversation provided time for her to reflect. Was that what she was doing—mourning her life away? Would Van be proud of her?

Emily took a deep breath. "The counselor assured me that when I began to question my feelings, it was time to give myself permission to move on. Living with or without pain, would never change the fact that Philip will always be in my heart. When I enjoyed some family activities, I was embarrassed at first. It was a weird sensation, but it was so liberating. I had to take baby steps, and the Lord helped me face each new day without dwelling on my loss."

Emily stood to refill the coffee cups. "I'm so fortunate. Philip was such a wonderful husband. All my memories of him are good ones." She patted Ed on the shoulder. "Not a week went by that my Jeff and his father didn't follow your career. He would've flipped if he had an inkling that Steady Eddie was his brother-in-law."

"I'm sorry we never met." Ed's eyes conveyed his regret. He finished the last of his cinnamon roll and licked goo from his fingers. "We could've supported each other in this whole twin thing. It would've been nice to have someone to commiserate with me." He winked at June. "How in the world are we going to tell these two apart? Even their mannerisms are similar."

"Your guess is as good as mine." June laughed. "All I see is double trouble ahead."

"We could always wear name tags to help you out," Cora quipped.

Emily leaned over to her sister. "Or, we could take full advantage of the situation, right?"

Ed returned to the aging photo album next to him. "Who's this, June?"

She smiled. "That's Jeff with his younger brother and sister, Reece and Rebecca." She pointed to another picture. "And this little tyke is our son, Jordan. He's fifteen now and should be home from football practice later. I hope you can stay long enough to meet him."

"Of course they're going to stay long enough." Emily pulled a scrapbook closer so Cora could see it. "You've got to see what Junie's done with my albums. She's a real scrapbook enthusiast, so I had her arrange them for me."

Emily proudly pointed to wedding pictures. "And this is our daughter, Rebecca, when she married," she ticked the groom's name off on her fingers, "LaMont Francois Laurent Bellamy IV. Isn't that a mouthful? Wait till you hear the dreadful names they gave their poor little girls. LaRue, LaVerne, and LaVinia."

Dr. Jeff arrived home laden with carry-out bags. "I figured since the Pegasi inadvertently got us together we should celebrate with souvlaki and baklava for all."

Ed and Cora burst out in laughter.

Emily looked puzzled. "No inside secrets in this family, Cora. Spill it, and spill it now."

"Wait." June closed her photo album. "I have to put the food in the oven, so don't tell any stories until I get back. I don't want to miss a thing. Jeff, why don't you change your clothes?"

Jeff excused himself to trade his suit for khakis and a sport shirt. Minutes later, he joined the festivities in the dining room.

June moved her chair over, to provide more legroom beside her. She also put him on camcorder duty to preserve every minute of the sisters' first meeting.

Laughter grew as Ed shared the shortened version of his restaurant experience. "It all started when I witnessed my wife coming out of the Pegasi in the arms of a young, handsome Casanova."

Heads turned to Cora.

Her face changed to candy-apple-red. "Just wait. It gets better."

"When I took her there the next day, everyone knew her. She denied it all. I thought she was lying through her teeth. What really got me, Cora left the table and the waiter said she'd been there often enough to have a usual order. When she returned, she ordered it."

Emily wiped her eyes with a napkin. "Chicken Souvlaki, right?"

"Complete with salata and Vanilla Bean Cappuccino." Cora added her side of the story. "Picture it." She threw her arms wide open and tried to suppress a giggle. "There we were, in a crowd of people gawking at us, and my beloved husband accused me of having, and I quote, 'a torrid love affair.'" She nervously laughed, and held her hot cheeks.

First a gasp echoed around the table, followed by snickers as all heads turned in Ed's direction. Jeff laughed out loud and scooted his chair back. "Wow, man. Do you have a death wish or something?" His camera zoomed in on Ed.

With one finger, Ed pushed the lens aside. "I'm hanging off the edge of a cliff here and you're going for a Kodak moment?" He turned to Emily and grinned. "It's your fault, you know. If you hadn't been walking around town with my wife's face on, this never would've happened."

"Hey, did you ever think that maybe she's using *my* face?" She winked at Cora. "Thanks for taking such good care of it, by the way."

"I had a little help from Velvety Dew moisturizing face spackle."

June gently pushed Emily's arm. "You two crack me up." She jumped to her feet. "Oh dear, I forgot about the food. It smells more than ready. I'll get our meal while you clear all these pictures off the table." She pointed to the kitchen. "Mom, would you get the iced tea?"

Jeff gathered the photos of his lively nieces. "I'm sure you've heard all about the La-La girls," he said, with a chuckle. "I hope Mom told you that Becky and LaMont didn't take our advice on naming their children."

Emily entered the room with a pitcher of iced tea and quickly replied, "Oh, I made sure to tell them that we wanted more traditional names for those precious babies, however they chose those dusty, old monikers they found in his family archives. That seems to be the fad these days." She handed Cora the placemats. "What about you, Sis? How many children do you have?"

A dull ache spread through Cora's heart. "We had one daughter. Vanessa."

Ed set a stack of plates on the table and took his

wife's hand. "Our only child died in a car accident at the age of thirty-five. We still have a good relationship with her husband, James, even though he's remarried. The visits with our grandkids aren't as often as we'd like since the family moved to Las Vegas."

Cora frowned and squirmed at the mention of James's remarriage.

Emily redirected the conversation as she put the tableware in place. "Why don't you tell us about your grandchildren? How old are they?"

That was all the encouragement Cora needed to produce a bulging purse-sized photo album comprised of the grandchildren's recent school pictures and holiday snapshots. Ed added a running narrative for each child.

When June returned from the kitchen with the main dish and salad, the table had been cleared and set. Jeff offered up a prayer of thanksgiving for the food and new family members.

As the Greek dish quickly made its way around the table, Cora observed each new relative. This was her—*family*. Emotion wedged in her throat. Not so long ago, her only blood relative had been snatched from her and she was drawn into the dark abyss of loneliness. How was it that two sisters, separated for years, could suddenly find each other?

Ed raised his breadstick. "Hey, Toots, this souvlaki is really good, isn't it? Can you believe how much easier this meal is to swallow than the one we had at the Pegasi?"

"Toots?" Emily's hand went to her mouth as she choked on her iced tea. A broad smile surfaced. "Is that what you want us to call you?"

"Only my husband is allowed to call me that."

Her sister grinned from ear to ear. "Not any more. I gotcha now, Tootsie."

Cora wiped her chin. "Touché, Eudora."

A puzzled look came across Jeff's face. "What's a Eudora?"

Ed laughed. "Your beautiful mother. She said it's on her birth certificate. Your family sure has a fetish for odd names."

"Yes, we do, Uncle *Steady*," Jeff agreed. "Would you mind passing the sugar, Aunt *Toots*? You two are so lucky to have such normal names." His emphasis on their nicknames brought a new wave of laughter.

A voice was heard from the hallway, and the door slammed. "I'm home, Mom. Who's car is out front?"

Jeff motioned for Ed to hide in the kitchen, then, excused himself from the table. "We're in the dining room, Son. I want you to meet someone."

As they entered the room, Jordan's young voice cracked, "Oh no! Grandma has a clone."

"This is Grandma's twin sister, Cora Timms. They were adopted as babies and just now found each other."

"Nice to meet ya, Aunt Cora." With his dad's nudge from behind, Jordan leaned over and gave Cora a quick peck on the cheek. When he stood, Ed entered the room. The boy's mouth dropped open. "Steady Eddie Timms! Way cool. How'd ya get him to come here?"

June's camcorder hummed as Jordan shook Ed's hand. He grabbed a breadstick and turned to his mom. "Can Tank and Mason come over and see Steady Eddie?"

"Maybe next time. Let's not overdo it on their first visit." June pointed to the kitchen. "Lose the pout and go get your supper before it gets cold."

"Tell ya what," Jeff added, "Uncle Steady and I are going to have coffee in the family room. You can eat in there with us."

The ladies loaded the dishwasher and discussed ideas for a family barbecue and reunion.

Cora placed coffee cups on the top rack and wiped her damp hands on a dishtowel. "Oh Em, I'm so excited about you staying with us for a few days. We're going to have so much fun."

June joined them in the kitchen and handed Jordan's dirty dishes to her mother-in-law. "Well, the men are busy making plans. I just heard the three of them schedule a golf date for this Saturday morning." She took a final swipe of the granite countertop.

"We have our own plans to make." Cora closed the dishwasher. "Let's join forces in the dining room and see what we can come up with."

As the ladies settled around the table, Jordan raced into the room. "Dad said I could have some more iced tea." He looked at Cora. "Uncle Steady was telling us about the guy who followed you home. How creepy is that?"

A momentary panic clenched Cora's stomach. "Yeah, it was creepy alright." Her gaze dropped to the table.

June took her son's arm. "Why don't you get your tea and go back in with the men? We have a lot of girl talk to do."

"Are you all right?" Emily reached over and held her sister's shaking hand.

Cora answered with a nod as her mind searched for answers. If George or his partner were still at large, she and Em would both be in danger.

17

It was after 10 pm when Cora and Ed finally pried themselves away from the Morgans' home. Cora found it impossible to stop her chatter about their new relatives.

"Can you believe how much alike we are?" She pulled a pack of gum from her purse and offered a stick to Ed. "Think you could tell us apart?"

"Need I remind you of the Pegasi fiasco?" Ed checked the side mirror as a semi rattled past them. "Think of all the people that have been confused by the two of you. George Shipley must've seen Emily at the Pegasi and thought it was you, just like I did. With good reason. I've never seen two people look and act so similar." Ed chuckled. "George had to be going berserk trying to pull off his scam."

She laughed along with her husband. "He was so angry on the phone when I didn't understand what he was talking about. It's been a bizarre situation right from the start."

"Today in particular." Ed pulled to a stop in the turn lane. "Although, finding that picture yesterday sure threw me for a loop. I thought you'd left me."

She studied the contour of his face as headlights of the car behind them illuminated the front seat. "Why on earth would you think that?"

"You've been acting so strangely, and then your dresser drawer was empty except for that picture." The traffic light changed and Ed made a left turn. "What else could I think?"

"So you came to the brilliant conclusion that I just packed up my undies and scampered off? Have bloomers will travel? Didn't you consider the fact I'd need something a little more substantial than that to wear?"

"Well, it *was* in the heat of the moment, Toots. I didn't think to look in your closet."

"You should have. What happened is I tossed all my stuff into the hamper, because George had his filthy paws on everything when he put the picture in." She shivered. "It still gives me the creeps."

Ed glanced her way and nodded. "Well, that makes more sense. Anyway, I'm glad you're still with me." He reached over and patted her knee.

"And to think, I was afraid of losing you, Eddie."

"Why? My unmentionables are still in the drawer where they belong." His hearty laugh filled the car. "You know, I think I've experienced every emotion possible the last few days."

Cora sighed. "Me too. I'm so glad it's over."

"Let's hope our minds unwind before we get home or it'll be ages before we can settle down. And we both know I won't be catching any Z's until you do."

She snickered.

"We're so exhausted, we'll both sleep like babies." Her laughter ceased as she reflected on Ed's accusations of that morning. Her tone was somber as she asked, "Hey buster, speaking of babies, exactly when did you think I'd have time to have a child behind your back? I know you were on the PGA Tour a lot, but honestly, Ed, what a silly assumption."

The comment momentarily silenced Ed. His voice was husky as he apologized. "I'm sorry. Evidence was mounting, and I jumped to the wrong conclusion. I've been a major clod."

"I should say so." She stared out the side window. "It really hurt when you accused me of having an affair. If the tables were turned, I'd like to think I would've trusted you."

"Forgive me?"

Her heart took a leap as she reached over and gently stroked the light stubble on his cheek. "Oh Eddie, of course I do." An undeniable attraction grew in her. Warm currents raced and melted the once icy hold on her heart. Cora grinned mischievously. "Now, let's get back to discussing that mysterious son you thought I had."

"Oh." His voice reflected guilt. "Well, can I be blunt?" He squinted over his glasses to see her in the darkened car.

"Go on, but measure your words carefully, and keep your eyes on the road."

Ed shifted in his seat and adjusted his seatbelt. "We didn't meet until you were nineteen. Then, yesterday, seeing that photograph in your drawer, I realized I might not have been the first man in your life. You even told me you bought coconut cookies for your son, so my mind immediately jumped to the wrong conclusion." He reached over, took her hand in his, and pressed his lips to her palm.

She felt the electricity of his tender kiss. "I understand. Actually, with everything going on, I was beginning to doubt myself." Cora remembered something else. "Hey, since we're clearing the air, wanna tell me about that big life insurance policy you took out on me?"

"For crying out loud, Toots, is this some sort of interrogation?"

"You betcha. I've had so many questions on my mind and we haven't been able to talk. Now, tell me about the policy."

"Aha! I thought you trusted me."

"Just tell me about it, Ed."

He took a deep breath. "Remember when I saw George and Roger at Sugar Dips?"

"How could I possibly forget?"

"Well, George was still feeling guilty about stealing from me. That's why he couldn't look me in the eye and left as soon as I went to their table."

"What's that got to do with the insurance?"

"When I got to work the next morning, Roger told me George was working for McFarland Group Insurance and was trying to sell him a policy at Sugar Dips. When I learned that was the reason they were talking, I took out the policy to help him."

"Oh."

"What did you think?"

"I thought maybe, well, never mind. It isn't important now."

Ed looked at her. "Did you think I had plans to knock you off and collect the money? Come on, Cora. We've got more money in the bank than we'll ever spend in this lifetime. Do I really need that penny-ante insurance money? Now, who's not trusting whom?"

"Busted!" she exclaimed with a throaty giggle. "Maybe we should change the subject?"

"Good idea."

Cora watched the lights as they approached the Saguaro Valley Complex. Thoughts of the photograph and the brother-in-law she never knew came to mind. "You know, that was probably Philip in that picture. It was so sweet to see him holding Em in his arms. Hey, why didn't we remember to give it to her this evening?"

With a heavy sigh, Ed searched his breast pocket. "You're not going to believe this, but I might've left it at the Pegasi."

"Well, you have to go back and get it. And while you're at it, would you mind getting a copy made, so I can give the original to Em? She'll be glad to have it."

"Right, I'll do that tomorrow. Do you want me to leave the copy in your dresser drawer?"

"I'll answer that with another question, dear," Cora said as the car pulled into their garage. "Do you want to wear your putter as a necktie?"

"Point taken." They shared a laugh as Ed helped her from the car. In one forward motion, he took her into his arms. His kiss was soft and searching.

Cora smiled as he guided her to the door.

Before they crawled into bed, Cora listened as Ed offered thankful prayers. First, for bringing his wife through traumatic times and for their newfound family.

"...but most of all, Lord, we thank You for restoring our relationship."

When the prayer ended, Cora thought she detected a playful flicker in Ed's eyes. Was there a deeper significance to his gaze? The implication sent waves of eagerness through her. She ached for his love, and reached out to him.

Ed gently gathered her into his embrace and held her tightly. Cora spontaneously wrapped her arms around his neck and experienced his heartbeat against her. She felt like a breathless girl of eighteen as he reached over and turned off the lamp.

As they snuggled, Cora's head fit perfectly in the recess of his shoulder and neck. She inhaled the familiar spicy scent of his cologne and was wrapped in the invisible warmth of his love. The anguish of the past few weeks dissipated as he tenderly pressed his lips to hers. She answered with a sweetheart's kiss.

⁊⸲⸳⸲⸲

In the wee hours, Ed still mulled over the day's events. He visualized the photograph of Emily and Philip and remembered the words on the back. "Does your old man know?" Was the man in the snapshot Philip? Exactly how did George fit into Emily's life? Where did the money come from and how did she end up with it? Was it blackmail? After meeting Cora's sister, it was difficult to think of her ever being a party to anything illegal.

Niggling thoughts continued to hound him. Something didn't add up.

18

Cora was up early the next morning to prepare for her sister's visit. After a quick breakfast, she washed grapes, sliced bananas and pineapple and added them to her fruit salad.

In the living room, she re-fluffed the throw pillows for the third time, and then glanced to the fireplace mantle. The tapered candles were off-kilter next to the framed photograph of Van and her family. How she wished her daughter could share in the day's excitement. Her heart ached as she looked into Van's face.

Cora blinked away the tears. It was time for a break. Emily would be here soon, and she didn't want to greet her sister with red-rimmed eyes.

She poured a glass of lemonade, dialed McGibbons's number, and crossed her fingers in hopes her neighbor would take the bait. Dahlia answered on the third ring. Cora spoke in her most serious voice. "Something's come up, Dahlly, and I desperately need my best friend to confide in. Could you come over for lunch today?"

"Oh Sugar, today? I'm up to my elbows in pie dough."

Cora suppressed a giggle and cleared her throat. "It's important, or I wouldn't ask."

"Oh…well, I guess I can have this here mess tidied up by twelve-thirty. Would that work?"

"You're an angel. I can't tell you how much I appreciate this." Cora hung up. She rubbed her hands together and basked in the thought of setting her friend up for a double-barreled surprise. Dahlia always pulled pranks on her, so it was time for the dessert maker to get her own just deserts. The chiming grandfather clock reminded her that she still had to whip up a coffee cake before Emily arrived. She'd have to get busy.

It was an hour later when she wiped the counter clean and the sweet aroma of hot cinnamon filled the air. Her mouth watered as she peeked inside the oven.

Cora eagerly waited at the window, and could hardly contain herself when her new relatives pulled into the drive. She threw the door open, and Emily raced to her. June, carrying Emily's two suitcases, followed her mother-in-law into the house.

The kitchen timer's buzz interrupted their emotional greeting. "Oh, my coffee cake's done." Cora motioned to the dining room. "Sit down, sit down, I'll be right back."

June patted her arm. "Tell you what, while you're in the kitchen, I'll get the photo albums." She faced her mother-in-law. "Would you help with the door, Mom?"

As Cora brought the coffee cake to the table, she saw her twin open the door. A man with a tool belt set a large box inside. Cora hoped to keep her twin identity a secret until later, so she backed into the kitchen.

The man's voice said, "Mornin' Ms. Timms. Do you feel safer with the new door locks? I made sure to get the very best." After a pause he added, "Well, gotta run. Have a nice day, now."

Emily giggled all the way to the kitchen. "He thought I was you, Sis. I didn't even try to trick him."

"That could be because I've never met the man."

"What?" Emily put her hands on her hips. "You mean I wasted a perfectly good 'come hither' look?"

With a hearty laugh, June guided Emily into the dining room. "Mom, you've only been here five minutes, and you've already tarnished Aunt Cora's halo. I can't take you anywhere."

"I think Em's going to enjoy what I have planned for later." Cora motioned for her guests to take their seats as she passed the servings of coffee cake.

After the carefree chatter, June drained her cup. "I'd love to stay for seconds, but I gotta run." She wiped her mouth and folded her napkin.

"You're leaving all ready?" Cora set her fork down and frowned. "You just got here."

Emily proudly stroked her daughter-in-law's hand. "Junie and her friend are directors of the 'Grannies-On-the-Go' program at the Senior Center."

"And, if I don't leave now, those grannies will be on the go without me." June kissed Cora goodbye, and then went to Emily. "I'm so glad your world has grown to include your new sister, but do us all a favor and behave yourselves, you hear?"

Emily looked at Cora with a conspiratorial gleam in her eyes and wrapped an arm around her shoulder. "I just wasted my best come hither look, Junie. I'm not about to make a promise I can't keep."

Cora added, "Would you be satisfied if we promised to pace ourselves?"

June laughed and threw her arms up as she headed for the door. "I'm washing my hands of the whole thing." She shook her head and left.

"Now that we're alone," Cora whispered. "We're going to have our first twin caper. My best friend's coming for lunch, and she doesn't have a clue about you. First, we need to make some minor adjustments." They hurried to the bedroom. "Here, Em, try on this blouse. She gave it to me on my...*our* last birthday."

Cora shut the closet door. "Be sure to call her Dahlly, like I do, or the jig's up."

"Dahlly. Got it." Emily fastened the last button, and went to the full-length mirror.

Cora stood beside her. "Now the only thing that needs changed is your hair style, Em."

"What?"

"Nothing major." Cora reached for a comb. "We'll just add a little more pouf and bangs. There we go. Now, you're me." She giggled. "Ready to put our prank into action? Let's go watch for our victim."

Emily nodded. "Do you realize even our giggles sound alike?" She followed Cora to the living room.

When Dahlia arrived, Cora swallowed her giggles, and eagerly hid in the kitchen. She watched the scene play out from around the corner as her proxy answered the door.

With a straight face, Emily welcomed Dahlia, who barged in without blinking an eye. "I know it's only been a couple days since I was here, but it seems like ages," she prattled. "So much has happened. Right after we hung up this mornin', I got me a call from QSN, ya know, Quality Shoppin' Network. Anyway, I'll be hawkin' my cookbooks an' a new line of aprons."

Emily's hand flew to her mouth.

"Ya look like someone slapped ya on the back while ya was chawin' tabacca. What's wrong?" The flamboyant host of Heapin' Helpin's TV show set the steaming pie with a crunchy-topping on the coffee table, and hugged the small woman close to her. "Did ya get another phone call?"

Emily coughed. "Ph-phone call? Uh, no, I-I don't think so."

Cora suppressed a giggle as her twin struggled back into character.

"I'll explain in a minute, uh, Dahlly. Make yourself comfortable at the dining room table while I take the pie into the kitchen."

"Hey, the table's set for three. Who else is comin'?"

"You'll see. I'll be right back." Emily hurried into the kitchen.

Cora burst out with titters and snorts as she hugged her sister.

"What's goin' on out there?" Dahlia called out. "Who's that with ya?"

"Just a minute, Dahlly."

"You're up to somethin'. I know you're up to..." Dahlia stopped mid-sentence when Cora and Emily entered the dining room.

Her mouth dropped. It was the first time Cora had ever seen her effervescent friend at a loss for words.

Dahlia's cackling laughter broke the silence. Soon tears ran down her plump cheeks. She looked from one lady to the other, and whipped out a hanky. "Well, I'll be hornswoggled. Will the real Cora please step forward?"

"That would be me. I'd like you to meet my long-lost sister, Emily Morgan."

Another guffaw pierced the air as the Texas cook pulled Cora and Emily to her, and in one fell swoop, smothered them both into her bosom.

With gasps for air, they finally pulled free.

"I haven't laughed this hard in a long time." Cora held the back of her chair. "Let's sit down, although I'm not sure I have the strength to eat."

"Horsefeathers! All that excitement put *me* on the growly edge of starvation." Dahlia scooted up to the table and plopped her usual super-sized portion of Caesar salad onto a plate. "I wanna know how y'all met, an' I'm talkin' details, ladies."

With a deep breath, Cora launched into her nightmare of menacing phone calls, car chases, and the disastrous lunch with Ed. She finished with how they found Emily's son, Dr. Morgan. "Jeff was the catalyst who brought the mishmash of puzzle pieces together. With one phone call, he arranged for us to meet."

Emily shook her head. "You and Ed shared bits and pieces of the restaurant story last night, but I had no idea you'd gone through so much before that."

"I can't get over ya findin' that pitcher of Emily an' Philip in your chester drawers." Dahlia took a second helping of fruit salad.

"Yeah, I'd sure like to see that," Emily said. "Was it a professional photo?"

"No, it was just a snapshot taken outdoors. It's a sweet picture, Em. He had his arms around you. When Ed gets home, let's remind him to give it to you."

The two women pummeled Cora with a flood of questions, and she did her best to respond to each one. Finally, she stood and picked up her empty plate. "Well, girls, I'm all talked out. And now that it's over, and Emily's here, I don't even want to think about it anymore." She took a deep breath. "Are we ready for tea and pie?"

"Before we get to the goodies," Dahlia said, "sit back down an' let me fill ya in on what Wendell Floyd told Jack at breakfast this mornin'. Mr. Sands, the complex manager called, an' said that the Santalises got therselves arrested last night." She took a sip of water.

Cora leaned back in her chair, and gasped. "Lupe and Mateo arrested?" She saw Em's confused face and quickly explained. "Lupe Santalis is our cleaning lady. Mateo is her husband. They've worked here for years." She looked back to Dahlia. "What on earth did they do?"

"Ya recollec' that mornin' when the cops came here to talk to ya?" Dahlia leaned forward as she relayed the details. "Lupe must've done somethin' fishy 'cause that Reed feller got his feelers up, an' checked her out."

"I never saw Lupe act so nervous, Dahlly. She rushed to the kitchen and tried to stay out of sight, but I saw her listening around the corner." Cora cleared her throat. "Do you think Lupe was the lady caller after all?"

"Well, I suppose it's possible. 'Nother thing, Sugar, Lupe does your laundry, so she coulda put that pitcher in your drawer."

Cora hit her fist on the table, "And those gritty footprints had to be Mateo's."

"You're prob'ly right." Dahlia nodded. "Jack told us the whole Santalis clan was here illegally, an' stayin' with Mateo an' Lupe. Well, ya coulda knocked me over with a feather. He told Wendell Floyd the whole kit 'n' kaboodle will prob'ly be deported."

Disappointment overshadowed the conversation.

Lupe was trusted unconditionally, more like a

friend than an employee. The betrayal ripped at Cora's heart.

"Don't feel so bad, Sugar." Dahlia reached for Cora's hand. "She didn't mean to hurt nobody, she was tryin' to protect her family."

Cora nodded in agreement. "I realize that, but it still hurts. This is a gated community and we're supposed to be safe. If we can't trust each other, what's the point?" She rubbed the back of her neck. "Can you believe something of this magnitude happening in this area? What's next?"

"Evidently ya haven't read this mornin's paper," her friend said.

"No. Ed took it to work with him. Why?"

"Well, hang on to your choppers. The Santalis scandal ain't the worst of it. The headlines said George Shipley kilt his mom an' then hisself."

Emily gasped. "Murder? Suicide?"

"Wendell Floyd said all along that ol' George was gonna snap one o' these days."

Shaken, Cora's hand went to her mouth. She swallowed to rid the ache in her throat. "Oh Dahlly, we sent the police to question George. Do you suppose that sent him over the edge?"

"The police questioned George? What are ya talkin' about?"

"They were going to question him about chasing me with his car."

Dahlia's eyebrows shot up in surprise. "Wait a minute. Ya mean he's the one who tried to run ya off the road? Ya didn't mention it was George."

"He was parked in Patrick's driveway when I got home, and Ed recognized his car."

"Me an' you suspected him right from the git-go,

'member?"

"Yeah, because he had our house keys and security code." Cora's chin quivered as she stood and leaned on the table "I'm worried about Ed's reaction to all this. I'm surprised he hasn't called me by now."

The silence only lasted a second before Emily spoke. "Maybe he hasn't read the paper."

"That's probably it." Cora sighed. "Ed always felt obligated to help him with family problems, and did his best to keep him employed at the golf course. This will really tear him up."

"I'm sorry, Sis. Ed must be a very patient man."

Dahlia nodded. "He did all he could to help. In the end, it was George's decision."

Silence followed. Emily pushed her chair from the table and stood. "How about if I put the kettle on for tea?"

Cora hooked her arm with her sister's. "Yes, let's get the dessert ready."

As they headed for the kitchen, Em jokingly called over her shoulder. "Dahlia, do you have a good recipe for Texas Tea?"

"Ya fixin' to make a pot o' crude oil, Yankee?"

Emily laughed at her own blunder and yelled back. "Never mind, ya ol' biscuit shooter. I found the tea bags."

Thankful for a reprieve from morbid thoughts, Cora wiped a tear from her eye and smiled.

Emily was like a shaft of sunlight piercing the dark.

"Hey! I don't cotton to sittin' in here by my lonesome." Dahlia joined them in the kitchen as the teakettle whistled. "Besides, y'all can't be trusted with your bag o' twin pranks."

Cora reached for the dessert plates in the cabinet. "Oh, Dahlly, I'm sorry." She giggled and looked at her sister. "Did that sound sincere?"

"Nope." Emily poured scalding water into the teapot and replaced the lid. "Sure wish I had known who I was tricking ahead of time. Imagine the shock of seeing my favorite TV star standing in front of me."

"Well, y'all best be watchin' your backs. Y'all got my dander up an' I'm gonna be lookin' for my chance to get even." The robust cook threw them a mischievous grin.

Cora snickered. "You'll know when she's really mad, Em. Wendell always says she gets like a bull on loco weed."

"Yeah, an' he would know. I've dented many a cast iron skillet on that knobby bald head." A boisterous round of cackling ensued.

They returned to the dining room to enjoy their dessert. The conversation changed from the topography of Wendell's cranium to Dahlia's upcoming cookbook and apron signing.

"I can't wait to get into this." Emily cut a bite from her spicy pie wedge, and slid her fork under it. She shut her eyes, closed her lips around the tasty mouthful, and let out a long, slow, "M-m-m-m-m."

Cora held her fork midair and chuckled. "I think she's given it her stamp of approval."

"That settles it." Dahlia smacked the table. "It's goin' in my cookbook."

Emily beamed with delight. "So when does this new bestseller hit the shelves?"

"Next July. It'll feature pies, an' I call it, *Flaky an' Proud of It*. My cookbook about grillin', *Totally De-Ranged*, comes out in a week. My publisher's got me booked for appearances mostly in Alabama an' the Carolinas." Dahlia sipped her tea and sighed. "An' then on to QSN. Looks like I'll be gone for quite a spell."

Emily leaned closer to the famous cook and set her cup down. "Wow! What an impressive itinerary."

"Think so?" The famous cook's response lacked gusto.

"Well, of course. What an exciting life. Could we go with you? When do we leave?"

Dahlia grinned at her new friend's enthusiasm. "We hit the road a week from today."

"Why sound so matter-of-fact about it?" Emily took a sip of tea. "You have such a huge following. Think of all that prestige."

"Come agin? It only sounds like a lotta glamour an' glitz. It's plenty o' hard work. There's newspaper innerviews with the same ol' questions. The story of how I began cookin' for ranch hands in Sweet Pickle, Texas, has gotten so old it's growin' whiskers."

Emily laughed. "Sweet Pickle, Texas? Is that a real place?"

"Sure is. I was all pigtails an' buck teeth back then." Dahlia paused for a sip of tea. "After them innerviews, I gotta sign books an' aprons at all the Kitchen Depots, an' still look as fresh as a daisy for TV. I'm plumb wore out just thinkin' about it."

An insecure feeling culminated in the pit of Cora's stomach. When Dahlia was home, she was Cora's physical lifeline while Ed was out each day. Her voice quivered as she nervously reached for her teacup. "Is Wendell going on the tour with you this time?"

"Well, yes an' no. He's goin', but there's a mystery solvers' convention in Charlotte. An' gun shows in

Mobile will keep him busy, too. He'll be outta my hair a good chunk o' the time."

With a shaky hand, Cora placed her cup on the table.

Emily's expression was etched with concern. "What's the matter, Sis?"

"I'm just being silly. The thought of Dahlia's long trip shook me up." Cora looked at her friend apologetically. "I'm sorry, Dahlly, now where did you say he was going?"

"Never mind. Relax, Sugar. George an' the Santalises won't be hasslin' ya no more."

"You're right, it must be a reflex." Cora reached for the teapot to refill her cup. "Feeling safe is going to take some mental adjustments, so be patient with me. Oh, the teapot's empty."

"We'll all be watching out for you, Sis. Our eyeballs are peeled."

Eyeballs. The word jolted Cora. The caller said, "You're in it up to your eyeballs." She glanced at the two women chatting as if they were lifelong buddies. Cora quietly went to the kitchen. Confusion made her head spin. Was Em linked to the caller somehow?

If there was a mistaken identity and a connection between Emily and George, they could be harboring a fugitive. She placed the kettle on a burner, and pulled out more teabags. *Oh, Cora Timms, turn off your imagination. Em couldn't be a criminal.* She took a cleansing breath.

Her relief was short-lived, as another doubt pounced on her reverie. If all her cohorts were out of the picture, Em would be the lone inheritor of the stolen money in that manila envelope. Cora ripped open another teabag as her mind continued to grapple with the theory.

The whistle on the kettle pierced her thoughts. She reached for the steaming kettle and looked down at the teapot. Good grief, how did she cram so many teabags in there? As she tossed the superfluous bags on the counter, another idea surfaced. What if her sister didn't have a reaction because she knew George and the Santalises weren't the callers?

Were the real stalkers still out there? Either way, she had to find out.

As Cora walked into the dining room with the freshly brewed tea, the grandfather clock chimed twice.

Dahlia pivoted in her seat to double-check the time. "Land sakes, is it that late? I got me a business call comin' in a half hour. I'd best hustle my bustle back home, gals."

Cora hugged Dahlia before they walked her to the door. "Now don't tell anybody about our twin-hood." She shook her finger. "Especially Wendell. We want to surprise—"

"No," Emily interrupted. "We want to *shake up* this neighborhood."

Dahlia gave them thumbs up as she left.

ॐॐ

It was later than usual when Ed arrived home for supper. Cora put the lid on the saucepan and turned the heat down. "I thought we could talk about the Shipleys before we eat."

Ed sat in an easy chair and smoothed his hair back with the palms of his hands. He leaned forward and placed his elbows on his knees. "It was in the morning paper, and Wendell came by the clubhouse to talk about it. I would've called you, but I didn't want to put a damper on Em's visit." He shook his head. "What a sad situation. I keep thinking I could've done more to prevent George from making so many bad decisions. I let him down, Toots, and he probably felt like he had nowhere else to turn."

Cora bent forward to embrace him. "Eddie, you provided help for the man over and over again. Maybe he needed professional care. You can't go back and change things. What's done is done."

Her words were razor sharp as they sliced into her own conscience. Vanessa was gone and nothing would bring her daughter back.

Ed sighed. "Yeah, I know. It's going to take some time to accept it. It just doesn't add up. George was a devout Catholic, and they feel suicide is a mortal sin. Was he really capable of taking his mother's life and then his own?"

"I guess he just snapped."

"Maybe that's the answer." He stood and kissed her forehead. "I'll be fine in a bit." He looked around the room. "By the way, where's Emily? Wasn't she supposed to be here today?"

"She's in the guest room unpacking. We've had a great time visiting all day. We'll tell you all about it over supper, but right now you need to get some rest."

"Good idea. I'll go say hi to Eudora on my way back to the bedroom. Call me when supper's ready."

Cora smiled at his humorous remark. Her husband was going to be fine. Meanwhile, Em's association with George and the stolen money had her stumped.

19

The next morning, Cora and Emily gobbled their bagels and cream cheese as they planned the day's events. Ed strolled into the dining room and stood behind Cora's usual chair at the table. He placed his hands on Emily's shoulders and gently squeezed. "Did you remember you have a doctor's appointment today, Toots?" He leaned over and planted tiny kisses on her neck.

Emily wiggled in her seat and patted the masculine hands that massaged her shoulders. "Oooh snookums! Have I ever told you what a fine hunk of a man you are?"

A brilliant red covered Ed's face as he jerked his hands away from Emily. He looked from one sister to the other. "Oh no," he moaned. "I do believe my peaceful existence has just spun out of control."

Cora couldn't hold back a burst of laughter. "Do you two want to be alone?"

He walked to his wife and thoroughly studied her face. "Now, are you Cora, or did you sneak in another sister?" He planted a big kiss on her lips. "Aw, who cares?"

Her arms swiftly encircled his neck. "I think you did it on purpose to get more kisses."

"Well, whichever one is my sweetheart, you have forty minutes before we have to leave."

"Oh no! I lost track of time." She jumped from her

chair, and began to gather the dirty breakfast dishes.

Emily touched her wrist. "You get ready and let me tend to this."

"Oh, I couldn't do that. You're my guest."

"I'm family and I insist." Emily turned her towards the bedroom and pointed. "Now move it."

Cora dutifully obeyed.

༈ ༺

Aware the days would be brighter now, Ed made note of the joyful state of mind his wife so quickly exhibited. She actually hummed as she left the room. Emily's presence breathed new life into her twin, and Ed knew his beloved wife was back.

He entered the kitchen and smiled at Emily. "I'm so glad you're here. I haven't seen Cora this happy in a long time."

"Believe me, God knew I needed her in my life as much as she needed me."

"I'm sorry we have to leave you here by yourself while we go to the doctor. Are you sure you don't want to go to Phoenix with us?"

"No, I'll be fine. I need to take a shower and then call June before she goes to work. She's anxious to hear all the details of our reunion. I can't forget to tell her about this morning's exceptionally warm greeting from Jeff's Uncle Steady."

"Am I ever gonna live that down?"

"In a word, no." They shared a laugh before Emily became serious. She told Ed about Cora's reaction to the McGibbons's upcoming trip. "So, would you mind if I offered to stay with her until they get home?" She added a mischievous wink, "If truth be known, it's not so much to help her, I just like your kisses."

"Well, don't get addicted." Ed chuckled. "All kidding aside, it would be wonderful to have you here."

As Ed watched the news, Cora waltzed into the room. She wore the sapphire blue outfit he had given her for their last anniversary. He proudly escorted her to the car.

∂∽∾

The front of the medical building held a large expanse of windows. Natural light filtered through the tinted glass which revealed a panoramic view of the vicinity. Ed placed a protective hand on Cora's back as they stepped into the empty elevator that would take them to Dr. Keith.

A foreboding sensation overshadowed Cora. She looked at her husband for a sign of reassurance. The ominous feeling intensified as the door closed and the elevator began its calm ascent.

"Something's wrong, Ed." Her voice was strained with anxiety.

"You're just worried about the results of your tests." He took her hand and gently patted it, then looked at his watch. "It's 11:00. In a half hour or so, it'll all be over. Everything's going to be fine."

Her shoulders straightened at his somewhat condescending tone. "No, it's more than just seeing the doctor. I've had this feeling—" Cora's sentence was interrupted as the elevator door whooshed open. Ed ushered her out while another couple entered the compartment and voices droned around them in the busy hall. She decided to wait for a more opportune time to express her concerns.

After a few minutes in the waiting area, Ed and Cora were sent to the examination room for her consultation.

Dr. Keith knocked on the door and walked in with Cora's file. The attractive doctor greeted them with a twinkle in his deep-set eyes. "Good morning." He shook hands with them and then waved the folder in the air. "Tests confirmed what I suspected all along, Mrs. Timms. No sign of Alzheimer's disease and let me assure you once again, you're not losing your mind, either."

With a big smile, Ed leaned over and hugged her. Their initial fears were alleviated. "See, I told you everything would work out."

The doctor cleared his throat and continued his assessment. "As I mentioned before, this is a diagnosis of exclusion. Before we can call it Alzheimer's, we have to rule out all other possibilities. The deciding factor is to check your language, problem solving, and attention capacity. We've done all the tests and scans, concentrated on your memory and counting skills since these were your biggest concerns. Everything came back well within the normal range."

Cora blinked. "You mean I'm normal? Even my math?"

"Mrs. Timms, you were able to do the math, it took you a little longer, that's all. With AD, you would completely forget what numbers are and what to do with them. Alzheimer's patients also forget how to prepare meals or participate in lifelong hobbies."

Cora studied his face as she sat back in her chair. She desperately wanted to believe him.

The doctor leaned forward. "Those are tasks AD

folks can't do at all. They forget the simplest things like how to wave good-bye or motion for someone to come." He looked up as the muscles in her face relaxed. "You mentioned the traumatic event of your daughter's death. Forgetfulness is common in the grieving process, Mrs. Timms. Often those who mourn feel disoriented and wonder if they're losing their mind. Let me ask you this, has there been further emotional strain in your life?"

Ed quickly answered for her. "Yes, there certainly has been, Doctor."

The physician offered a compassionate nod. "The weight of anxiety causes many problems, depression being one of them. The loss of your daughter, coupled with this new emotional strain, is enough to throw you into a tailspin." He looked over her chart again. "We know your symptoms came on all of a sudden. Alzheimer's is gradual and progressive."

"Stress has been causing the forgetfulness?" Cora asked. "Things are calming down, so my problems should be coming to an end. You'd think I'd be dancing around the room." She shrugged her shoulders. "Then why do I still feel apprehensive?"

Dr. Keith gently replied, "First, go easy with physical things and get plenty of rest for a week or so. Once you're relaxed, your mind will settle down. I'll give you a prescription to help with your depression and anxiety. Be sure to tell your family doctor and if things don't improve after a month, he can adjust the dosage."

Cora's expectation of a dismal future may have been erased, but she sensed something was still wrong.

They thanked the doctor for his time and advice, and then found their way to the receptionist's desk.

While Ed took care of business, Cora impatiently waited, eager to be home and begin a new life with her sister.

Then it hit her. *Emily*. She grabbed Ed's arm as they walked to the elevator. "Something's happened to Emily. I need to call her."

"You and your woman's intuition," he teased.

Undaunted, Cora continued. "Remember the night Vanessa had her accident? Well, it's that same sick feeling I had just before we got the call."

He lifted his hands in surrender. "By all means, we'll call home if you feel so strongly about it."

Cora was determined not to give him a moment's peace until her fears were mollified. After all, she had been right about Vanessa. She looked for her cell phone. "Where did I leave it this time?"

"Here, use mine."

She grabbed the phone and opened it. "Oh no. There's no signal. Now what?"

"OK, calm down. Maybe we'll get lucky and find a payphone. Hey, there's a custodian. I'll ask him."

The elderly man shook his head and pulled a cell phone from his pocket. "These things are really handy and come in different price ranges. I'm sure there's one to fit your budget."

Cora thanked the man, and nervously punched in their home number. She chewed her lower lip and looked at her husband. "There's no answer. We've got to get home."

"Now wait a minute, Toots, maybe she's taking a shower or out walking and ran into Letitia. You know how she can talk your leg off." Ed paused and added, "Emily has a cell phone. Call her on that."

"I don't know her number," Cora wailed and

handed the phone back to the custodian.

Ed thanked the man and turned to her. "Calm down. Jeff's office is in this building. We can get her number there."

Within a few minutes, Ed and Cora stood in Jeff's waiting room. The receptionist took them to his office.

The young doctor listened to their concerns. "She's doing fine. I called her earlier. She told me a neighbor came over with her dog and a plate of brownies, and then nearly talked her ear off."

"Letitia." Ed and Cora said in unison.

20

Ed was in a hurry to get back to his office at the golf course. He pulled into the driveway and waited for Cora to get into the house.

She was relieved to get home. The premonitions about her sister had been so strong; she needed to actually see Emily, in order to satisfy her intuition.

"Em! I'm home. Where are you?" As Cora neared the guest room, the shower could be heard along with Emily as she sang a rousing rendition of "The Man on the Flying Trapeze."

"O-o-o-oh, he flies through the air...with the greatest of e-e-e-ease..."

Cora giggled and went to get some much-needed coffee. She filled her cup and headed for the bedroom, eager to ditch the itchy outfit Ed got for her. Now that he saw her wear it twice, the prickly dress was destined for the back of her closet, along with the matching shoes. Her bunions were in an uproar. As much as she hated to admit it, those duck slippers were quacking her name.

She was still in her slip when the bedroom door popped open. Her heart jumped to her throat. "Emily! You scared me to death."

Emily laughed. "I'm sorry. I heard a noise in here and thought it was a boogieman."

"And you came dressed like that?" Cora pointed to her sister's terry bathrobe and fluffy pink Barbie slippers.

Once they regained composure, Emily sat on the end of the bed. "So, what did your doctor say?"

Cora put her satin robe and duck slippers on. "Good news." She took a sip of coffee and explained the doctor's findings. Suddenly she stopped. "Did you hear that?"

"It's probably Ed."

"No, he dropped me off because he had some work to do at the golf course." Cora looked at her twin. "Think we should check it out?"

Emily nodded and whispered, "We need a weapon just in case. What have you got?"

"Oh, Em. I can't think of anything, except a can of hairspray."

"That'll work. I'll put it in my pocket and I've got my cell phone, too. We can call 9-1-1 if we need to. Let's go." Emily grabbed Cora's hand. "Stay with me."

Quack-quack!

"Take those dumb ducks off. He'll hear you."

They were in the middle of the hall when a loud crash followed by a man's booming voice came from the other end of the house. They froze and waited for further commotion. Cora held her half-filled coffee cup in one hand and duck slippers in the other.

Together, they tiptoed through the kitchen and into the hallway, just outside the office. With one eye, Cora peered through the crack of the partially opened door. Books and objects covered the floor. A shiver ran down her spine as she saw a man about their age. He wore a denim jacket and mumbled while he attempted to break into Ed's desk.

She held her breath, and leaned closer to the opening. Come on buddy, look up. I wanna see your mug. His curses became audible, and she backed away.

Emily peered in. She turned to her sister, pointed a finger in the air and tapped her temple.

What was she going to do? Cora wasn't good at charades. She watched in amazement as Emily held her phone up and pressed a button. Photographs. She took his picture.

The intruder opened the desk and rifled through each drawer with reckless abandon. Obviously, the man didn't find what he was after. He stood and stretched his back.

As he turned, his craggy features came into view. With eyes as big as hubcaps, Emily grabbed the sleeve of Cora's robe and snapped another picture.

With the door still ajar, Cora juggled her almost empty coffee cup and her slippers. The two backed away as the man continued to explore, oblivious that several photos had been taken.

Cora stared, engrossed with his ardent search. He yanked out the middle drawer, dumped the contents, and then tossed it on top of the cluttered desk. Ed's golf bag pencil holder fell off and a jumble of pens and pencils littered the floor.

"The pencil holder." He rushed around the desk and picked it up. His pudgy forefinger dug into a zipped pocket. He pulled out a key and headed for the safe.

Cora realized the danger they were in, and tugged on Emily's arm. They had to get away. Emily carried the cell phone with the incriminating photos close to her. They took two steps.

Then it happened…the cell phone rang.

Emily's flinch bumped her sister's hand and Cora dropped her cup to the tile floor with a crash.

They were toast.

A gruff voice yelled. "Who's there?"

Emily whispered, "Hide." They scurried to the kitchen, and Emily left the ringing phone on the counter.

Cora ran for the pantry. They barely squeezed into the small enclosure as sounds of the intruder drew closer. Fearful images of a physical attack sprang to Cora's mind. She managed to shut the squeaking door behind them, not a second too soon. She drew a deep breath. Through the louvered slats, they observed the beefy man bolt into the kitchen and survey the room.

His sinister eyes darted about. They watched him pick up the cell phone from the counter. Would he see the pictures? Emily gasped, and her hand went to her chest.

Cora felt the shadowy cubicle close in on her. That was when she noticed Emily's breathing had become labored. Did she need her medicine?

Jeff said that it would bring on an incapacitating headache. Should she take the nitroglycerin anyway?

Only Em could make that decision. When her sister's hand went into her pocket, Cora instinctively knew she was after the pill…or the hairspray.

Her attention returned to the hefty man.

The intruder's shifty eyes locked onto the pantry door. He slammed the phone on the counter, then turned and left the kitchen. Cora eased the death grip on her slippers. He was gone.

Emily was fidgety. She whispered, "Did you see who that was?"

"He doesn't look familiar to me."

"Well, I know him from somewhere. I bet he was in cahoots with that guy that killed himself." She clutched her chest. "I've got to get out of this pigeonhole."

"I don't think it's safe to leave yet. Can you wait a few more minutes?" Cora held her wristwatch up to the slats in the door. The barely sufficient light allowed her to see it was almost one o'clock.

Emily placed a tiny white pill under her tongue, and leaned against the shelving.

Would a headache follow? This pantry was no place for Em to be immobilized. They needed to move soon, before the severe pain rendered her helpless.

Cora struggled to put her slippers on. She'd have to remember to tiptoe to keep the ducks quiet. She spoke softly, "Now's our chance. If we can just make it to the front door, we can go to Dahlia's for help. Wendell and Jack will be there eating lunch. Ready? Let's go."

Cora pushed on the door. It stuck. A fresh panic clinched her heart. *Don't scream. Be brave for Em.* She took a deep breath, then, pushed harder, and the creaking door compliantly yielded. Cora stopped short, and waited for a response to the squeaky disturbance.

When all was quiet, she assumed it was safe, and took a tentative step forward. With desperate determination, she ventured out of the pantry. A box of macaroni fell to the tile floor with a loud crack. Emily backed deeper into the pantry as little elbows flew far and wide.

From the hallway came a hoarse whisper. "Corrah."

Her heart plummeted right to the soles of her duck slippers. She glanced in the direction of the voice. The intruder abruptly appeared, ready to strike. Cora's slippers quacked as she dodged him. She reached for the counter to regain her balance. A firm hand grabbed her arm. Crushing fingers dug into tender flesh.

"Let me go!" She flailed and clawed at his rugged face.

His grip increased as he stepped behind her. "Nice try, Cor-rah," he growled. "All you had to do was give me the envelope."

In the hallway, she writhed in the futile attempt for freedom.

He yanked her right arm behind her.

Her bones felt brittle as he delivered a sharp wrench.

Finally, he trapped both her arms and backed her tightly against himself. "Don't try that again," he warned through gritted teeth. "Or you'll be sorry."

"Wh-what are you going to do to me?" Cora weakened at the intensity of his strength.

Without warning, Emily fell from the pantry, and landed in a heap. The hairspray can rolled into the middle of the kitchen floor. Cora moaned. The nitroglycerin pill had taken effect.

"What the—?" He ignored Cora's continued pleas, and half-dragged her back to the kitchen. Her foot twisted on the broken cup and a shard pierced her ankle. Cold metal touched her neck. Hard and threatening.

He released Cora with a warning. "I've got a gun. Move and I'll shoot her." He grabbed Emily from the floor and threw her over his shoulder, and then he waved the gun at the garage door. "My van's out there. We're all going to go quietly without attracting attention. Got that?"

With a gun pressed in her back, Cora led the way. She had to protect her helpless sister from this monster. Once she came to, they'd make their plans for escape. That was their only hope. A still, small Voice spoke to her. *Fear not, for I am with you.*

21

Bright sunshine streamed through the window of Ed's office at the Saguaro Valley Golf Course. His assistant, Roger Clark, whistled in disbelief. "What a wild story." He chuckled. "I would've given my eye teeth to see the fallout from that scene."

"Lunch at the Pegasi was a real roller coaster ride, let me tell ya," Ed added. "But finding Cora's twin sister has been a Godsend. I haven't seen her this happy in years."

"Have you celebrated, yet?"

"No, not yet. We haven't had time."

Roger laughed. "You should take them back to the Pegasi. I'll alert the media."

"What a great idea. I'll do it." Ed's eyebrows lifted. "Don't you dare call the press."

"Aw, why not? Think of it as free publicity. I can see the headlines now: Steady Eddie Timms Scores a Double Bogey."

Ed laughed and looked at his watch. "I'd better call home so they don't plan supper." He dialed the phone. "Hey Rog, there's Pastor Luke coming for his lesson. He's all yours."

"Oh, I see how it is, stick the lowly assistant with the putter-challenged preacher." Roger chuckled. "By the way, is this a good time to ask for a raise?"

Ed tossed a golf ball at the door as his mischievous employee ducked out. He dialed his home phone number. When he got the answering machine, he left a quick message. "Hey Toots, call me a.s.a.p. Love ya." He looked around to check for an audience. Even with no one there, he still covered the mouthpiece, cleared his throat, and whispered, "Kissy-kissy."

A half-hour later, he phoned the house again. Cora hadn't mentioned any plans when he dropped her off. She couldn't go anywhere, he had the car, and hers was still in the shop. Where were they? Letitia's? Well, he couldn't call *her*, she'd never hang up. After the third unsuccessful phone call, he decided to contact Wendell. He always bragged about having his finger on the pulse of the community.

The security guard was glad to check in on Cora at the house. He immediately returned Ed's phone call to report his initial findings. "I'm inside an' been yellin' for 'em, Ed, but I don't hear nothin'. You're prob'ly right, they must be out walkin'. Maybe that ol' magpie, Letitia, is bendin' their ear. If so, we won't be seein' hide nor hair of 'em for a while." He hesitated then added, "I reckon I could mosey on over there an' see."

"Would you mind?"

"Well, just wait a minute. I'm in the kitchen, now. Your pantry's open, Ed, an' a box of macaroni's dumped on the floor, an' a can of hairspray, too. Hey! We got us a cell phone on the counter," he announced. "Prob'ly Em's, don't ya think? I'll just take it over to Letitia's with me."

Suddenly Ed heard Wendell let out a sharp whistle. "Ah-oh. I see a broke cup an' spilt coffee in the hallway."

The disquieting information alarmed Ed. His stomach churned. Was there a struggle? Or did one of them get hurt? Maybe he should alert Sam.

The Texan's voice intensified. "This ain't no good. I see some blood on the floor."

"Blood?" Ed's heart was in his throat. Was it Cora's or Emily's? "How much blood?"

"Can't rightly tell since there's coffee there, too. Woo-whee! This really gets my detective juices flowin'. Too bad Jack had to go get hisself a new drain snake. Boy howdy, is he missin' out." Wendell chuckled. "Oh well, Jack's loss is my gain. I'm headin' for the bedrooms now."

Ed heard him knock on a door. "Don't forget to look in the closets and bathrooms, Wendell."

"Nope, they ain't here, neither. Lemme go check your office."

As Ed visualized Wendell boot-scootin' down the hallway, he considered all the ramifications of the Texan's search. He turned and saw the pro-shop manager nearby. "Hey Larry, I need you to call 9-1-1 and send the cops over to my place. I think there's been a break-in."

Wendell's loud voice on the phone recaptured his attention. "Woo-whee! Ed, I hate to tell ya this, but everything's catty whompus in your office."

Ed's mind raced as the news sunk in. "Don't touch anything, Wendell. I'll be right there."

"What do ya mean, don't touch nothin'? I'm a highly-trained security guard here, an' this ain't my first rodeo," Wendell complained. "An' don't ya forget I know all about police procedures. I worked at the department for 30-odd years."

Ed rolled his eyes. He was aware that custodial work was as close as his friend ever got to actual investigating. Still, the Texan was proud of his link to law enforcement. "Just let the police handle it,

Wendell. I'll be right there."

It wasn't long before Ed saw the damage in his home office. The doorbell rang, and he made his way back to the living room. Wendell, a policeman's worst nightmare, opened the door.

"Howdy." Wendell scratched his ample belly as Ed joined them. "I'm the senior secur'ty officer here. I done checked the house."

"What do you mean you checked the house?" The police sergeant asked.

"Just what I said. Ol' Ed called me first 'cause I'm the senior secur'ty guard. He couldn't reach the missus or her sister on the phone. He was worried 'bout 'em an' wanted me to check things out 'cause Cora's sister has herself a heart problem. I've been all over the house an' it looks like a buckin' bronco's been let loose."

The policeman frowned at him. "Did you touch anything?"

Wendell took his clearly identifiable John Wayne I-got-it-all-under-control stance. His voice took on an air of importance. "Why is ever-body worried 'bout me touchin' stuff? I know this here is an official crime scene, an' I ain't been contaminatin' no evidence."

Three police officers pushed their way past Wendell and into the house. The sergeant looked at Ed. "Are you Ed Timms?"

"Yes, I am." He impatiently answered the officer's many questions.

Later, Wendell stood next to Ed in the far corner of the living room. "If I only had me a tad more time, I coulda found vital evidence."

The two men watched the police go about their investigation, with the presence of the security guard obviously going unnoticed. Wendell muttered, "They might be makin' me stand in the corner like a whooped pup, but, I'm gonna stay two jumps ahead of 'em. I got me an idea. Yessiree. They'll be singin' therselves 'nother tune when me an' Jack crack this here case."

Ed tried to change the subject. "Where did you say the handyman was?"

"Aww, he's stuck at the plumbin' store. He needed a new drain snake. That ol' Letitia's drain got plugged with poodle hair again. She scalps that dog every other month, like clockwork." He frowned at Ed. "Ya, know, if ya weren't so famous, we wouldn't have but one cop here an' I'd have me a better chance to do my sleuthin'."

Ed smiled. Talk about dodging a bullet. He quickly pulled the plug on that thought when a bloodcurdling scream came from outside. Was it Cora?

A split second later, the policemen stormed past them and charged out the front door.

Wendell grabbed his Stetson and ran outside with Ed on his heels.

Their elderly neighbor, Letitia Bockman, was in her driveway. Her high-pitched voice screeched as she pointed to the policemen who ran into her garage. Then her feet stomped out an Irish jig and loose skin flapped under her flailing arms. What was going on?

Ed had never seen Letitia in such a frenzied state.

One of the policemen called, "Hey Sarge, better come see this."

The police sergeant leaned over and put his arm around Letitia's frail shoulders. With a stern look, he motioned for Ed and Wendell to join them. "Stay here with her." He headed for the garage.

Letitia shook uncontrollably. "I was just taking my

garbage out and Tinkle-Belle started scratching at those boxes in the corner. Then I saw it." She shivered. "I saw it."

"Well, what was it?" In one smooth move, Wendell whipped a notepad from his rear pocket and repeatedly clicked his pen.

"It was a bloody hand." Her voice quivered. "Eewwwww!"

"Can ya describe it for me?"

"Eewwwww!" The feeble woman's feet repeated the Irish jig.

Ed jerked Wendell aside. "They'll need to question Letitia. Let's get her calmed down so she can think." He hugged her close. "Don't worry, Lettie, everything will be all right."

"You gotta be pullin' my leg, man." Wendell shook his head. "This has to have somethin' to do with the Saguaro Sidewinder Case."

"The what?"

"Ya know, Cora's case." Wendell pushed his Stetson to the back of his head. "Ya 'member that night she said she saw a murder but none of us could find a body? Well, right chere it is."

Ed stared at the garage. Was Wendell right? Did Cora actually witness a murder? Why hadn't he believed her? Where was Cora?

Letitia was questioned while both the Timms' home and hers were cordoned off with yellow CRIME SCENE tape. It was hung along the sidewalk and across the driveway to keep curiosity seekers at bay.

Blue and red lights flashed as the neighborhood crawled with law enforcement.

A police photographer came with a meticulous criminologist, and both homes were searched for clues.

Phoenix area detectives soon joined the primary contingent of police in the search for Cora and Emily.

22

The kidnapper had removed their gags and left them alone in a dimly lit motel room. Cora, bound with nylon cord, sat stiffly on a wooden chair lodged between a wall and an unmade bed. Her heart raced and terror welled in her throat as she checked the rope for any slack. Powerless to move her hands, the probability of escape seemed hopeless. With every ounce of strength gone, she allowed her head to rest back against the nicotine-stained wall. What place was this? Well, one thing for sure, they hadn't been swept off to Shangri-La.

Pungent odors in the room filled Cora's nostrils. Potent cigar smoke mixed with mold, mildew and probably jungle rot intensified her fear. Could a person get black lung disease from this revolting Petri dish?

She glanced over to her sister. Unconscious with a debilitating headache, Em was sprawled face down on the grungy mattress. The thought of the poor soul breathing in disgusting micro-organisms gave Cora the heebie-jeebies. She'd have to check Em's hair for cooties and other specimens of wildlife.

Beneath her duck slippers lay orange shag carpet riddled with burn holes. She also recognized toenail clippings and wads of hair. Dampness and age had pulled the rug free from the walls as if it attempted its own escape from the filth.

Cora gasped as the door opened and the

kidnapper stormed into the room. The hefty man leaned over and jerked her bindings, then went to the other side of the bed to make a call on the old rotary dial phone. The short cord tethered him to the nightstand, and offered only a scant three-foot area for his livid pacing.

His temper flared as he dictated his bidding. "Get to room 19 at the Catchpenny Motel now, Rita." He lit a cigar clenched in his teeth, and listened impatiently before he bellowed his response. "Yes, I know it wasn't our original plan, you dimwit. There are two of them and they walked in on me. Can't tell one broad from the other. I had no choice but to take them both. Just consider it plan B and get your can over here on the double. I'll expect you in fifteen minutes. If I get back to work on time, they'll never suspect us."

He slammed the receiver onto the cradle, swore, and shook his head with disgust at his hostages. "I'm not sure which one of you got me into this with your stupid code of ethics. If you hadn't squealed on me, I wouldn't have been behind bars for ten years."

Cora closed her eyes and inwardly grimaced at the ranting and raving. She offered no response to his accusations. He was the one who served ten years, and since she wasn't the squealee, it had to be Emily who turned him in. So that's why he tracked her down. Cora couldn't imagine what the man did, but the good news was her twin wasn't the Bonnie to his Clyde after all. She released a sigh of relief.

Curses spewed from the man's mouth as he ran chubby fingers through his hair in exasperation. "Not only do I have to wait on Rita to get her lazy carcass in motion, I have to sit here and watch your sister pretend to have a stroke. You women always cause me grief."

Cora peeked as the man dialed the old phone again. Who was he calling now?

"Why isn't your answering machine kicking on?" He swore, slammed the phone down and kicked the mattress. "Can't you do anything right, Cor-rah?"

The kidnapper turned to the antiquated TV perched on a flimsy stand. He inched his way around the bed and pulled the knob that turned the set on. As it slowly hummed to life, he plopped into the torn recliner. The artificial leather creaked as he shifted his weight to find a comfortable position.

He looked at Cora. "What are you smiling about?"

She blurted, "It won't work."

"Shut your pie hole. 'Course it'll work. You think they'd leave a useless set in the room?"

She cringed and lowered her head. This motel didn't spring for bug spray. Did he honestly think they'd get cable?

The set sputtered, followed by grating static and a screen-full of electronic snow. He looked at Cora and pointed at her mouth. "Pie hole, lady, pie hole."

His explicit language turned the air blue while he wrestled his stocky form out of the sagging chair. He turned the TV off and went outside. His vocabulary was obviously limited since he used the same four-letter words repeatedly.

Within a few minutes, he returned with a portable radio, and placed it on the windowsill. The man opened the tattered drapes a bit, then pushed the chair closer to the window as a news report blared from a local station. He muttered and glanced outside while his backside searched for the same ruts he'd rested in before.

With the captor's attention diverted, Cora

continued to assess the meager surroundings. The assessment wasn't good. Cobwebs dangled directly overhead in a complex pattern. Clearly, the motel owners hadn't consulted Martha Stewart for any cleaning or decorating tips.

From the corner of her eye, she caught a glimpse of an unidentifiable insect as it skittered across the floor. Was he a scout for a whole battalion of buddies? Her skin crawled. If only her hands were free to scratch...everywhere.

In an effort to ward off the creepy sensation, she again concentrated on a possible means of escape. She looked at Emily. Oh, she needed her help. What was this brute going to do to them? No doubt about it, this was a perfect setting for murder and the less time spent here, the better.

If there was anything to this twin telepathy thing, now would be a good time for it to kick in. She sent concentrated brain waves to the quiet form on the bed. *Wake up, Em.* Cora nudged the bed with her knees.

Emily's head turned slightly. She winked at her.

Hey, maybe there was something to that twin stuff after all! Cora gave a half-grin and mouthed, "OK?"

Em replied with a nod.

Cora tried to send another subliminal suggestion through the airwaves. She squeezed her eyes shut. *Stay still, Em. Feign unconsciousness.* She searched her sister's face for an answer.

Emily smiled and squinted.

The chug of an ailing car engine drew the man's focus to the window. A door slammed and soon they heard a timid knock.

The kidnapper unbolted the door and allowed the woman to enter.

"*¡Hola!*" the señorita said. She took a sip from the Java Joe's cup in her hand and flung her fuchsia-colored purse onto the bed.

While he waited, the senior partner-in-crime had built up a head of steam. "You stopped for coffee?" he shouted and knocked the Styrofoam cup from her hand. Brown liquid splattered on the wall. With ham-hock hands, he grabbed the girl's upper arms and jerked her further into the room. "You knew I had to get back to work to cover my tail."

He pitched the young woman sideways. She landed awkwardly on the floor, and cracked her head on the nightstand. The phone fell off with a crash. Anger flashed in woman's dark brown eyes as she rubbed her throbbing hairline. She stood and bit her lip. She spoke softly in her rich, lilting accent, "*Perdón, mi amor*. I hurry fast."

He roughly pushed her away. "It wasn't fast enough. Don't let it happen again. If this thing is going to work, you have to be reliable. You made me late and now I'll have to explain myself."

"Do not be in such *mal* humor, *amado*. You can count on me."

"Remember, if I go down, I'm takin' you and your illegal family with me. Just watch every move those two make and don't let them talk you into anything, understand?"

Rita stared at Emily bound on the bed. "What is with *dama antigua? ¿Ella es doliente*?"

"How many times do I have to tell you? You're in America, speak English. And no, she's not sick." He made a dismissing gesture. "That's a sympathy act. Just ignore it."

Rita squinted and bent down to observe Em more

closely. "She is breathing?"

"Forget her and listen to me." He handed his partner the gun. "Here, don't be afraid to use it. Remember, we've got five million riding on this deal. You'd better not be the one to let the ball drop." He checked his watch. "I still have to deliver a ransom note. Simpleton, over there, didn't have their answering machine on."

Cora listened to the dialogue, and her mind quickly came to attention. Five million? Ransom? She peeked at them from her seat of confinement. Of course there'd be a ransom. She and Em had been kidnapped. But, five million smackers? Wow!

A cloud of dense cigar smoke circled the heavy man. "Everything's in order so don't do anything stupid. I'll be back soon." The ex-con left in a huff and slammed the door behind him.

Rita used the barrel of the .38 to hold back the curtain as she watched out the window. Squealing tires announced her accomplice's hasty departure. She muttered, "*Adios, bandido.*"

Cora sighed. Good. He was gone. One kidnapper down and one to go. She needed to stay calm and think of some way to escape. As bad as their predicament was, Cora was relieved that her sister had regained consciousness and just one female now stood guard.

The amateur criminal shuffled across the floor and grumbled about the purpling goose egg on her forehead and her never-ending bad luck. "I do not trust him. Not *uno momento.*" She marched to the radio, and turned the set off.

In the gratifying stillness, Cora decided it was time to size up the enemy. One thing for sure, the beautiful señorita enjoyed bright colors. Rita was 30ish and had a petite frame much like her own. That was good. At least, size-wise they were on a level playing field.

As Rita leaned over to get her bright-colored purse from the bed, Cora spotted slight discolorations on her neck. Concealed bruises. How much abuse had this poor child been through? She was in over her head and needed help.

Their new captor flopped on the worn recliner, searched through her purse, and pulled out a pill bottle. She shook it, and then angrily threw the empty container at the door.

Cora continued to give her the once-over. The woman's bleached blonde ponytail had crow-black roots which advertised overlooked hair appointments. Her lethal-looking fingernails were covered with red chipped polish and her makeup was unusually heavy. No doubt to hide the bruises. Not exactly the fresh-scrubbed look of the girl-next-door.

Emily's bloodcurdling scream jolted Cora from her thoughts.

Rita's fuchsia purse flew into the air, its contents rained on the bed.

"Cora, roach on your foot!" Em yelled.

The granddaddy of all cockroaches scaled up Cora's slipper. It was slightly larger than a bar of soap.

Cora screamed a perfectly pitched trio with the other ladies. Even with legs bound, she managed to kick her slipper two feet up.

"¡Ay-yi-yi-yi!" Rita screamed. "¡Cucaracha!"

Gunshots rang out. Glass shattered. The TV died its second death. The lamp bit the dust, and the lovely señorita faced seven years bad luck when the mirror splintered into smithereens.

Finally, the giant cockroach went belly-up and

gave one last kick.

Stillness hung in the air as the dust settled. As if repulsed, Rita tossed the smoking gun onto the bed next to her empty fuchsia purse and Emily. She shuddered, wrung her hands, and wiped them on her jeans. An anxious expression surfaced as she paced the floor.

Emily cleared her throat, which broke the awkward silence. "Your partner sure left you holding the bag."

"Do not worry, *dama antigua*. It is under control." Rita's tone was bitter and defiant. "Once we have *dinero*, he will kill you like that man and his mamá. Then we will live in *abundancia*." She stopped short. The stunned look on the señorita's face indicated that she'd blurted too much information. She crossed her arms over her multi-colored shirt, and quickly turned her head.

"So he's going to kill us?" Cora asked. "And you think he'll let *you* live?"

Rita's eyes darted about the room. "We have many plans."

"I bet he said you'd live in a fancy house or a big mansion, didn't he?" Cora hoped to make the young woman think. "I'm not sure what you're expecting, but this dive is an example of how you'll live. Once you've murdered someone, you'll be a fugitive, constantly on the run and looking over your shoulder. Is that what you want?"

Rita picked up the gun and pointed it at Cora. "If you do not shut up I will get rid of you now. *¿Comprende?*"

Cora sighed. Obviously that approach didn't work. Rainbow-girl needed a reality check. What was going to sway her? She closed her eyes. *Dear Lord, if You're really there, we desperately need Your help. Please give us wisdom and a way to escape.*

Emily looked at the girl with caring eyes. "It's hard to imagine a pretty lady like you with that burly old coot. You could do so much better. Your whole life could improve."

"You do not know about my life. He say he love me.Besides, why you care?" She wedged the .38 into her waistband.

"You're holding us hostage and threatening to kill us, but we still care what happens to you. Others have helped me when I didn't deserve it. That's God's love at work. Real love is patient and kind." Emily paused. "Calling you names and slapping you around doesn't sound like love to me. This man is using and abusing you to get the money. When you get it, you'll see it won't buy the kind of love you're looking for. Only God can give pure love."

A hateful sneer came to Rita's face. "Five million dollar will buy new life. No more debt, and no more bad job." She frowned and pointed to Emily. "And no more religious kooks!"

Cora shook her head. "Greedy people like him are all alike. He has no intention of giving you your share of the money."

"You do not know. Keep your mouth shut." Rita rubbed the tender spot on her forehead.

Obviously this new injury took a toll on the young woman. An angry man who manipulated everything would be stressful enough, but this unplanned kidnapping must've pushed her over the edge.

Rita rubbed her head and cringed as if the action caused great discomfort. "My head aches," she complained.

Headache? Did she say headache? A mischievously brilliant plan popped into Cora's mind. Was this their open door? As if on cue, the twins looked at each other.

Cora cleared her throat, and tried to keep as subdued as possible. "Em had a doozy of a headache when we first got here. Well, you know, you saw her. Couldn't stand the light or the noises. And all the smells, well, let's not go there." For a moment, her guilt almost convinced her to ditch the idea. Her heart raced. She had to do it. This might be their only chance.

"You think I am fool?" Rita looked at her skeptically, then pointed to Emily. "The old bandido said she was not so much sick."

"He wouldn't have caught us if I hadn't been ill," Emily said.

"What did you do for pain?"

"I took one of my little pills. Within five minutes I noticed a *big* difference!"

Rita's eyebrows shot up at the mention of drugs. "Is it *prescripción*? You got more?"

"Oh, yes. I have to keep them with me all the time. I never know when I'll need one."

Cora noticed Emily's mouth quirk as if to fight a smile.

"Give me this pill."

"No, no, no. It's a prescription meant just for me. I couldn't possibly give you one. Maybe you should go to the corner drug store and get something for yourself."

"I take any *prescripcións*. I want this pill, now." Rita sternly patted the gun in her waistband.

"You certainly drive a hard bargain. There should

be some in my robe pocket, unless they fell out when your friend threw me on the bed. Untie my hands and I'll get one for you."

The captor held her head and eyed Emily suspiciously. "What? I am *loco*? You will kill me and run, *sí*?"

"I couldn't overpower you if I wanted to. Just look at me. I'm a shriveled up old lady. I've been tied up on this bed for hours and my bladder's bursting. My legs are so stiff and sore, it'll be hard to stand let alone make a run for it. Let me go to the bathroom while you take one of my pills." Emily waited for Rita to answer.

"The pain is too bad. I...I cannot think."

"If you don't want my pill, fine, but I've really got to go." Emily squirmed for effect.

"How I take wonder *aspirina*? *El augua* stinks."

"You don't have to use water. They're very small," Em reassured. "Just let it dissolve under your tongue. That's what I do."

Rita reluctantly loosened the nylon rope that bound Emily's hands and feet. "I will trust you." She pulled the gun from her waistband. "Do not *escapar*. I will shoot."

After Emily dispensed a nitroglycerin pill, she scooted to the foot of the bed and stood.

Cora watched her lean against the wall for support and shuffle unsteadily into the bathroom. The medicine might not worsen Rita's headache, but it was worth a try. A smidgen of hope formed in her chest.

Without hesitation, Rita placed the tablet under her tongue.

A few minutes later, Emily called from the bathroom, "How are you feeling, Rita?"

"*¡Ay! ¡Caramba!*" Rita's gun fell to the floor as she

slumped into the faux leather chair. With muffled moans, the suffering woman grasped her head. The drug-induced pain had struck.

"Em, now!" Cora yelled. "Come untie me and let's get out of here."

Emily poked her head out the bathroom door, and cautiously looked at Rita. She knelt to untie her twin's ankles. "You've got a gash on your foot. What happened?"

"I got cut on that broken coffee cup when ol' Sasquatch caught me." When Cora was freed from the ropes, a searing pain rushed through her foot as she stood for Emily to untie her hands. "Where's my slipper, Em?"

Emily scooped the limp duck off the floor. Her finger went through a bullet hole. "Poor little thing's been shot through the quacker."

Cora grabbed her slipper, jammed her foot inside, and stepped down. *Phttt!*

With a giggle, Emily glanced at the chair-borne Rita. "Oooh. Her face is gray."

A tinge of guilt pricked at Cora's conscience. "I hope she doesn't suffer any permanent damage from your medicine."

Emily frowned, grabbed Rita's glow-in-the-dark purse and retrieved its scattered contents, and then shoved the loaded gun in, too. "We can't worry about that now. This is self-preservation and as they say, all's fair in love and war."

23

Cora eyed the telephone before she left the room and was tempted to use it until Rita stirred in her chair. Fearful their kidnapper would rally, she opted to find another phone. With one last look at their foe, Cora hobbled outside. Her slippers protested. *Quack...phttt! Quack...phttt!*

In spite of their dangerous situation, Emily snickered. "Oh Cora, leave it to you to bring a whoopee cushion to the party." Suddenly, she stopped dead in her tracks and pointed to the only vehicle in the parking lot. "Tell me that's not our get-away car."

There, in all its blazing glory, sat a fluorescent lime green car.

Cora groaned. "How are we supposed to make an inconspicuous escape in this thing?" She plopped into the driver's seat, fumbled with her robe, and searched for car keys in the confiscated purse. "Where are they? Oh, wait, maybe they're in this little zippered pocket." She pulled out a cell phone and looked at Em.

Em squealed. She grabbed it from Cora's hand and poked buttons with her finger. "Well, it's dead. We'll have to find a pay phone after all."

"I'm still looking for the keys." Cora shook the bag. "I hear them jingling. Here they are."She tossed the over-sized bag into Emily's lap and inserted the ignition key. A heady rush coursed through her. Then, her stomach dropped as she reached for the automatic gearshift. She looked heavenward. "Oh, no. It's a stick shift. I can't drive this thing."

"Hey! Calm down," Emily urged. "I learned to drive with a stick, surely I can remember enough to fake it to a telephone. Let's trade places."

A hasty, but modest, Chinese fire drill followed.

"Let's see, I want reverse. Here it is. Now clutch, shift...and away we go." A loud clunk sounded from the rear as the car jerked backwards, shuddered and died.

Emily threw a frantic glance at the motel room. With shaky hands, she shifted back to neutral. "I can do this." She took a deep breath and repeated the steps. Her next endeavor was as discouraging as her first, but the third attempt was successful. Em found first gear and the lime green auto finally made a jaw-rattling bunny hop out of the parking lot of Catchpenny Motel.

Cora glanced to the rear of the car. "What's that noise?"

"Well, we can't worry about it now."

The road sign caught Cora's attention. "This is Old Yucca Road! I've seen this on the news. Oh Em, it's a high crime area."

Her sister's eyes grew large. "Lock the doors."

Cora's mouth dropped at the sight of vacant buildings, painted with graffiti and gang signs. "Look how rundown this place is. I think it used to be the main drag through Saguaro Valley until the downtown stores moved to the shopping malls."

Emily pulled the lime green car to a halt at a bent stop sign pitted with bullet holes. "Sis, we're on the lam. While I concentrate on keeping this bucket on the road, you need to be on the look-out for a payphone."

"Point taken." Cora looked up and down the chipped, uneven sidewalks and spotted a payphone in her peripheral vision. "There's one down this side road. Let's see if we can find a secluded place to park this thing."

The right rear fender rattled as Emily pulled into an empty lot behind the now defunct Shady Sadie's Pawn Shop.

The sisters, clad in bathrobes, walked up the nearly deserted street. *Quack...phttt! Quack...phttt!* Cora limped as they approached the phone booth in front of E-Z Finance and Dusty's Bar and Grill. The smell of greasy food and frying onions hung in the air.

The phone booth door squeaked as Emily stepped inside. "I'll call Jeff." She frantically dug through Rita's purse for change. "He'll know what to do." The bag was a conglomeration of cosmetics, medicines, and...the gun. Old, crumpled tissues cascaded to the floor as she pulled out a driver's license. "Rita Santalis. Santalis? Isn't that your housekeeper's last name?"

Cora took the card. Her shoulders slumped as she stared at the ID. "I hope this is just a coincidence."

Emily found Rita's coin purse, opened it and scraped together enough change for one call.

The blaring jukebox from Dusty's Bar and Grill grew louder. "I can't hear a thing." Emily kicked the trash from Rita's purse out of the booth and closed the door. Before long, she joined her sister. "That was a waste of time. Jeff's out looking for us. He was in such a hurry, he forgot to take his cell phone. I couldn't find enough change to make another call, so we'll have to venture into one of these fine establishments."

Cora gulped and looked at the businesses up and down the street in search of the best option. "There's

The Tat House Tattoo Parlor and an old, deserted bus station next to the Wet Your Whistle Liquor Store. Oh, Em," her voice quivered. "I don't want to go into any of them."

They decided on The Tat House, and walked around a homeless man asleep next to an old, scruffy, malnourished dog. Inside the tattoo parlor, they came face-to-face with a middle-aged Goth-chick.

Her black, spiked hair, several tattoos and facial piercings were bad enough, but it was her feline-inspired contacts that overwhelmed Cora.

The woman's cat eyes were heavy with layers of black mascara and liner. "Well, well, well. Looks like you silver foxes are finally getting hip to our lifestyle." She scooped up her tarot cards and shuffled them. "So, are you here for a tat, a pick-up, or a reading?"

Cora grabbed Emily's arm. A pick-up? Was this a dating service? She could only imagine what kind of specimen Catwoman would come up with. Or was she hawking pulverized bat wings and eye of newt?

"Oh honey," Emily said, "we're not here for that sort of thing."

The woman dealt the first row of cards. "Don't you want to know about your love life?"

"Actually, we just came in to use the phone."

"Customers only. Unless you want a tat, you'll have to go somewhere else." She squinted her cat eyes and held up her piercing gun. "Or, I'll do a piercing for ya. Just name the body part."

Emily's eyes grew wide. "Umm, no thank you, dear. We'll go elsewhere." The sisters turned and scurried out the door. "Sure lights up a room, doesn't she?"

The Wet Your Whistle Liquor Store was next in

line. They took a deep breath, and nervously crossed the threshold. *Quack…phttt! Quack…phttt!*

The lady at the cash register wore a tag that proclaimed the name Rhapsody. Cora glanced around, relieved the shop had no patrons.

The old floorboards groaned as Emily walked to the counter. "Could I make an important phone call without a purchase?"

"Long distance?" the clerk questioned as she studied their strange attire.

"That all depends. Is Phoenix long distance?"

Rhapsody shook her head and pointed to the telephone on the counter.

"Jeff wasn't at his office, so maybe I can get June at home."

When June failed to answer, it was Cora's turn to call home. The line was busy and she was near tears.

"Wait, wait, wait!" Emily exclaimed. "I left my cell phone on your kitchen counter." She dialed the number. "It's ringing. Hello? Who's this? Oh, Wendell McGibbons." She let out a sigh of relief, and her voice trembled. "You're Dahlia's husband. This is Emily Morgan, Cora's sister. Cora's here with me, I'll let you talk to her." She motioned for her to come closer and handed the phone to her.

"Wendell? Wendell? This is Cora."

"Cora? Everybody's lookin' for ya!" Wendell's voice boomed. "Where are ya?"

"Can you put Ed on the phone?"

"He's bein' innerviewed by cops," Wendell replied. "An' they won't let me in the house."

Crestfallen, she uttered, "Oh, can you at least get a message to him some way? This is a matter of life and death."

"Like I said, they won't let me in. By the way, we found Patrick."

"Oh good. Look, I don't have much time to talk. We're in real trouble and need help right away." She covered the phone and turned to look at Rhapsody who couldn't help but overhear. "What town is this?"

The clerk's face showed concern. "We're in South Basin, the oldest part of Saguaro Valley."

Cora relayed the information to Wendell. "Now, you'll need to tell the police all this, so you'd better write it down." She sighed and rolled her eyes. "Yes, I'll wait for you to get more paper, but hurry." She impatiently tapped her fingers on the well-worn counter.

Emily moaned. "It's twenty after four, Sis." She nervously looked out between the bold lettering on the storefront window. "The nitroglycerin pill must've worn off by now. Rita's going to be hot on our trail."

"Hurry Wendell." Cora glanced at her throbbing foot. "Oh, my ankle's bleeding again."

Rhapsody brought her a chair and a bottle of water for each of the sisters. The clerk twisted off a cap and handed it to Cora. "You look thirsty. I'd better get the first-aid kit for that cut, too."

Cora smiled. "Thank you, dear." She took a welcomed drink while Rhapsody left the room. "Wendell? What's taking so long?"

"All these reporters an' I can't find no paper. Wait a minute, there's that wind-bellied newspaperwoman." Wendell's voice grew intense as he called out, "Hey there, Vi. This is important, can I use your notepaper?" His volume lowered. "Cora, ya still there?"

"Yes, I'm here. Do you have something to write on? Good. Now get this down right because I won't be able to call you back. Rita Santalis is one of the kidnappers. Right now she's indisposed at the Catchpenny Motel, but I don't know how long she'll be there." She paused to give him time to write the information down. "Tell Ed and the police we've managed to escape, and to please hurry before Rita catches up with us."

"Right, got it. The cops are crawlin' all over this here place. When I tell 'em about this, we'll all get there quicker'n a hiccup."

"Listen, we can't stay here, so we'll start for home. How do we get there from here?"

"South Basin. Let's see. Get on Ol' Yucca Road an' it'll take ya clean to the north side of town. You'll see signs for the Saguaro Valley complex. Just foller 'em." Wendell stopped to think. "Wait a minute. There's too many news people here. Ya might get trampled. So tell ya what, we'll meet ya at Lickety Splits Ice Cream. It's on the way. While they go after the kidnappers, I'll escort ya back here."

"Great. We're in a lime green car, can't miss it." After Wendell's confirmation, Cora hung up and turned to Rhapsody. "Would you call the police and send them to room 19 at the Catchpenny Motel? A young lady may need medical help there."

Emily looked out the front window and then snatched the fuchsia handbag. "Never mind, Rhapsody. There she is."

The supportive clerk pointed to the back door. "Go this way and I'll distract her." She shoved a box into Cora's hand. "Take this first-aid kit with you and hurry."

The sisters ducked out the back exit and with the clerk's help, they successfully eluded the felonious señorita.

❧❦

Finished with the police interrogation, Ed looked out the living room window. Reality hit when he saw the sun shine on the yellow tape that kept a flock of reporters at bay. His chest stung with anguish. Their neighbor, Patrick, had been found murdered. Cora and Emily were missing.

Where were they? Would he ever hold Cora in his arms again? Why would the Lord bring them through two years of grief and sorrow only to take her away from him? A soft prayer formed in his heart. *Please, Lord, put a hedge of protection around my wife and her sister.*

Ed released a deep breath as his gaze settled on a familiar white cowboy hat as it bobbed through the crowd. Oh, no. Wendell. Just what he needed.

The Texan stooped down to enter the cordoned off area. Then, maroon-haired Violet Ashton, with her ever-present cigarette, followed the leader.

Wendell must've lured the newspaperwoman into one of his harebrained plots.

Ed rubbed the back of his neck. The temptation of his name in print would only spur the cowboy into a gumshoe tizzy.

Reluctantly, Ed went to the door to receive the confident couple as they approached the uniformed policeman at the door.

The officer crossed his arms and refused to let them pass.

Ed stayed out of Wendell's view and strained to hear what they were up to.

"I'm sure yer chief's gonna want the highly confidential details in my possession. I got it straight from the horse's mouth, that them women ain't far from here. Now, let me speak to yer chief." In spite of Wendell's spiel, the policeman took another step closer, which forced them off the porch. "Well, if that ain't a kick in the caboose." Wendell turned to Vi. "Officer Knob Head, here, just blew it big time. Jack ain't comin', so I gotta do it by my lonesome."

"Not necessarily." Vi patted her companion on the back. "I'm still here."

Wendell scowled at the news reporter's presumption. "Stop the mule train, woman. I don't recollec' nothin' about you taggin' along."

She patted her camera. "I'm sure, my friend Mr. Kodak can change your mind." Vi shaded her eyes from the bright sun, and pointed to the street. "Wait a minute. There's a policeman in his squad car. Let's tell him and maybe he can get the ball rolling."

With purposeful strides, Wendell and Vi headed for the poor, unsuspecting cop.

Ed rushed out the door. Why did Wendell always have to get his fingers into every pie? Of course, the old boy meant well, but he doggedly got in the way of progress with his exaggerations. Now Vi wanted to get into the act. Ed felt the need to shorten their reins, so he quickened his steps to catch up.

As the motivated couple approached the squad car, the clean-cut officer jauntily tilted his head down and glared over his reflective sunglasses.

"Wow!" Vi raised her camera and shot a few frames. "Talk about poster-boy good looks."

"Well, he don't do much for me. I think he oozes the charm of a slimy reptile myself." Wendell laughed.

"Besides, don't ya think you're a little long in the tooth for him?"

"Shut up, or I'll misspell your name in my article."

Wendell cleared his throat to get the officer's attention.

The cop blatantly turned away and shut the car door.

Wendell poked his head inside the passenger window of the cruiser and cleared his throat again, this time with more gusto.

Finally, the policeman glanced their way with an agitated scowl.

The security guard made a quick introduction. "Hey there! The name is Wendell Floyd McGibbons an' this here shutterbug is Vi Ashton." He lowered his voice. "I figured out where Emily an' Cora's at."

The cocky policeman raised his hand to silence the man who interfered with his official call. Once his report had been completed, the cop shuffled through some papers, and still disregarded the intruders.

Ed came up from behind and put his hand on Wendell's shoulder. "Let's not bother the police with a wild goose chase. They're trained to find missing people. Let them do their job."

The perturbed security guard leaned back inside the window and checked the cop's name tag. Wendell stood, crossed his arms and looked down at him.

Ed smiled.

Wendell used the gesture he said gave him a psychological edge.

"Officer Reed?" Wendell's security badge glistened in the sun as he tapped it. "Looky here, boy. Law enforcement's what my family's all about. My daddy an' his daddy afore him was Texas Rangers.

Know what that means?" He stepped forward. "It means we don't back down."

"This isn't a game of cowboys and Indians," the cop said. "Kidnapping is serious business and I'm not in a game-playing mood. So, go find your bingo buddies and get out of my way, old timer." It wasn't clear what Officer Reed mumbled as he raised the window, but the implication wasn't overly cordial.

Ed felt sorry for poor Wendell. Dismissed. Just like that. Psychological edge and all. The man in cowboy boots and Stetson and his knobby-kneed, chain-smoking sidekick didn't make much of an impression.

Vi took another puff of her filter tip and clenched her jaw. She pushed Wendell aside, and pounded on the cruiser window. The cop rolled it down and left a crack for her to speak through.

Her assertive voice was just above a whisper as she glared at the officer. "This man has pertinent information about the kidnapping case. It would behoove you to listen to what he has to say." A vigorous bout of coughing cut her tirade short. She backed up and shoved Wendell towards the police car.

The arrogant cop smirked. "*Behoove* me?"

Apparently validated by the female reporter, Wendell leaned down to look the officer in the eye. "I know where them women are. They're gonna meet us at Lickety Splits."

Reed's condescending smirk reappeared. "Let me get this straight. The kidnapped women are sitting in an ice cream parlor not five miles from home gulping down a tutti-frutti while waiting on *you* to save them?"

"Uh, yeah."

Ed rolled his eyes. Oh, Wendell, Wendell, Wendell. When was he ever going to give up?

Reed stepped out of the squad car.

Wendell slowly tipped his head back as the officer stretched to his full height of over six feet.

"Alright, Lone Ranger," the impatient policeman said. "Since you know where they are, why don't you go pick them up? Take Tonto along so she can send us smoke signals when you find them. Oh, and while you're at it, bring me back a mocha shake."

Poor Wendell, shot down again.

The young officer made him look like a fool.

Ed's presence hadn't helped one iota.

Wendell shifted his weight from one foot to the other. "Lone Ranger an' smoke signals? Well, now, ain't we the comedian? Just go ahead an' poke fun, Reed. You'll be whistlin' another tune, later."

"Remember, you had your chance," Vi added.

"Ain't our fault we know more'n you." Wendell abruptly turned to Vi. "If brains were leather, that boy couldn't saddle a flea. An' ya can quote me on that." He yanked a hanky from his pocket, and swiped his forehead. "Wish Jack could help me with this here rescue."

"Why can't he help us?"

"Aw, he's busy pullin' clipped poodle hair from Letitia's bathtub drain, 'bout now." Wendell glared at the presumptuous woman. "An' what do you mean 'us'?"

Her darkly penciled eyebrows arched as if she were endowed with considerable leverage. The aggressive reporter answered. "Look, even a kick in the pants can be a step forward. I was a member of the White House press corps for thirty-eight years. If you want due credit..." Vi winked at Ed and lit another cigarette with the end of the last one. "I have contacts in all aspects of the national media and beyond, so it would be to your advantage to let me tag along and take pictures for my article."

Ed sighed. At least this wild goose chase would keep Wendell out of the way. He had to hand it to Vi, she sure knew just the right buttons to push.

"Pitchers an' national media?" Wendell contemplated the offer for a nano-second. "Ye-haw! Let's get the show on the road, then." He turned and stomped to his Jeep Grand Cherokee parked in his driveway.

Vi flipped her cigarette on the ground and crushed the ember beneath the toe of her low-heeled shoe. "Wait for Tonto, *Kemo Sabe*!" She wheezed as she ran to catch up with him.

Ed walked back to the house as Wendell's Cherokee squealed from the cul-de-sac. He shook his head. "Hi yo, Silver!"

24

Cora watched mile after mile of arid landscape whiz by, and hoped to catch sight of something…anything familiar. Her nose twitched. "Oh, no." She grabbed Emily's arm and pointed to the hood. "Look! Steam."

"It's overheating." Emily pulled to the side of the road. The car jerked to a stop and the loose rear fender fell off. "We're not going anywhere in this rattletrap."

The be-robed twins took a deep breath and grudgingly stepped out of the car. Cora bumped her foot on the door and winced in pain. "Ouch." The deep gash on her ankle throbbed even more. "Em, come help me fix this bandage."

"That looks awful, Sis. You may need stitches when we get home. I'll double-wrap it for now. Hand me the first-aid kit Rhapsody gave us."

While Cora put her bloodstained duck slipper back on, her twin surveyed the area. Emily found no shield from either sun or abductors. "I'm sorry, we have no choice but to walk."

"We're going to get burned to a crisp out in this sun."

"You're right." Emily went to the back of the car. "I'll look in the trunk to see if she has an umbrella. You grab our water and don't forget the purse." The trunk opened with a pathetic groan. "No umbrellas. Sorry. Umm, Cora-dear, how much dignity do you have left?"

Cora frowned. "And why would you ask?"

"Because I've got good news and bad news. Good news is we have protection from the sun." Emily stepped into Cora's line of view with an over-sized sombrero on her head. "This is the bad news."

"Oh great." Cora read the advertisement on the hat. "Happy Hot Birthday from Paco's Tacos? And what, may I ask, are those hangy-down things?"

Emily giggled. "Peppers. So, do you want the red ones or the green ones?"

"Just gimme a stupid hat."

"Here, take the green one. It compliments your fetching frock."

Plastic peppers dangled before their eyes as they began their trek. Cora's slippers continued their annoying *quack* and *phttt* with each step she took. For a half-hour they trudged through the relentless heat waves that hovered across the asphalt road.

Cora noticed a cloud of blowing dust on the horizon. She grabbed her sister's arm and pointed. "Uh-oh. Looks like we have company. Think it's a good guy or a bad guy?"

"Your guess is as good as mine."

Cora's heart raced as the vehicle drew closer.

An SUV pulled up alongside them. Wendell rolled down his tinted window. "Well, if it ain't Thelma an' Louise. I thought we was gonna meet at Lickety Splits."

The frazzled women lifted their sombreros and sighed with relief. Cora was first to speak. "I'm so glad to see you, Wendell. The car died, and we've been so afraid the kidnappers would catch up with us."

Wendell hopped out of his Cherokee and helped

them into the backseat, while Vi Ashton captured the rescue on film. The colorful sombreros were stacked in the seat between them.

Vi lowered the camera and retrieved her notebook. "Where were you held hostage? Do you know who the kidnapper is?"

"It was the Catchpenny Motel. I'll never forget that nasty place." Cora shuddered. "There were two kidnappers."

"The gal's name is Rita Santalis." Emily looked out the rear window. "Where are the police? Weren't you going to bring them with you?"

"Well, we talked to one cop." Wendell huffed. "All capped teeth an' phony charm, that boy was, he didn't believe us. Once we pull up with both of you in tow, he'll be whistlin' a different tune."

The maroon-haired reporter grabbed her camera and ordered, "Wendell, I need shots of that getaway car. Then, swing by the Catchpenny."

Cora came up off her seat. "Don't you dare take us back to that roach motel. Just get us as far away as possible."

"Rita's looking for us," Emily said. "If El Bandido is with her, we'll be shot on sight."

A deep groan came from the driver's seat. "Ya got yourself a point, there. S'pose we ought-a think it through a tad more, Lady Reporter?" When no answer came, he said, "How come you're so quiet all of a sudden?"

"Just thinking about where to send this headline story. I still have connections at the Washington Post and a few other choice newspapers and magazines. My anchorman-friend in D.C. will be excited to get a firsthand account of the kidnapping, too. From there, it could go global." A conspiratorial glance was passed between the driver and reporter.

"Yee-haw! Move over, Dahlia Sue. Ya ain't gonna be the only celebrity in the fam'ly."

"I can see the headlines, now," Vi said. "Famous cook's spouse cooks kidnapper's goose."

"Aw, you're killin' me, here."

Vi laughed and removed the lens cap from her camera as the Cherokee pulled to a stop beside the lime green car. "Well, first things first. I need to get pictures of the car, and then the motel. I'll have you pose in some."

It was Emily's turn to come up off her seat. "You've got to be kidding. You're risking four lives just to get a picture for the paper?"

"Tell ya what," Wendell offered. "If anybody even looks shifty, we won't stop. We'll just make it a drive by so Vi can shoot her pitchers." He chuckled. "Could call it a drive-by shootin'." He adjusted the rearview mirror and glanced at the exhausted women's reaction. "Lay low, gals, an' I'll get ya home safe, an' that there's a promise."

A few miles down the road, the dead silence was interrupted by Vi's prolonged bout of coughing. With shaky hands, she tucked a cigarette in her mouth.

Wendell threw the self-imposing passenger a look that could curdle milk. "Don't smoke in the Cherokee."

"I don't see any 'no smoking' signs."

"I got asthma. That's why I ain't a Texas Ranger like my daddy an' his daddy—"

"Yeah, yeah. Afore him, I know." Vi took the cigarette from her mouth and pointed out the windshield. "There's the Catchpenny." The reporter poised her camera with the telephoto lens and snapped pictures of the rundown motel.

Emily reclined in the back seat while Cora wriggled down to a more comfortable position. They grabbed their sombreros to hide their faces while Vi's camera clicked repeatedly.

"Now, Wendell, get out and let me get a shot with you pointing to the sign."

When the photo session was finished, the Cherokee hit the road.

Vi quizzed the sisters for a firsthand account of the remarkable saga. "Do you remember anything else?"

"Yes," Cora said. "Remember the Shipley murder/suicide? I heard the man say he was the one who actually killed them."

Wendell wrinkled his nose. "Why, that stinkin' polecat. They ought-a skin him alive. I knew all along that George wasn't the kind of guy to kill hisself. An' he loved his mama."

Vi ravenously recorded the information provided by the sisters. An hour later, the aggressive reporter had the story, and the photos needed for her front-page exclusive.

The SUV made it back to the gated community without any complications. Wendell turned into the cul-de-sac. The Cherokee was blocked by the overabundance of television vans and police vehicles.

Curious residents were intermingled with the swarm of photographers congregated on the sidewalk and driveways. Cora and Emily hunched in the backseat of the SUV, their eyes peering above the window's ledge.

A denim-clad figure caught Cora's attention. She fought back a tide of panic and pointed, "I don't believe it. That's him over there!"

Emily glared in that direction. "Oh Cora, you're right."

Vi raised her camera. "I've got him in my viewfinder."

Wendell looked. "Ya mean Sam?"

"No, silly. The man next to him. He's the one who kidnapped us." Cora maneuvered herself in the backseat. "Em, keep calm and duck down!" She feared the commotion would cause her sister's fallible heart to falter. If the palpitations got bad, she'd need a nitro pill...and Rita still had them.

"That's Jack. Aw, can't be him. You're pullin' my leg, right?" Wendell questioned. "I don't wanna doubt ya, but I can't hardly believe it. Jack has breakfast with me every mornin'. He's even been helpin' me solve this here mystery."

"You're a fine judge of character, Lone Ranger." Vi continued to take pictures of the alleged kidnapper. "I, on the other hand, ladies, don't doubt you for a second."

Wendell turned to the backseat. "You're double-dog sure it's Jack?"

"Yes, we're sure," Emily declared. "I've got pictures of him ransacking Ed's office on my cell phone. That's tangible evidence. Please tell me you still have my phone, Wendell."

Wendell patted his leg. "It's right chere in my pocket. I'll give it to ya in the house. Ya say there's pitchers on that phone? I sure didn't see none."

The reporter turned in her seat and stared wide-eyed at Emily. "You took pictures of Jack in Ed's office? I can add those to my article."

"Unless the Lone Ranger deleted them."

Vi moaned. "Don't even *think* that. Wendell, I need

that phone right now."

"Can't ya wait 'til we get to Cora's?"

"I need to send copies of those pictures to my cell phone. I won't be able to do it later because the police will confiscate it."

With a slight hesitation, Wendell handed over Emily's phone.

"It'll only take me a couple clicks. There! It's done."

Wendell fidgeted behind the wheel as he honked the horn to get past the crowd. "There ain't no way we're gonna get through here." He put the Cherokee in reverse, and slowly backed out of the cul-de-sac.

"Where are we going, Wendell?" Vi asked.

"There's more than one way to pluck a buzzard. We're goin' in the back way."

Vi clenched her teeth. "There is no back entrance, Wendell."

"Sez who?" He sniffed. "Just wait an' see."

The car turned onto Shifting Sands Avenue, and raced to the clubhouse of Ed's golf course. Wendell smirked and nodded to the golf carts. "Ya need to trust me, Scoop."

"Fine. I stand corrected."

"Just make sure ya spell my name right in that hoity-toity article of yours."

The sisters crammed on their sombreros, and climbed in the back of the cart. The foursome took off down a path en route to Cora's backyard. The ladies white-knuckled it as they bounced through the rough and skirted the greens on the fifth hole.

Over the next hill, the eighth hole was in play. Wendell's comb-over dangled over his ear, and he licked his fingers a couple times to smooth it back into place. "Playin' through!" he yelled to the golfers.

Emily and Cora pulled the sombreros further over their eyes.

One of the disgruntled men shouted, "Get that cart back on the path."

Wendell veered to the left, and nearly hit one of the players. "Official po-lice business!" he hollered loudly over his shoulder. "Carry on."

The golf cart jerked up the last small hill and rounded the top. When Wendell released the pedal, their front wheel entered the edge of a sand trap. The passengers braced themselves as the small vehicle lurched to a stop.

"Great, A. J. Foyt, now what?" Vi asked sarcastically. "This trek across the golf course is taking too long. I need to get this article out ASAP."

A huge smile stretched across Wendell's face. "Cora's place is just over there a piece. We'll be there in two shakes." He stomped on the gas pedal, smacked the steering wheel, and let out a war whoop. "Boy, I wish I had me a sirene 'bout now."

Three gaggles of golfers stood along the perimeter of the course, and watched the commotion in the neighboring complex. The astonished group turned and stared as the cart charged through the well-manicured grass.

Wendell steered into the backyard and pulled up to the patio.

A sigh of relief arose from the feminine trio.

They stood under the awning as Wendell hollered and banged on the kitchen door.

Someone shouted from the side of the house, "There they are!" The feeding frenzy began. The entire herd of zealous journalists stampeded in their direction.

Quick-thinking Vi held up her suit jacket just in time to protect the sisters from the invasion of cameras. Flash bulbs glared like strobe lights. Rapacious journalists simultaneously barked questions in their direction.

∽◦◦∾

Drawn by the commotion, Ed ran ahead of the police captain to join Dahlia in the kitchen. Jeff and June followed. Much to everyone's surprise, two Paco's Taco sombreros were at the door.

Wendell's head popped up behind the hats. "Open up." His mouth split into a cheesy grin as he turned and waved to the photographers. "I told ya I knew where they was, Ed. I brung 'em home safe an' sound."

Dahlia wrestled with the newly installed lock and opened the door. "Well, if you gals ain't a sight for sore eyes." She grabbed her husband's arm. "Stop muggin' for the cameras an' get your bones in here, Wendell Floyd."

The Texan strutted into the kitchen, proudly leading his human trophies. Vi closed the door to block the clamoring members of the media.

"Cora!" Ed's large hand gently cradled her face. "I thought I'd lost you."

She stood on tiptoe, touched her lips to his and melted into his embrace. "Oh Eddie, I thought they'd find us dead in that squalor."

He held her tight. "Why didn't you call the police instead of Wendell?"

"Oh...I don't know. Guess we panicked." She scratched her head. "All we could think of at the time was contacting you and Jeff. Em remembered she left her cell phone on our kitchen counter, so we called that, thinking you would answer. How could we know Wendell had her phone in his pocket?"

The crowd migrated into the living room, as Vi's camera snapped in quick succession.

Jeff kissed Emily on the forehead. "You really had us worried, Mom."

"Are you feeling alright?" June asked.

Emily hugged her son and daughter-in-law again. "Oh, I'm exhausted. I've got to rest. First, Cora and I need to give the police our statement."

The sisters told their stories to the police. They named Jack Thurston and Rita Santalis as their kidnappers, and also mentioned it was possible that Jack murdered the Shipleys.

Wendell turned and grabbed a cop's arm. "We just saw Jack standin' next door in front of Letitia Bockman's. There was always somethin' shady about that feller. I just couldn't put my finger on it."

Instantly, Captain O'Hara sent his men out the front of the condo.

Vi and Wendell were in hot pursuit.

Then, Emily handed her cell phone and Rita's purse to O'Hara. "The pictures on my phone will give you all the evidence you need. The bag belongs to Rita."

"I appreciate your help." Captain O'Hara quickly folded his notebook and headed for the door. "We'll be in touch."

25

For the first time that day, Ed allowed himself to relax. Cora was home, and he couldn't stop gazing at her. Who would've guessed that Wendell actually knew what he was talking about? If only he had believed the man.

"Just look at ya in them dirty robes. I can't hardly believe y'all been gallivantin' around like that." Dahlia cackled as her strong arms surrounded the sisters. "Ya look famished. There's food over on the table an' I'll crank up the BrewMeister."

Emily turned to her sister. "I don't know about you, but my old carcass smells pretty gamy. I need a shower before I can think about food."

"By the way, Em, I saw some jumpy things on that motel pillow. Remind me to check your hair for bugs."

"Eewww! Now, I'm twice as itchy. Thanks a heap, Sis."

Cora grabbed her arm and they hobbled down the hall. "Hey! We even smell identical."

Ed called after them. "Wait. Take this trash bag for your robes, slippers and anything else you may have on."

"That's a good idea." Dahlia gave a hearty laugh. "We don't need a herd o' bedbugs gallopin' around here."

Ed felt a warm hand on his shoulder.

"How are you holding up, Uncle Steady?"

"Do you realize how fortunate we are, Jeff?" Ed wiped his eyes and smiled. "God spared their lives, and chose to bring them back home to us."

Their conversation was interrupted when mayhem broke loose outside the living room window. The police had cautiously surrounded the area as friends and neighbors backed away from Letitia's front yard. This offered Ed and Jeff a clearer view, even though members of the media continued to hold their ground.

"Looks like the cops have zeroed in on him." Jeff's voice shook in anger. "I want to get a better look at this guy. Wanna go with me?"

June bit her lower lip and linked her arm with Jeff's. "We nearly lost your mom and Aunt Cora. Please stay in the house where it's safe."

"We'll be fine, don't worry." Jeff's gaze softened as he kissed her forehead. He turned to Dahlia. "We'll only be a few minutes. You ladies keep the coffee hot and the pie warm."

June's arms hung limp as she watched them leave.

"Do you see Wendell anywhere?" Ed scanned his front yard as they inched their way through the large gathering. As they approached the edge of the property, Jack casually stood next to Letitia and Tinkle-Belle.

Fury, like Ed had never known before, nearly choked him. His hands formed tight fists. This man terrorized his wife for weeks.

A hush fell on the crowd. The police closed in on their suspect, revolvers drawn.

Jack instantly seized Letitia Bockman. His arm went across her frail shoulders as he pulled the older woman in front of him as a human shield. She screamed. He lifted her off the ground as he backed up.

Tinkle-Belle ferociously snapped at Jack's heels. The dog grabbed his pant leg, shook it violently, and threw the man off balance.

Letitia's arms and legs thrashed in self-defense. Her artificial pearls catapulted into the air.

Wendell unexpectedly appeared from the back of the house. Ed's mouth gaped in disbelief as the Texan crept up behind the kidnapper. Of all the times for him to become a hero.

"Let her go, Jack." Wendell's voice boomed and his arm snaked around the man's throat. "Nobody bluffs Wendell Floyd McGibbons an' gits away with it."

Jack gasped for air and relaxed his grip on Letitia.

She dropped to the ground with a yelp.

Three policemen quickly moved in to apprehend the offender.

The dog's aggressive snarl indicated she had no intention of releasing her human tug toy.

Cheers and whistles erupted from the onlookers as Officer Reed cuffed the prisoner. "I'm placing you under arrest for the kidnapping of Cora Timms and Emily Morgan. You have the right to remain silent..."

Cameras continued to roll while the policeman finished the Miranda Rights and led the cursing handyman to the squad car.

Letitia's large poodle yipped and pranced in circles as the EMS Team quickly wheeled a gurney to the elderly woman's side.

Friends and neighbors clamored around their beefy security guard. Ed hugged the man and patted him on the back. "Good job, Wendell. I'm proud of you, buddy."

Jeff squeezed in beside his Uncle Ed. "Yes, I want

to thank you for saving Mom and Aunt Cora. You're a brave man."

Wendell puffed out his chest and wiped his eyes with the heel of his hand. "Pshaw, 'tweren't nuthin. Ya know, my daddy and his daddy afore him woulda done the same thing."

"You were amazing." Ed threw his arm around Wendell's shoulder. "I think your daddy and his daddy would be real proud."

The security guard frowned. "Thank ya, but that ol' Reed feller still gets credit for cuffin' that varmint."

"You're forgetting something," Vi added with a wink, "I've got the whole story and close-ups of you as the real hero." She lit a cigarette. "Now, while the other reporters are still scratching to get their stories, I'm going to sneak away with my complete exclusive. And, as a favor to you, Lone Ranger, I'll leave Reed's name out of it."

"Thank ya, ma'am." Wendell grinned. "You made a great sidekick, Tonto. Smoke signals an' all."

Ed's thoughts tumbled as Vi disappeared into the crowd. How odd. Who would've thought Washington DC's elite could coexist peacefully with one of Sweet Pickle's finest?

Captain O'Hara approached, notepad in hand. "I have a few more questions for Mr. McGibbons."

"Let's go back to my place," Ed suggested. "I think we all need a cup of coffee."

Wendell answered questions as Dahlia served coffee and pie all around.

After the police captain left, Ed walked the now-famous security guard and his wife to the door. As the couple took one step outside, the media converged on them.

Wendell raised his Stetson to the crowd, and smiled at the scrawny man with the camera perched on his shoulder. His face radiated with pleasure as several microphones were shoved under his nose.

Ed moved out of view and continued to listen as the persistent reporters fired questions at his friend.

"Word has it you were friends with the kidnapper. How does it feel to find out he's a criminal?"

Wendell threw his hands into the air to halt the questions. "Let's take it one at a time." He turned to one reporter, cleared his throat and looked directly into the TV camera. "Well, Noble, as y'all know, I was the first officer at the crime scene..."

The crowd followed Wendell and Dahlia home.

Ed grinned. He closed the door and went to check on his wife.

Eleven o'clock that evening, Ed turned on the TV, eager to catch the story on the local news. He plopped on the couch beside Cora and put his arm around her. "I hope your sister's watching this."

Cora nestled closer. "I wish Em had stayed a few days longer."

"Remember, she needed to see her doctor first thing tomorrow."

They watched the news report on a robbery in Phoenix, then, the anchorman referred to the field reporter, Noble Dunnichey.

"Thank you, Lance. I'm here at the Saguaro Valley Retirement Complex, where a rash of murders has taken place. According to what we've learned, and this is based upon unconfirmed reports, local handyman, Jack Thurston, has been arrested for the double homicide of George Shipley and his mother, Gertrude. He's also being held for the kidnapping of Cora

Timms, wife of legendary golf pro, Steady Eddie Timms, and her identical twin sister Emily Morgan. Detective Wendell Floyd McGibbons, who rescued the twin sisters, had this to say:

"Well, Noble, as y'all know, I was the first officer at the crime scene. That's when I found Mrs. Morgan's cell phone. She called me on it an' told me where they was. The perp was hot on their trail. It was plainer than ears on a mule, them poor ol' gals needed some rescuin'. Me an' Vi Ashton told that Officer Reed feller that we knew where they was, but I reckon he weren't interested. He told us to go ahead an' pick 'em up." Wendell offered a toothy grin and nonchalant shrug. "So we did."

The camera spanned back to the reporter. "As that crime was being solved, another appeared. The decomposing body of local resident, Patrick Hyde, was found in the garage of Letitia Bockman. Mrs. Bockman and Mr. Hyde are both neighbors of the Timms. The police are now looking for a connection with Hyde's murder, the kidnapping of the sisters, and the Shipley double murder. If any of our viewers have any information concerning these events, please contact Saguaro Valley Police." The reporter took a deep breath. "That's about it from here. I'll be standing by in case of further developments. For KARP-TV Newscenter, this is Noble Dunnichey in Saguaro Valley. Back to you in the studio, Lance."

Ed turned off the recorder and shook his head. "How did Emily ever get tangled up in Jack's mess?"

The next day Cora was contacted by the producer of a popular television show. She called Emily, and they agreed to allow their story to be highlighted on *Mysteries of the Rich and Famous.*

News of the filming crew's arrival in Saguaro Valley flooded the neighborhood.

Ed and Cora were soon swamped with non-stop phone calls.

The gated community buzzed as the paparazzi, camera-toting friends, thrill seekers, and everyday looky-loos descended on their front lawn.

Wendell was designated to record the program when it finally aired. The entire Timms-Morgan family reluctantly promised not to watch the show because part of their reunion celebration would be to view it together.

৵৽৻

Six weeks later, it was an evening like every other in Meadow Falls, Indiana. Neville Neubauer poured a glass of apple juice and went to the living room to watch his favorite TV show. The announcer provided a short teaser before the program began. The picture on the screen immediately caught his eye. He bolted into an upright position in his recliner.

"Tonight on *Mysteries of the Rich and Famous*, the wife and sister-in-law of celebrated golf pro, Steady Eddie Timms, kidnapped at gun point by murderer. The harrowing story, next."

When the commercials ended, the announcer continued, "It was a mystery that spanned nearly six decades."

Neubauer watched the program for a short time and then reached for his cordless phone.

26

Cora was elated when Dahlia and June, being first-rate organizers, promptly agreed to arrange the first Timms-Morgan family reunion. However, she had been disappointed that it took six weeks to coordinate everyone's schedule.

When October finally trickled into November, their excitement intensified as they readied for their extended families to merge.

A few days before the reunion, Cora called Dahlia with the final headcount. "There will be ten Morgans attending." She counted on her fingers. "Emily, Jeff, June and their son, Jordan. Em's younger son, Reece, is coming from Boston. Her daughter, Rebecca, her husband LaMont, and their three girls are flying in from Canada. I can't wait to meet them all."

Cora added that Vannie's former husband, James Hollabaugh, promised to bring his family a day early. "Ed and I are thrilled to spend an extra day with our three grandkids. It's been months since they moved to Vegas."

"I lost track, now how old are them kids?"

"Jason's sixteen. Can you believe he's actually driving now? Heather's fourteen and Todd just turned thirteen."

"Oh Sugar, it'll be so good to see your grand-sprouts again, seems like years."

"Yeah, well, that's the good news. The bad news is

James' new bride will be tagging along." Cora's stomach knotted and her enthusiasm waned at the anticipation of Jocelyn's presence. As always, she'd have to put on a front to keep peace in the family. There had to be creative ways to avoid the girl and not appear aloof. At least she had a whole three weeks to prepare for an award-winning performance.

∂◦◦

Cora checked another day off the calendar, and then turned to Emily. "Can you believe the family reunion is actually tomorrow?"

"Your house looks like a party waiting to happen. The balloons add that extra dash of panache."

Cora nodded. "If it wasn't for Dahlia and June's expertise in food and decorations, balloons and hot dogs would be all we'd have."

"You've known Dahlia for a long time. She's such a busy woman, you don't think she minds all this extra work?"

"Are you kidding?" Cora giggled. "She thrives on stuff like this. Haven't you heard her singing and whistling?" She grabbed the mayo and mustard from the refrigerator door. "We'd better get the deviled eggs done before Dahlia gets back."

Cora had finished peeling the hard-boiled eggs when the phone rang. By the time she hung up, her joyful mood had plummeted, and she retreated to the bedroom for time alone.

Several minutes later, there was a knock on her door. "How are you doing, Sis?"

"I'm a bit overwhelmed, Em. I'll be out shortly." Cora dabbed her eyes and blew her nose, as she struggled to gain control of her emotions.

Emily peeked inside. "May I come in?"

"Yes, of course." Cora quickly turned away and brushed the wrinkles from her pink blouse. The last thing she wanted was for Emily to see her tears.

"Dahlia just got here." She sat on the bed. "That phone call must've upset you. Was it one of those awful calls you had before?"

"No, it was James. He said they're in town and checking into their hotel rooms."

"Oh, good."

Cora avoided her sister's eyes. "I'm not sure I can handle this thing with Jocelyn."

"Our reunion is a once-in-a-lifetime event." Emily took Cora into her arms. "We can't let a problem with James' wife ruin it for you."

"James said he's going to drop Jocelyn here then pick up the kids at the mall, later." Cora released a shaky breath. "She should be here any time."

"Why don't you rinse your face with cool water, then, we'll have some coffee and talk about it."

They went to the kitchen and sat on stools at the counter while Dahlia poured three cups of coffee.

Cora looked at her sister. "I honestly thought I'd come to terms with Jocelyn being a part of the festivities. Now, my resolve is crumbling." She covered her face with her hands.

"Sis, I understand that Jocelyn will never replace your daughter." Emily nervously sipped her coffee. "Dahlia says she's a charming young lady, so I don't understand why she upsets you."

As she studied the tile floor, Cora fidgeted, embarrassed that she'd revealed her animosity. With a swift glance up and a swifter glance away, she contemplated her reply. "Fine, you want to know all the reasons?" Her eyes narrowed. "James and that perky adolescent married only a few months after Vanessa died."

"Yes, I know, and you feel like he's cheating on her, right?" Emily countered.

"Of course. He was so attentive to Van. I thought they had a perfect marriage. Then after her death, James up and married the first young thing that crossed his path. He quickly changed from a grieving widower to a lovesick teenager. Disgusting. It's a betrayal to her memory."

Dahlia's tenor voice cut in, "Is there a timetable for grief, Sugar?"

"Well, it's certainly more than a couple months." Cora paused. "It makes me wonder, d-did he know Jocelyn *before* the accident?" It was out. That nagging suspicion she had never verbalized. "You know, there could've been something going on and none of us knew it."

"Give them the benefit of the doubt." Emily patted her hand. "Was Vanessa happy?"

"She was always happy and full of zest. Van doted on those kids and always said James was her knight in shining armor."

"Then ya can be thankful she had such a wonderful life," Dahlia said.

Cora nodded and sighed. "That's what Ed always tells me."

"A lot of folk can't lay claim to that."

"Was Van ready to be with the Lord?" Em asked.

"Yes, she was at teen camp when she gave her life to the Lord. We were thrilled to watch her grow closer to Him through the years."

"I'm glad to hear that, Sis. Since she was such a loving wife and mother, don't you think she'd want someone to care for her family?"

Cora's voice intensified. "It was only eight months before the pimple-cream model lured James to the altar. What kind of respect is that for a loving husband to show?"

"Sometimes in our grief, we do things out of the ordinary." Emily leaned over to put her arm around her. "We don't know his heart, so let's not speculate on all the reasons behind his decision."

Dahlia held her cup midair and looked over her shoulder. "Did y'all hear somethin'?"

The twins shook their heads. "I reckon I'm just hearin' things again. Anyway, I knew Vanessa, an' she'd want them babies to have a mama."

Cora dabbed her eyes. "Yes, I know. However, James' new trophy wife had to have the big house in Las Vegas and he gave in. That move took them so far away, I feel like I lost the rest of my family. It's just Ed and me, now."

Emily placed her hands on her hips. "Well, I like that," she teased. "No, it's not just you and Ed. Look at all the friends you have in this community and you do have a drop-dead-gorgeous new sister, you know."

Cora's eyes gravitated to Emily's as a spontaneous giggle escaped.

"An' look at that brood of kinfolk she's brung with her." Dahlia released a throaty chuckle. "Ya ain't never gonna be alone again, girl."

"That's right. We'll get together all the time," Emily assured her.

Cora knew they meant well, but she longed for her own grandchildren. Emily's relatives were still strangers and not substitutes for those babies she'd bonded with from birth. She wrapped slender fingers around her cup and peered into the tepid coffee.

With a serious tone, Dahlia added a spiritual reference. "Ya also have God. He's never left ya. Just look how He's protected ya here lately when your life was in danger."

"Good point. We could've been killed," Emily agreed. "The Lord never promised that believers would be free of problems, but He does promise to make a difference in our lives when we trust Him."

"I know all that," Cora replied. "Exactly where was God when Vanessa had her accident? He allowed her to die instead of protecting her."

Emily's answer was gentle. "He did protect her, Sis, just not the way you wanted Him to. The Lord cared enough to gather your sweet daughter in His arms and take her out of her pain."

The words pierced her conscience. Cora shifted restlessly. *He did protect her, just not the way you wanted Him to.* She looked at Em, then, turned her head.

"Unfortunately," Emily continued. "As long as we're on earth, we're subject to the frailties of human life. He promises that we don't have to go through it alone. We just have to trust and lean on Him."

Dahlia refilled their cups. "Here's another thought. My baby died 'fore I could hold her. Oh, Sugar, bask in all them years ya had with Van an' stop wrappin' yourself in the mem'ries of her death."

Silence hung in the air as they drank their coffee. A few minutes later, the grandfather clock chimed, and broke into their thoughts.

Emily carefully set her cup down. "Sis, have you ever tried to look at Jocelyn's point of view? Marrying into a ready-made family of teenagers has to be hard. The poor girl can't be expected to be the perfect mom, yet."

"Yes, but the fact remains she's far too young to know what those children need," Cora argued. "Did you know her dad's that movie producer playboy, Gregory Cassell? And her mother's actress Kiki Lane, who's divorcing her *fifth* husband? What kind of morals are my grandchildren being exposed to?"

"You're right about her being young, but that doesn't make her a bad mother, and neither does her family background," Emily countered. "That's why it's vital for us to pray for her."

Cora twisted in her seat as her sister's wise counsel hit home. Pray for Jocelyn? She and God hadn't been on speaking terms since Van died.

"You can play an important part in helping her become the kind of parent your grandchildren need," Emily added. "If you let God use you."

A choked cry came from the living room, then Jocelyn darted to the bathroom and slammed the door.

The three women stared at each other, their mouths agape.

"Oh the poor li'l thing must've been here the whole time. I bet she heard everything ya said." Dahlia slid off the stool and hurried to calm the young woman.

Emily hugged her sister, then joined Dahlia.

Cora's heart pumped with deep shame. Tears filled her eyes as she became conscious of the obvious pain her words caused Jocelyn.

This wasn't just about the loss of Van. Two years of bitterness had resulted in a judgmental attitude for James and his young wife. It also drove a wedge in her relationship with Ed. Worse yet, she felt separated from the Lord's presence, which kept her shackled in pain. She had been its prisoner for too long. This negativity hurt everyone and it was past time for an attitude adjustment.

She lowered her head and whispered, "Dear Heavenly Father, I've been wrong and need Your forgiveness. I've hurt everyone around me, including my grandchildren." Tears streaked her face. "Like the Serenity Prayer says, help me accept the things I can't change and please give me strength to change my bitterness towards James and Jocelyn."

As Cora wept, she felt the spiteful restraints break away. Her heart lifted at the first genuine prayer she'd uttered since her daughter's accident. The warmth of the Lord's forgiveness and healing presence enveloped her.

Filled with the urgent need to apologize, Cora took a cleansing breath. Would Jocelyn forgive her? She sheepishly tugged at her blouse and joined the vigil at the bathroom door.

Cora's vision blurred with tears as she gave Dahlia a hug and whispered, "Don't worry. Everything's going to work out." She knocked on the door as Emily and Dahlia went to the kitchen.

"Jocelyn?" No answer. Compassion swept over her. She called again, this time with a gentler voice. "Josie? I've made some terrible mistakes. Let's talk. Please?"

The lock turned and the door opened slowly. Jocelyn released a shaky breath and looked at the floor.

The older woman held out her hand and led her into the bedroom for a private chat.

Cora cleared her throat. "I'm not sure how to

begin—"

Jocelyn's voice was clipped as she interrupted her. "Look, I was standing there a *long* time and heard everything you said about me. There was no affair."

"I should've known." Cora sat on the satin comforter. "My only excuse is that Van's death hurt me deeply. I couldn't handle James' sudden remarriage. It's like he forgot about her."

Jocelyn paced alongside the bed. "We met when I modeled for his advertising agency and that was after Vanessa was gone." She stopped and looked at Cora. "I was amazed at how James handled his loss. He still had a joy and peace about him."

"He had to be strong for the children," Cora rationalized.

"No, it was real. He had the hope and inner contentment I wanted in my life. I had so many questions and he always took time to answer." She reached for a tissue on the night stand. "Our first date wasn't quite what I expected. He took me to church. Later, he introduced me to his pastor's wife. She told me things I'd never heard before, like explaining the Gospel. After a few months, I realized what was missing in my life. That's when I gave my heart to the Lord."

Taken aback by the revelation, Cora replied, "I'm sorry I judged you so harshly." She looked into Jocelyn's dampened eyes. "I understand now it was undeserved and I'm so ashamed. Will you ever forgive me?"

Jocelyn ignored the apology and lashed out. "As for us moving to Vegas, I guess that *was* my fault. My mother lives there and I was stupid enough to think we could have a relationship now that I'm an adult."

The older woman cleared her throat. "Oh honey, I didn't know that's why you moved. I was feeling sorry for myself and missed my grandkids."

Jocelyn's sad eyes pierced through Cora's heart as she replied, "James' folks aren't living and I've never had a close relationship with either of my parents. In fact, I never experienced any kind of family life until I met James. Did you know I grew up in a Swiss boarding school?" She brushed away the tears that filled her eyes. "James spoke so highly of you and Ed that I prayed you'd be surrogate parents for me." She turned and covered her face.

Speechless, Cora stood as intense sorrow invaded her spirit. She drew Jocelyn close and held her tight until the sobbing girl relaxed in her arms. As they sat on the edge of the bed, she whispered. "I'm so sorry, honey."

Jocelyn released a deep, unsteady breath. "I wish we hadn't moved so far away, Cora. It didn't work out like I thought. The kids are with their new friends, and James has to work long hours, so I come home to an empty house." She twisted a strand of her blonde hair. "Except for one time, he invited his boss and wife for supper without telling me. I'd been painting, and met them at the door in shorts, a tank top and bare feet. They were dressed up and expected a fancy dinner like Vanessa used to make." Jocelyn moaned. "It was terrible. I just had a few hot dogs and hamburger patties on hand."

"Oh my!" Cora exclaimed. "What did you do?"

"I sent Jason to the grocery store to get some potato chips and buns while I changed into something more suitable. After the impromptu cookout, James' big excuse was that Vanessa didn't mind if he brought unexpected company home for dinner. He was nice about it, but I could tell he was disappointed in me."

As her sympathy peaked, Cora patted the girl's hand. "So, you're not a domestic diva, yet. I've got a secret for you. Van always hated when he did that, too. Dahlia taught her how to freeze meals ahead of time for those surprise occasions. You could do that, too."

Jocelyn nodded and continued to unload her frustration. "The kids are always telling me their mom did things this way and didn't do it that way. She did everything better. How can I possibly live up to Wonder Woman?"

Cora lowered her head. "And my attitude and snarly remarks didn't help either, did they?"

"And now I find out you think I'm some gold digging adulteress who purposely laid a trap for James?"

Ouch. The comment hit Cora between the eyes and it hurt. A long silence ensued as she regretted the months wasted in rejecting someone who needed her. Now she understood what James went through. He wasn't being unfaithful to Vanessa; he needed someone to fill the hole in his heart. And love-starved Jocelyn sought after the emotional and spiritual security he represented. "I was lashing out at the easiest target." She put her arms around Jocelyn. "I feel so bad, please forgive me.

"Vanessa's death consumed me." Cora took a tissue from the nightstand and wiped her eyes. She took a deep breath, and wrapped her arms around the girl's shoulders again. "When James remarried so soon, I became bitter and spiteful. There's no excuse for how I treated you, Josie. Please tell me we can start over."

Jocelyn awkwardly returned the hug. "My whole

life has been filled with my parents' not wanting me. I hope you really mean it, Cora, because I can't handle more rejection."

The depth of suffering Cora had caused increased her anxiety and regret. Her throat tightened with emotion, and she broke down once more. "Oh honey, both our hearts have been broken. We need to help each other heal."

"I'd like that." Jocelyn's eyes anxiously searched Cora's. Finally, the corners of her mouth crinkled into a smile, and her voice dropped to a whisper. "Yes, let's start over."

Cora prayed as the two women clung to each other. Her freed spirit soared, and she was eager to share her victories with Ed.

27

Saturday morning dawned clear and sunny. Late autumn breezes tugged at the colorful balloons that swayed blithely on the patio. It was a perfect day for a family reunion.

Cora and Emily were up early, and Dahlia arrived shortly after with her tasty contributions for the dinner.

Countless pictures were taken of Cora and Emily, as their smiles cut across the lost years. Introductions were made as their guests arrived.

Tears pricked Cora's eyes at the sight of her grandchildren. She threw her arms open wide and pulled the teenagers close. "I've really missed you kids." She smoothed Heather's long, dark hair as they walked into the living room. "I like your new hairdo. Did Josie help?"

"Yeah, and she helped me pick out this new outfit, too."

"Stylish." Cora turned to her youngest grandson, Todd, who sported a hint of a mustache. "You look so debonair." She looked at sixteen-year-old Jason. "I hear you're driving."

The lanky teen grinned and kissed her cheek. "Dad was gone, and I was stressing about the written test. Josie helped me study, and I got all the questions right."

Within minutes, Dahlia went into drill sergeant mode, and barked orders to the men who positioned picnic tables in the yard. She withdrew to the kitchen while their task was accomplished. "Get that BrewMeister cranked up, girls, an' don't skimp on them scoops." Dahlia sighed and pushed up her sleeves. "I need me some high octane this mornin'." She looked out the kitchen window. "It's sure quiet out there. Now where'd the men-folk go?"

"I believe your troops went AWOL." Emily laughed. "Jeff told me they're playing golf. Just nine holes so they'll be back by noon."

Jocelyn and Heather entertained the La-La girls in the den, while their mommy and Aunt June prepared the picnic tables.

Dahlia continued to busy herself in the kitchen.

Cora and Emily filled serving dishes, in various shapes and sizes, and placed them in the refrigerator.

"Josie," Cora called. "Would you do me a favor? Our neighbor, Letitia called and asked for someone to pick up the dessert she made for us. Would you go for me? I don't have time to chat with her today."

"Sure, I'll be glad to." Josie turned to her stepdaughter. "Want to go with me, Heather?"

The teen shrugged her shoulders. "Let's see if we can take the munchkins with us. It might get rid of some of their pent-up energy."

Cora carried a stack of dishes out to the patio while Rebecca and June discussed the seating around the picnic tables.

Rebecca picked up her sister-in-law's camera. "Hey! Are you sure you brought enough film?"

"Becky, this is the 21st century. I'm using a digital camera. It doesn't use film." June carefully took the dishes from Cora. "That baby has enough space to capture the whole family several times over with no problem."

The whole family.

Grief surfaced and once again, Cora's shoulders drooped. Her entire family wouldn't be together because Vanessa wasn't here. The feeling of loss emerged with a vengeance. Her heart was crushed.

Cora's eyes misted as she watched her granddaughter play with the dog next door. The fourteen-year-old girl looked so much like her mother. She had Vanessa's easy smile and dark hair that tumbled about her shoulders.

For a moment, Cora imagined it was her daughter. It was difficult to pull away from the bittersweet scene and face reality. Vanessa was gone. She had to accept it and not allow the enemy to take her prisoner again.

She turned to see the concerned looks of Emily and Dahlia at the door. Cora smiled and squared her shoulders slightly. "I'm fine." She took a deep breath, and clapped her hands. "Let's get busy, girls. Those men will be back from golfing soon and they'll be hungry."

ॐॐ

Golf clubs clattered and men's voices grew louder as the golfers scurried into the backyard. All the men patted Jeff's back, to congratulate him on his successful last round.

"I taught him everything he knows," Ed playfully announced.

Jeff gave a winsome smile. "Yep, I learned it from all those years of watching you play on TV, Uncle Steady."

Emily and Cora stood on the sidelines to sort out

the various relationships represented within the group. The initial awkwardness of this family of strangers didn't last long as they discovered the uniqueness of their blood ties.

The lively La-La girls entertained with preschool songs and newly learned tap dance steps.

Cora and Emily giggled at the delightful innocence of the three little sisters in look-alike dresses. A round of applause filled the air as the youngsters ended their mayhem of missteps.

All the excitement provoked Letitia Bockman's French poodle into a round of howls. An invisible fence kept Tinkle-Belle contained as she danced along the property line.

Dahlia placed her fingers in her mouth and gave a shrill whistle. "Hey, y'all!" she called. "It's time to mosey on inside an' watch your television show."

Everyone stood to make the trek into Ed's den. Wendell put up his hand to stop them and announced, "Be sure an' watch close when they innerview me. I got to tell 'em about my daddy an' his daddy afore him bein' Texas Rangers."

Dahlia frowned at her crowing spouse. "Ya didn't cough up that ol' hairball again, did ya?" She stepped away from the door to let the group inside.

"Well, I think it added a li'l somethin' to the piece," Wendell turned to check the heat of the sizzling grill. "I'll be ready for the chicken in about fifteen minutes, Dahlia Sue."

Inside, the children and teens huddled on the floor in front of the TV while the adults squeezed together on the furniture. Dozens of eyes were glued to the set. Everyone was ready to view the McGibbons' tape of the twin's segment on *Mysteries of the Rich and Famous*.

Members of the family waited excitedly to see themselves on the nationally aired program.

Cora noticed when June nervously checked her watch. A few minutes later, the family historian tiptoed out of the room. Where was she going? As the show's theme music swelled, Cora's attention was drawn back the television.

A fervent command arose from the back of the crowd, "Hey! Turn it up, I can't hear."

"Shhh!" was the reply. A photograph of Cora and one of Emily filled the screen as the announcer's deep voice blared, "It was a mystery that spanned nearly six decades. Cora Timms, wife of legendary golf pro, Steady Eddie Timms, and her identical twin, Emily Morgan, were separated and given up for adoption at two years of age. They grew up only ninety miles apart, not remembering their twin existed.

"Ed and Cora Timms live in this high-end complex outside of Phoenix. The pleasant community is home to over three hundred senior adults who co-existed peacefully...until one stormy night, when Cora thought she witnessed a murder in her own backyard. Days later, the decomposing body of the Timms's neighbor, Patrick Hyde, was found in a nearby garage. This would be the first of three murders to ravage the serene neighborhood.

"The story took an unexpected twist when Emily, who lived in Grand Sands, Arizona, came to Phoenix to visit her son, Dr. Jefferson Morgan."

The scene on the television changed to show Jeff as he sat on the corner of his desk. "You can imagine my surprise when Steady Eddie Timms came into my office with my mother. When I got close enough to hug her, I realized she wasn't Mom. That's when we discovered Mom and Cora were identical twins."

The show's host added, "For some time, the sisters had been mistaken for each other throughout Phoenix and the surrounding area. Convicted embezzler, Jack Thurston, was no exception. He worked with one of the sisters at Mathelcorp in San Francisco. She and her husband had been close, personal friends of Thurston and unknowingly played a key role in his embezzlement scheme."

Emily and Cora held hands while Thurston's intricate plot was exposed to the viewers. A bird's-eye view of the California prison aired. "For ten years, Thurston had been incarcerated here at Stockton Correctional Facility for Men. While serving time, he learned that his now-widowed friend had remarried and moved out of state.

"Weeks after his parole, Thurston found an article promoting Saguaro Valley Retirement Complex. A photograph of Steady Eddie Timms and his wife, Cora, caught his eye."

While the announcer gave further details, Emily leaned over and whispered in Jeff's ear. He replied with a simple shrug.

"Thurston," the announcer said, "naturally assumed she was Mrs. Morgan, the former employee and close personal friend from San Francisco."

Emily grabbed Cora's elbow. "Wait! What did he say about me?"

"Shhh!" came a choir of voices from the back of the room.

The program reverted back to the Saguaro Valley Complex. "Thurston secured a job as a handyman in the community where the Timms's live. Soon, he was harassing Mrs. Timms over the phone, trying to obtain his property, which he thought was stored in their home safe.

"When Mrs. Timms didn't comply with his demands, he increased his fear tactics and recklessly pursued her on the way back from Phoenix one evening. Cora Timms was nearly run off the road. However, she was able to break away from her stalker on the outskirts of a nearby town. When she arrived home, the stalker's car was parked in her neighbor's drive. Mr. Timms recognized the auto as being that of George Shipley, his former employee. This blatant effort to put his wife in danger alarmed Steady Eddie enough to contact the police. Officer Norman McNulty was there to answer the call."

Gasps were audible throughout the room as film footage of two covered bodies were removed from the Shipley's home. Officer McNulty appeared on-screen. "When we went to question the suspect, we found the bodies of both Shipley and his eighty-two-year-old mother, Gertrude. They had been fatally shot and rigor mortis had already set in." McNulty's jaw clenched, his eyes slightly narrowed. "This was proof that they were dead prior to the car chase, and that Shipley hadn't been Cora Timms' stalker."

Mug shots of the criminals were shown as the announcer added to the story. "According to the police, Thurston's accomplice, Rita Santalis, acknowledged that he murdered Patrick Hyde and the Shipleys. In an effort to throw suspicion onto the dead man and off himself, Thurston used Shipley's car to tail Mrs. Timms."

Greek music filled the air and viewers were transported to the Pegasi Cafe.

Emily squeezed Cora's hand as the dark-haired

reporter stood in front of the bubbling Pegasus fountain. "Pegasi waiter, Ben Shafer, told of the confusion when he had mistaken Mrs. Timms for her sister." He held the microphone up to the waiter's mouth.

"You should have seen Mr. Timms' when I told him his wife was here every week." the waiter grinned and added, "With Dr. Morgan."

The announcer's voice grew soft and mysterious as he faced the television camera. "This revealing bit of information led Steady Eddie and Cora to visit Dr. Morgan, who fortunately held the key to the puzzle. Once the mystery was solved, the twins met for their first tear-filled reunion in many years.

"The next day, Mrs. Morgan went to her sister's home. While alone, the ladies heard noises in the house and discovered Thurston ransacking the Timms's home office. Unbeknownst to Thurston, Emily Morgan used her cell phone to take pictures of him. Later, he found the women hiding in a food pantry. Emily had taken medication for a heart problem and the ensuing headache rendered her helpless. There was a struggle. It was then the twins were kidnapped and held hostage in room 19 at the Catchpenny Motel."

One of Vi's photos of the repulsive room appeared on the screen. That picture changed to the be-robed twins, sombreros, duck slippers and all.

Cora moaned and covered her face with her hands. "I can't watch."

Emily nodded. "Sorry to say, they got this part exactly right." She smiled at June, who returned to the room.

Wendell's voice boomed throughout the den. "OK, here it is. This is where I get to talk. Listen, he calls me detective."

"While doing his preliminary search," the reporter said, "Detective O'Givens found the cell phone with the incriminating evidence."

Wendell stomped his foot. "Aww, he got my name wrong an' I even spelt it for him. I didn't catch that whilst I was tapin' it. No wonder I ain't been gettin' no calls."

Then, Wendell, in his Stetson, appeared on camera. "Once't I found Emily's phone, I stuffed it in this here pocket. Later, she called me on it an' asked me to come get 'em."

"Weren't you afraid the kidnapper would catch up with you?" the correspondent asked.

"Naw. I was raised to be a lawman. My daddy an' his daddy afore him was Texas Rangers. I got their blood a'gallopin' through my veins."

As the camera broke away from Wendell, the local police station came into view. A motorcycle roared past while the announcer stepped into the building. "Mrs. Morgan's cell phone was found and surrendered to the police. It held enough evidence for the Saguaro Valley police to arrest Thurston on breaking and entering. Charges for kidnapping the twins, and the murders of the Shipleys and Patrick Hyde were quickly added.

"While abducted, Emily Morgan's quick thinking thwarted her former friend's attempt to follow through on his death threats of her newfound brother-in-law, Steady Eddy Timms."

Emily stood up. "Wait! Former friend? They're still getting us confused, Cora. I never met Jack Thurston until that first day I came to your house. Remember he thought I was you."

"What are you talking about, Em?" Cora asked. "He hasn't worked here that long, and I'd never met him. I've only heard about him through Wendell." She frowned. "You have to be Jack's old friend."

"No, it's not me. I've never been to San Francisco, and I certainly didn't work at Mathelcorp. Besides, that beast kept calling me Cora. So, I just naturally assumed he mistook me for you."

Ed turned the television off, "Let me get this straight. All this time you've had to discuss a relationship with Jack, and you've never brought up the subject?"

"We wanted to put all that negative stuff behind us," Emily explained. "It was important to learn about each other and just enjoy being together."

Cora nodded. "After all the phone calls and crazy things going on, bringing up our kidnapper was the last thing we wanted to do." She cleared her throat. "That still leaves us with one unanswered question. If it wasn't either of us working for Jack, who was it?"

A voice came from behind. "It was me. I worked for Jack."

28

Dead silence filled the room as all heads spun to see the speaker.

First Emily, then Cora shrieked, as they focused on the new couple June ushered in.

The long-lost siblings were thunderstruck at the appearance of another duplicate face.

The unforeseen turn of events brought everyone to their feet.

"Triplets!" Dahlia's forceful voice hollered. "If that don't beat all. Your mama had herself a litter." She went to the back door and called for her husband to share in the celebration.

A sly smile came across June's face as she announced, "Cora, Mom, I'd like you to meet Dr. Vincent Bedford and his beautiful wife, Nora."

Without a moment's hesitation, Nora rushed over and latched on to her two identical and bewildered sisters. All at once six arms crushed three bodies while kisses, tears and squeals caused an electrical charge of excitement to crackle throughout the room. Cameras and camcorders went into action.

Ed walked over to the white-haired man beside June. "Well, hello there, brother-in-law." He put his hand on his guest's shoulder. "Guess we should get acquainted. My name is Ed. Shall I call you Vincent or do you prefer Vince?"

"Everyone just calls me Doc." The pudgy

gentleman offered a hand. His dark eyes smiled behind wire-rimmed glasses.

The McGibbons joined in the celebration of family as the Bedfords were embraced by their welcoming relatives.

Dahlia sniffed the air. "Smells like ya best get back out to the grill while I make sure the triplets sit together at the table." She raced around the kitchen, and gathered two more table settings.

Wendell flipped the last of the grilled meat onto the platter and handed it to his wife. He whistled for the crowd's attention, and then took a deep breath and bellowed,

"Chicken's off the grill, coffee's in the pot; get up an' get 'em, get 'em whilst they're hot!"

Everyone laughed at Wendell's announcement and found their places at the food-laden tables.

Dahlia clapped her hands. "Ed, you're the head of this here household, why don't ya lead in the blessin'?"

Ed stood, cleared his throat and offered thanksgiving for their extended family and blessings for the food.

Serving dishes were passed along as the hungry guests filled their plates. Platters and bowls fell into a smooth cadence and the group settled to wolf down the feast.

While they ate, Nora asked the family to call her Nonie, a nickname given to her by a neighbor boy. "Chip called me No-No when he started to talk."

Doc added, "That later changed to Nonie and the name stuck. Seems everyone thought it suited her bubbly personality."

She then revealed how they learned about her sisters. "Doc and I were on a short mission trip to

Bolivia. You can imagine our surprise when we got a call from our friend, Neville Neubauer." Nonie took a drink of water. "He told us about the segment of Cora and Emily on TV. Once we returned to the states, I tried to get in touch with you right away. It was nearly a week before I could get June on the phone."

Doc cleared his throat and touched his wife's shoulder. "Nonie told me that Jack had been her boss and was a friend of her first husband's. She remembered an obscure envelope she'd found in the safe years ago."

"What I didn't know was, Jack had given an unmarked envelope with a key and fake ID to my husband." Nonie wiped her mouth. "My husband must've put it in our safe but forgot to mention it to me before his fatal heart attack." She sighed. "Eight months later, I discovered Jack's embezzlement scheme and blew the whistle. I didn't connect it with the strange envelope in our safe."

"It turns out," Doc said, "the key was to a safety deposit box that held the embezzled money, but with that fake ID, we didn't know who it belonged to. The only fingerprints belonged to Nonie's first husband. Anyway, it took the police several weeks to tie up the loose ends."

Ed listened intently, then, excused himself from the table. Within a few minutes, he returned with the old photo that had been left in Cora's drawer. He asked his wife's sisters if they knew the man.

Nonie took the photo from Emily. "That's a picture of me with my late husband, Art."

The name caught Cora's attention. She almost choked on the potato salad. She grabbed a napkin, and exclaimed, "Art? That must be what the caller meant."

She highlighted the story of Jack's frequent references to art. "He wasn't talking about our paintings and sculptures, like I thought, he meant your husband, Art."

"Do y'all realize," Dahlia said, "If Nonie here hadn't turned that buzzard in all them years ago, chances are y'all never woulda met?"

The Timms' looked at each other. Ed remarked, "That's a good way to think about it. Gives some purpose to all the craziness, doesn't it, Toots?"

"The Lord does work in mysterious ways," Emily added.

Lighthearted chatter continued while Letitia's cake and Dahlia's pies were passed around the table.

The family learned that Nonie was the daughter of missionaries and grew up in what is now known as Belize in Central America. She shared several childhood tales, from the antics of Howler monkeys to horrifying incidents of evil shaman practices. The group sat in awe of the diverse adventures of her youth.

After dessert, the three exhausted La-La girls went down for a much-needed nap.

The adults took their coffee and moved into the great room to view the Morgans' extensive collection of family photographs.

Cora made a special effort to sit next to Josie.

Emily handed scrapbooks to Doc, then looked at Cora and said, "We've not seen very many of your family pictures. Won't you get them out for us?"

Cora hesitated. "I haven't seen them in a long time. They're only in plain photo albums, not beautiful scrapbooks like June's." She turned to her husband. "Ed, could you get our family pictures from the top shelf in my closet?"

"You should see my collection," Nonie assured her sister. "They're all in shoe boxes."

"Mine were too, until Junie got her hands on them," Emily said with a laugh.

James proudly smiled. "Josie's started an album for each of the kids. Of course, the boys aren't into it, yet, but Heather appreciates it."

"Could you help me arrange all our pictures in albums, too? Maybe that's something we can work on together." Cora patted Josie's hand. "You could come for a weekend."

"That's a great idea," James said. "Guess the kids and I can feed ourselves."

Josie nudged Cora and gave a sly wink. "Don't worry about that, I'll have all your meals in the freezer."

"If I could have everybody's attention," Ed announced. "I have a special gift for my wife." He handed her a beautifully wrapped present.

With a questioning look, she accepted the heavy package. "Oh Eddie, what have you done? This better not be anything embarrassing." She opened the box and lifted a bronzed object.

"What...on...earth...is...this?"

"Bookends, Toots!" Ed laughed at his joke. "I had your duck slippers bronzed and mounted. Push the button at the base."

"Quack-quack!"

Laughter exploded. Then the slippers/bookends were passed around the room.

When it ended in Jeff's possession, he begged, "Please hide those things before the La-La girls wake up."

Cora took the ducks, and handed them to her grinning husband. "These will look smashing on the bookshelf in your office, Ed."

The doorbell resonated and everyone held their breath as they glanced around the room.

"Cora, Nora, Eudora, I bet that's your sister, Flora!" Jeff shouted.

"Oh, say it isn't so!" Ed took a deep breath and opened the door.

Vi Ashton stood with camera in hand. "I got an urgent call from the Lone Ranger." She pointed to Wendell. "He said a shot of the triplets would make a great sequel to my first article."

Wendell herded the trio in front of the living room fireplace, and stood behind them. "C'mon ladies, say cheese."

"Wendell Floyd," Dahlia called. "Get your hide outta the pitcher."

"It's alright, he can stay," Vi said. "After all, a promise is a promise." She shot a few frames. "Perfect. Now let's have the sisters sit over there and look at those photo albums."

"I want one of me with Em an' Cora," Wendell announced. "After all, we was the ones to crack this here case. Ya know, you gals are purty good at crime solvin'."

Emily nodded. "Thank you. It was stressful, but now that I think about it, it was kind of fun. Let me know when you have another case begging for your attention." She joined her sisters and smiled for the camera.

Once the short photography session was over, Vi thanked them for their time. Then with a wrapped piece of Dahlia's pie, she waltzed out the door.

Cora placed their family photographs on the coffee table next to the Morgans' collection. She dabbed her eyes. With a sweep of her hand she said, "Look at all the years we've missed. Let's make a pact to be together as much as possible, now that we've found each other."

"I agree to that wholeheartedly." Nonie winked at her husband.

Vince Bedford spoke. "As a matter of fact, we've given this a great deal of thought and prayer since we found out about her siblings. It's high time this old boy retired and took up golf with the great Steady Eddie Timms."

The sisters squealed in delight as Dahlia let loose with a war-whoop.

Excitement bubbled throughout the room.

"Nonie wants to be close to her family. We'd like to move into this complex. I see a couple condos for sale across the street. Are they just like this one?"

Wendell piped up. "Yep, they're the same. Now, this here part of the complex is a tad bit older, but just behind 'em are some brand spankin' new units with more square foot. Might give ya a bit more wiggle room."

Cora leaned closer to her newest sister. "How soon can you move in?"

"It'll take a few months."

"My son, Daniel, has agreed to take over my medical practice in Meadow Falls." Doc explained. "He's wanted to sell his Chicago practice and relocate his family to Indiana for some time now. They're excited about the move back to his home town."

Nonie's voice was timid as she spoke up. "I hate to ask a favor so soon, but would my two favorite sisters come and help me get ready for the big move when it's time?"

They nodded their heads vigorously as Emily responded, "Just try and stop us!"

Dahlia cackled. "I'm guessin' wild horses couldn't keep 'em away."

"I can't believe my ears," Cora said. "To think only a couple months ago we didn't know each other existed. Now the three of us can get together all the time."

Emily agreed. "This is wonderful news. I'm not that far away." She shifted in her seat. "Junie, you'll see a lot more of your old mother-in-law."

"Perhaps more than you think." Jeff grinned and scooted to the edge of his seat. "Before we go any further about the condo, there's something I need to tell you." He looked at the Bedfords. "Sorry, Uncle Doc, but one of the units across the street is already taken. June and I put a deposit down a couple weeks ago."

Emily stared at her son in disbelief. "You did what?"

"Well," Jeff cleared his throat. "Mom, I know you're reluctant to move from the home you and Dad shared for so long, and you've always told me not to put you in Shady Hills next to the cemetery. Well, this isn't a nursing home. It's a beautiful retirement complex where you can still come and go as you please. Since both your sisters will be here, wouldn't you like to live next to them? We'd sure be proud to make it happen for you." He grinned. "We don't want to pressure you or anything, but the deposit's non-refundable."

"Oh, Em!" Cora squealed. "How generous. You're

going to take them up on it, aren't you? Please, pretty-please?"

Emily hesitated for a minute. Everyone held their breath. "I'm dumbfounded," she finally said. "This is all so sudden. I don't know what to say."

"Just say yes." Jeff put an arm around his mother. "You know we've wanted you to move closer to us for ages. Now seems like the perfect time and place. So what do you say, Mom?"

Nonie took Emily's hand. "Can you imagine all three of us reunited like this? Think of all the memories we're going to make."

"How can I turn down such an offer? Let's do it!" Emily exclaimed.

The triplets stepped into a three-way embrace. A shoebox filled with snippets of the Timms' lives fell to the floor.

As Cora and her sisters retrieved the fallen photos, she noticed the note card beneath her shoe. The picture on the front was of the college that Van had attended. It was addressed to Ed's mother in Vanessa's distinctive script.

Ed saw his wife's shocked response and took the card from her hands. He read the note aloud. "Dear Grandma Bertie, this quote by Peter Marshall was given to me by one of my professors when Grandpa died. It's really helped me and I thought it might help you, too. 'Those we love are with the Lord, and the Lord has promised to be with us. If they are with Him and He is with us, they cannot be far away.' Your loving granddaughter, Vannie."

Cora fell into Ed's arms. If the card had surfaced a few days ago, she would've completely shut down. However, once she surrendered her overwhelming grief and bitterness, the Lord replaced the anguish with His peace. He had even blessed her with two identical sisters who would be neighbors. It was more than she ever dreamed possible. And then, there was Josie, a special relationship she was determined to cultivate.

God's love and acceptance surged through Cora and she finally knew all was well. The Lord was more than merciful and His presence, sweet.

Thank you for purchasing this Harbourlight title. For other inspirational stories, please visit our on-line bookstore at www.pelicanbookgroup.com.

For questions or more information, contact us at titleadmin@pelicanbookgroup.com.

Harbourlight Books
The Beacon in Christian Fiction™
an imprint of Pelican Ventures Book Group
www.pelicanbookgroup.com

May God's glory shine through
this inspirational work of fiction.

AMDG